THE FIRST CONCEPTION

Rise of Eris
(The Conception Series Book 1)

BY
NESLY CLERGE

ALSO BY NESLY CLERGE

When the Serpent Bites
(Book 1 of The Starks Trilogy)
Readers' Favorite 2017 International Book Awards Gold Medal Award

When the Dragon Roars
(Book 2 of The Starks Trilogy)
Readers' Favorite 2017 International Book Awards
Silver Medal Award

When the Phoenix Rises
(Book 3 of The Starks Trilogy)

End of the World: The Beginning
(Book 1 of a Serial - Amazon #1 Bestseller)

The Anatomy of Cheating

ACKNOWLEDGMENTS

My sincere thanks to my editor, Joyce L. Shafer, for continuing to believe in and supporting my storytelling abilities, as you did from the start. Thank you for helping me get to the finish line for each novel adventure.

Tierra Guy, not only are you my significant other, you also provide straightforward critiques amplified by encouragement and enthusiasm. My efforts and accomplishments are enriched by your presence in my life and contributions to my writing efforts.

Kay Smillie, you've been with me from the beginning of my writing endeavors, and are always the first person I look to for comments about and reviews of my published novels. Your feedback and diligence are invaluable; your support of my efforts are far more than significant to me. I count my blessings that you're my #1 fan.

I owe a debt of gratitude to my Goodreads reviewers and fans, whose comments assist me in more ways than I can list here: Diane Lybbert, Rebekah Brown, MD, Lynn McCarthy, Kimberlie Lashley, Julie Green, Tamara Lewis, Brenda Telford, Patricia Brooks, Shannon Fairley, Maxine Groves, Dee Cherry, Irene Appleby, Anthony Richard Parsons, Dianne Bylo, K Morton, Lorraine Sithole, Torrie Angel, Tracy Watson Fisher, Laura Cerone, Russell Dent, Linda Strong, Veronica Joy, Nicki, Lesley Marino, Sue Ward, Kostas Kinas, Sue Leonhardt, Roberson Lapierre, Renee Cherry, Dreama Akers Poore, and Hensie Lapierre.

Shayla Eaton, because of your exceptional marketing skills, you make things happen. Thank you!

I also have profound gratitude for the input of these esteemed authors: Rebecca Mcnutt and C. P. Bialois.

PROLOGUE

Viewers around the world ceased whatever they were doing as BREAKING NEWS flashed on the screen of every TV and electronic device. The year—2015. The time—5:21 p.m. on the West Coast of the United States.

Recognized by most, a woman with spiked magenta hair, ivory complexion, and brimming turquoise eyes stared into the camera.

"Good evening, viewers. I'm Sasha Aspen, with a Global Media breaking-news announcement. Make that a heartbreaking announcement.

"We've just received word that Amber Lake, our miracle woman, the only woman on our planet to conceive in the last five years, has suffered a miscarriage.

"As you know, some of the brightest minds have been unable to determine what initially caused this—there's no other way to say it, conception catastrophe—or why even in vitro fertilization, our last hope, continues to fail."

Tears spilled onto her cheeks. "It's been four years since the last child was born anywhere. If this does not change soon, our human race faces inevitable extinction."

She gave her head a hard shake, flashed gleaming white teeth in a broad smile and said, "We now return you to your program. This is Sasha Aspen, wishing you a better tomorrow."

The inevitable extinction of the human race.

I'm here to tell you it's something more. Much more. How did we get to this point, you may ask? It's best if we start from the beginning.

Who I am is Katherine Eris Barnes. My name means nothing to you now. But it will.

Sometime around mid-July, 1977, my father did what was required to cause his sperm to infiltrate my mother's egg, creating that first spark of the zygote that resulted in my not-so-immaculate conception, and me, who made my entrance into the world mid-April, 1978.

Several years later my father made the career choice to become a drug addict. Then an inmate. I was seven at the time. Mom demonstrated strength for about five minutes and divorced him when I was eight. We never heard from or about him again. Nor did we inquire—we, being my mother, Sally, and myself.

His absence was a relief but proved to be only a temporary reprieve.

Knowing my mother's behavior patterns, I seriously doubt their union ever had anything to do with love, despite the frequency with which he climbed on top of her. I used to bury my head under the bedcovers and read aloud to myself from one of the many books about molecular biology, genetics, or geometry, borrowed from the school library. I stumbled over some of the larger words, fingers plugged in my ears, to avoid hearing his grunts as he did the old push-and-pull. Nor did I want to hear her sounds in response.

The first time I heard this barnyard event was in our rat-trap apartment in the Cabrini-Green housing projects located in the Near North Side of Chicago, referred to by locals simply as C-G. Hearing these strange sounds, I climbed out of bed and went sleepily to their open door. Revolted at what I saw, I returned to bed and barely spoke to either of them for days. When I finally admitted what was bothering me, my mother shrugged. My father said I should get used to it, and the idea of it. That one day I'd find out how much I enjoyed it.

As with nearly everything else, he was wrong.

It was later that I learned how generous a man he was. That he didn't limit sharing his *joy-juice*, as he called it, with just my mother. Not long after he retired from a life of idleness to a cell in the Joliet prison, I discovered that a woman didn't have to be married to a man for him to crawl on top of her. Or beat her.

My mother always could pick them. There were times when I wondered if she drove up to the nearest mental ward and yelled out the window, "Got any new ones in?"

That apartment no longer exists, thankfully. The building was razed in 2011. A far easier task to cleanse that property than my life. Or my memories. I still chuckle when I recall that in 1981, the then-mayor moved into C-G to prove it was a safe place to live. She lasted three weeks. My parents lacked her option to relocate.

As a child, I approved of my first name, resented my middle name, pondered how we arrived at our surname. It's anyone's guess why my African-American mother gave me two Greek names in front of the Old English surname that, as far as I could learn, came from an old Norse word that means warrior. I never once saw her read any of the classics, or any printed word on a page other than the phone book, much less demonstrate any knowledge or interest in Greek gods or goddesses. She didn't even like Greek food, not that she ever tried it.

However, it would be years before I appreciated the appropriateness of all three names. They became my secret inspiration.

As to why my African-American father allowed those first two names, I don't think he gave a damn. I wasn't much more to him than the product of a good time had by him. For all I know, he has a number of such *products* running around, though I doubt any of them turned out as well as I did.

Katherine means pure, in case you were unaware of this. That's nice and all, except it didn't take long for me to discover that neither my mother nor others in my early years, or later, for that fact, had any intention or inclination to keep me that way.

As for Eris, I initially resented being named after the Greek goddess of strife and discord. Right up until the moment when I realized it was appropriate after all.

Homer wrote this about Eris, "Strife, whose wrath is relentless ... she who is only a little thing at the first, but thereafter grows until she strides on the earth with her head striking heaven. She then hurled down bitterness equally between both sides as she walked through the onslaught making men's pain heavier."

Homer knew what he was talking about. In part. My wrath *is* relentless. And I do intend to make men's pain heavier in a way they can't fathom. But I never measured up to the original goddess as far as size went. I was small as a young girl and, though round in the places where women usually are, remain petite now that I'm older. A distinct and dangerous disadvantage. At least, in my reality.

At some point in life, most of us wonder about the nature of reality. Quantum physics tells us there is no such thing. That peering at the smallest particle under the largest microscope reveals there's nothing there. But there is something there. We see, hear, taste, smell, and touch what we call reality. Initially, what I read about this topic led me to believe reality is all in the mind.

With one exception: that theory or concept is extraordinarily difficult to accept when you're being abused.

Plato said that in the universe, "things are taken care of far better than you could possibly believe." All you have to do is look around at the confusion, the chaos, and the hideous acts people perpetrate on one another to realize that his statement is a load of nonsense. And if you're willing to be honest, most of the discord is perpetrated by men.

Until now.

Now, I'm on the scene.

Some might say I sound like a woman scorned. Believe me—it's way beyond that flimsy, often-used expression. Men have long dominated women, possessed and oppressed them. Have taken advantage of them in ways some don't risk imagining.

Some of us don't have to imagine.

Like me.

Reasons given for this inequality included that women are mentally and physically inferior, therefore, need a *strong man* to look after them. They should see what kind of strength is required to carry a child, to relinquish their bodies for nearly a year, while they grow another human inside of them. Let's see how they'd manage *that* while maintaining the beliefs about themselves they hold so dear. What woman hasn't wished this on a man at least once in her life?

Warriors? Ha! They love war because it boosts their egos and their assets.

Providers? Like the manner in which my sperm-donor father and subsequent men provided for my mother and me? No thanks.

Adept thinkers and hunters? Certainly. Especially when what they're thinking about is how to hunt a defenseless woman.

Or a defenseless child.

If these are the qualifications required to rule the world, well, it explains why the world is the way it is.

Long ago, adding insult to injury, men posed as religious leaders and doubly enforced this belief system. Raised themselves up, subjugated women. Forced everyone to believe or accept their superiority until it was assumed a "fact" of life.

Time for this erroneous posturing to disappear into antiquity. This is the twenty-first century, after all.

I'm no longer a child. Or disillusioned. Women have made strides in some measure, in some locales. Despite our meager advances, only a few countries have had women rulers. We're allowed positions of power, but only so much. We're allowed better salaries, but only so much. We're allowed—some of us—certain freedoms. But only so much.

Frankly, I've had it. It's time to make them pay.

And if I could find him now, I'd start with the man—Mom's boyfriend number six in two years—who slipped into my darkened room when I was ten.

CHAPTER 1

Tummy-down on my bed, I was desperate for the sun to set so the temperature outside, and in, would lower even a few degrees. The window on the front wall of my room remained stuck shut. No one attempted to fix it, no matter how often I complained.

I'd found a rusty metal geometry compass discarded near a storm drain and took it home. Some would have left it there, while others might have kicked it into the drain. I was thrilled to have this mathematical tool and cleaned it up as best I could.

I twirled the compass in circles and read aloud, "Geometry bridges the One and the Many. A circle is the most perfect form known to man and in nature. All shapes are within it and are derived from it."

What is that racket?

I marked my place in the book, flung open my door, and marched into the living room that opened into the kitchen. "Mom? What's going—?"

I said this as the fist of my mom's latest boyfriend—Buster—made contact with her jaw, sending her sprawling against the crappy, crud-covered kitchen cabinets.

How I wanted to kick him but didn't dare go near him. "You leave my mom alone! You're nothing but a gross pig. You should be wallowing in mud somewhere and eating what you defecate."

He turned and snarled. "Get yo' smartass self back to yo' room. 'Less you want some of this."

"We don't want you here." I pointed at the only door to our apartment, wishing him transported to the other side of the peeling paint and buckling wood.

He looked at my mother. "She right? You want me to go?"

My mother licked her bloodied lips. "No, baby. You know I want you to stay."

He grabbed her by the wrist and yanked her into him. "Then you need to show yo' man just how much."

He sneered at me as he dragged Mom to our ratty sofa and unzipped his pants. "Wanna watch, Little Katie?"

"It's Katherine. Not Katie."

"Maybe you oughta let your mama show you how it done then take over for her."

He pulled *IT* out. Grabbed my mother by her hair and said, "Little Katie think she so smart. Let's see how fast she learn the only thing she need to know."

My mother took hold of *IT*. "No, baby. This all mine." Her head swiveled in my direction. With one normal and one swelling eye aimed at me, she said, "Get on back to your room. Leave us be."

I left him standing in front of her, her holding *IT* in her hand, while she told him how great he was.

She went quiet.

He moaned.

I glanced back.

Nearly made me puke.

***

Why didn't my mother come when I yelled for her? What is she doing that's more important than saving me? Buster's hand over my mouth makes it hard for me to breathe.

Stop touching me there!

Even in the dark, his eyes and face are scary—it's like he sees me and he doesn't.

His beer-breath stinks.

Get off me. You're too heavy.

It's too hot. You're too sweaty.

I don't want you here.

I don't want to be here!

I close my eyes and mentally go where I feel safe. I rewrite what he's doing to me:

When you use a pencil, use it firmly. Keep it steady. Move it deliberately and with no hesitation. Keep the point sharp.

TOO SHARP!

Why am I wet down there? Did he make me pee?

I stay with the words I've read, while he does what he's doing. Turn it into geometry. Anything but this. I'm drawing starfish and beehives in my mind to block out what he's doing to me. And what he's doing to himself with his other hand.

"Lit-tle Ka-tie. Had to start with my finger 'cause you too small. Maybe you grow big enough by next year. Maybe I stick around so you can find out what the real thing feel like. You'd like that, wouldn't you? Nod your head, Little Katie. I said, nod your head, you little bitch."

There's no eraser big enough for this mistake.

CHAPTER 2

Which is the better buy? A six-pack of batteries for $8.99 or a ten-pack of batteries for $10.25?

This math question had nothing to do with the vocabulary pop quiz my fifth grade teacher had scribbled on one side of the blackboard. The math question had been left on the other side, from the eighth grade class that used the room the prior hour. My teacher had been too lazy to erase it, I suppose.

I couldn't tell if any student had gotten the answer right. The answer wasn't included on the board. But I knew it. I'd had to learn how to figure out such things. Because even at ten years old, I had to become the adult at home.

Sometimes my mom shops for food, but most of the time, I'm the one who has to make sure we have something to eat. I got over my embarrassment about using food stamps in a hurry—I was too hungry. Her lazy boyfriend never gives us a dime, but sure keeps one shelf in the fridge filled with beer cans. Makes me wonder if that new gold chain around his neck is real or if it'll turn green after he sweats on it enough. Shouldn't take long. His skin is always hot and moist, like he just walked through steam.

I don't mind doing the shopping. It's a good way to get away from them while they grunt and squeal in the bedroom, which seems to be almost all they do. If they even bother to go into that room. That's why my old mattress, dragged in from off the sidewalk, has imprints from my body all over the top. That's where I stay, sitting up or sprawled, door closed, more than any other room in the apartment.

Each morning, long before either of them even think about waking up, I slide from my bed, tiptoe to their room and close the door. As quietly and as quickly as I can, I scrub their cooties from the toilet seat and tub and take my bath. I run the water at nearly a trickle so I don't wake them up. After I dress, two bologna sandwiches are made by me, put into a small paper bag by me. I dress and leave early, sometimes while it's still dark out.

You might think it's scary to walk by myself at that time, but it isn't. Anyone who was up to no good the night before is asleep. Besides, it's scarier to be inside when they, especially *he*, get up. As I said, she really knows how to pick them.

The time by myself in that early part of the day is the only time I feel like I can breathe. It takes several minutes to get away from the stink in the projects. Then it's more open, with more green things to look at or touch. If it's early enough and not cloudy, I see stars overhead. Study their geometric configurations above me in the velvety midnight-blue sky. And there's the special place I go to watch the sunrise. There, I eat one of my sandwiches and remind myself to hang onto hope.

I looked that word up the first time I read it—hope. I'd never heard it spoken by anyone around me. *Desire accompanied by expectation.* I could see how that could be interpreted a lot of ways. But I knew what it meant for me. Or could. No matter what anyone did to me, I wasn't going to ever, *EVER*, give up.

"Time's up. Pass your papers to the front."

I don't dare look at my teacher. He isn't going to be happy with me about this pop quiz.

"All right, class. Use the rest of the time as a study period."

Mr. Sanchez shuffled the papers and put them in a stack at the middle of his desk. He plopped his pudgy body into the chair, grabbed a red pencil, and began to go through the quiz sheets. I opened my textbook, stood it on my desktop so I could peer at Mr. Sanchez over it, and pretended to read. My stomach felt like I'd swallowed a plump pigeon that wanted out of that dark, confined space.

I knew he got to my paper because he raised his eyes to glare at me. I blinked hard, trying to see the words on the pages of my book. My face grew hotter and hotter as I waited for him to yell at me.

He didn't. Instead, he placed my paper face-down on his desk and to the side. Head down, but eyes aimed at him, I studied his face as he studied the back of my paper. I swallowed hard and let go of my breath when he went back to marking the tests.

Every couple of seconds, I checked the hands on the clock that seemed to have forgotten how to move.

The bell rang. I snapped my book closed and grabbed my other books so I could hurry to the bathroom before my next class.

"Katherine Barnes."

I skidded to a stop halfway to the door. "Yes, sir?"

"Come here."

I shuffled toward him and stopped in front of his desk.

He jabbed his finger against my paper. "What's the meaning of this?"

"Sorry, Mr. Sanchez."

He marked a big red F on the blank front of my quiz paper. "I don't understand you. You didn't even try. Just doodled on the back of the page. I wanted answers, not drawings of flowers, honeycombs, stars, and boxes in perspective."

"The word doodle implies absent-mindedness, something a silly person does. Leonardo da Vinci and some other famous people doodled, and look how they turned out. Besides, I read that doodling is a tool for self-discovery and discovery of the world around us."

"Be that as it may, Katherine, when I give a test or quiz, I expect my students to turn in answers. It seems the only answer you gave was to the math problem on the board for eighth graders. You also got it right."

I shrugged. "It was easy."

"Easy or not, why'd you do this?"

No way was I going to tell him I couldn't put my mind on anything like vocabulary because I was hurting *down there*. The only thing that brought me comfort was my precious geometry. I glanced at the wall clock above his head. Only a minute left before my next class. I was going to be late.

"Mr. Sanchez, could you give me a hall pass? Please?"

"What for?"

Head down, I said, "You know." I crossed my right leg over my left as I stood there wishing I was almost anyplace but here.

I needed to change the wad of toilet paper I'd stuck in my underwear prior to his class. The last thing I wanted was for the liquid still oozing from between my legs to leak onto my clothes or desk seat.

He stared at me, but his eyebrows were back over each eye instead of over his nose. From the middle drawer, he pulled out a hall pass, filled it out, signed his name and held it out to me. "You're my brightest student. Anything wrong? Anything you want to talk about?"

His eyes stayed fixed on me. I snatched the pass from between his fingers the way a stray cat once took a piece of bologna from mine. "No, sir."

After a few seconds more of staring at me, he sighed and said, "Get going."

I zoomed from the room.

CHAPTER 3

Earlier that morning, when I'd made my sandwiches, there wasn't much bologna or bread left. It was up to me to get more after school. Good thing that's all we needed, because that's all I could carry along with my books. Homework in every subject. I was probably the only student who didn't complain. Nothing like the perfect excuse for going into my room and not coming out until the next morning.

Cabrini Greens & More, the neighborhood store, was small, but its bins and shelves stayed crammed with items, all the way up to the ceiling. Anytime I needed something from up top, like paper towels or toilet paper, one of the stock clerks had to get whatever down for me with a grab-pole too long for me to manage yet. Mr. Johnson, the owner, said I'd grow into it. I hope he's right. Being small is a definite disadvantage at times.

Mr. Johnson is the oldest person I know, and he never seems to move off the wooden stool positioned behind the check-out counter. He's only ever been nice to me. So, I don't mind the smelly cigar always stuck in the corner of his mouth. He lets it dangle there, except when he flips ashes into a rusty coffee can on the other side of the cash register.

With his gravelly voice, which always sounds sweet to me, he said, "How you doin' today, Miss Katherine?"

I shrugged. "How are your joints?"

"Tellin' me it's gonna rain."

I glanced out the glass front and up at the sky. He was right. I hadn't noticed the dark clouds forming overhead. Can't notice the sky when you're keeping your head down.

Mr. Johnson folded then stuck one of those big plastic trash bags into my paper bag. "Just in case you need it."

"Thanks. I'll return it if I don't use it."

"Keep it. Never know when you'll need it for rain. Or something else."

The sky roared like a lion I saw at the zoo during a field trip for school. No one in my family ever took me anyplace. Not the zoo. Not the botanical gardens or a museum. If not for school and books, my imagination would never go anywhere.

I made it home without using the plastic bag, but it was close.

Buster wasn't there. I put the bologna in the fridge and the bread in a cabinet. "Where is he?" I asked.

Mama sniffed like she had a cold. "Why you wanna bother him?"

"Why do you stay with him?"

"Gives me somethin' to do."

"What about getting a job?"

"Too busy givin' 'em." She snorted and swiped at her lips with the back of her hand.

I crossed my arms and stared at her, waiting for her to explain that confusing statement to me.

She sucked on what was left of a cigarette until the white paper turned to gray ash, leaving only the brown filter smoldering between her fingers. She stubbed it out in a cracked saucer. Mom leaned on the table as she stood. The ash- and butt-filled saucer slid close to the edge as the table shifted down on one leg. The folded paper towel I'd positioned under the shorter leg was missing. Again.

Crumpled beer cans filled the garbage pail. I figured *he* must be getting more at the liquor store around the corner. Maybe one of those big, noisy, greasy, grimy, stinky, slimy garbage trucks would flatten him on the street. Or see him for what he is and load him into the back. Do that compacting thing and squish him until they can't tell him from the rest of the trash.

"When will he be back?"

Mom turned bloodshot eyes toward me, but didn't look at me directly. "Leave him be."

"Borrowing from your words, I want *him* to leave us be."

"Fix yourself somethin' and take it to your room. And don't come out."

"Don't worry."

"You sassin' me?"

I sighed. "No, ma'am."

"Better not be." Mom held out a hand. "Gimme one of them colas."

I handed her one of the small plastic bottles from the six-pack on the counter and reached for the handle of the tiny freezer at the top of the fridge. "I'll see if there's any ice."

Mom sneered. "I ain't gonna drink it." She shook the capped bottle, wobbled to the bathroom, and slammed the door behind her.

Grownups confuse me.

As I made a peanut butter and jelly sandwich, I heard my mother curse and mutter to herself from behind the bathroom door. And I heard *him*, laughing and bellowing his jive-talk to someone, which meant it wouldn't be long before he was back inside, polluting my air. He's so full of himself it makes me want to puke.

I grabbed my sandwich and school things and beat it into my room. Dropped my books and stuff onto my bed and ran back to the kitchen for one of the four metal folding chairs at the table. Shut my bedroom door just as he opened the apartment door.

The aroma of fried chicken wafted through the gap between my door and the floor. My stomach gurgled. I opened the door a crack. Saw the bucket on the table. No way was I going out there, not even for a wing.

Since when did he bring food here? I figured he must have stolen it from some poor person walking out with his or her order. Maybe robbed the Colonel, himself.

My eyes slid to the small school calendar stuck to my wall. Mom would have gotten her welfare check, cashed it, and given him the money, as she did every month. It was a wonder the exertion of going to the mailbox downstairs and the bank hadn't worn her out.

I locked my door and positioned the chair back under the door handle, like I'd read in a novel. That done, I sat cross-legged on my bed as I ate my sandwich. Opened my favorite library book to where I'd left off and read as I chewed. It's the same book I used to check out over and over.

At first, the school librarian said I couldn't borrow it more than twice in a row. I checked on it every day for a month. No one but me ever read or requested it. After pleading with her, she agreed to let me check it out as often as I liked, as long as no one else wanted it. Eventually, she asked if I wanted to help out in there during my lunch hour—shelving books and such—in exchange for the book. That was last year.

I hide the book under my mattress every night, though it's not like anyone but me is going to wash the sheets, which I do in the tub, but only in the early hours, and only when I know he'll sleep late on the weekend. After I press and twist out all the water I can in the tub, I drape my sheets over furniture in my room to dry. It's a chore to get this done. It's also why the intervals between washings can be longer than I'd prefer.

I refuse to touch my mother's sheets, or even go into her room. Both have a funky smell. Her sheets have stains everywhere. I don't think she's washed them since even before my not-so-immaculate conception when my combination DNA began to emerge into shapes and patterns that would result in me.

I turned to one of my favorite chapters:

> *Shapes and patterns are everywhere around us. If we know how to "read" them, we learn more about nature and how shapes serve us in our daily affairs. Like, why are some things round? Why do hurricanes, curls, pinecones, galaxies, shells, and whirlpools function as spirals?*

Here's what I read about that once. The spiral is nature's most efficient way to encompass the most information in the shortest distance or most compact space. Like DNA. See what I mean about why geometry and nature fascinate me? You don't learn just one thing when you look at a spiral, you learn a whole bunch, especially if you look around.

Ever watched a fern unfold? I watched one do that in a school science film once. Time-lapse photography, they called it. And I realized everything is in motion. All. The. Time.

However, some people seem stuck in place. And some people's actions cause us to lose our balance. Then we wobble in place like a slowing toy top until we figure out how to stop them from throwing us off our center point.

I hadn't had time to grab something to drink before *he'd* returned. Peanut butter stuck to the roof of my mouth. No way was I going out there to get something to drink. Thank goodness I'd used the restroom before I'd left school. Probably won't be able to go until they start up with their nasty stuff again and forget I exist or pass out from drinking and whatever else they get up to.

Amid all this chaos, and because I'm smarter than the two of them together, I'm considered the freak.

Go figure.

My eyes flew open. Had I heard something, or was I dreaming?

I lay stiff, unmoving in the dark. Then I knew.

Someone flushed the toilet.

Footsteps tromped toward my door. They stopped on the other side.

I sat up in bed, trembling. Pulled the sheet up to my chin.

No. No. No.

Someone fiddled with the doorknob. Yanked on it. Fists pounded against my door the same way my heart pounded inside my chest.

"Unlock the door, Little Katie."

I can't breathe.

With each connection his fist makes with my door, I quake.

I heard my mother call him. He told her to get her ass back in the bed.

She ignored him. I know this because I heard her say from the other side of my door, "C'mon, baby. Come back to bed. Mama wants more of what Daddy gives her."

"You done got enough."

"Unh-uh. Lookit over here. Look at what I'm shakin' at you. C'mon, now. You know you like to spank this. She ain't got nothing you want, baby. You a *big* man. This big girl's business."

"I'm gonna give you the business."

"That's right, baby. Now, let's go back to bed."

"Nuh-uh. Right here. Against the door."

"Let the child sleep. She got school in the mornin'."

"What I tell you 'bout dissin' me, bitch?"

"I ain't dissin' you. I tryin' to give you more good stuff."

"An' I tol' you to get yo ass outta my business."

The scuffle started. Even with my fingers in my ears and my pillow over my head, I can't block out the *whumps* and *thumps* against my door a few feet away. Or the disgusting things he says to her. Or what she says back—pleading with him. Weak-willed.

I guess there's only so much a person can stand. When I heard Mama scream, I scrambled from the bed. It took longer than I meant for it to, to move the chair and unlock the door with hands that wouldn't stop shaking. By the time I reached them in the kitchen, he had Mama cornered on the floor in the kitchen. She held her arms crossed in front of her as he'd kick, curse, kick, curse. Tears streamed down her face, but she didn't make another sound.

I started to run at him but she saw me and gave a subtle shake of her head. When I nodded defiantly in response, she looked up at him and said, "Let me do what always calm you down, baby."

He hesitated then went still. Mama, moving slow, got to her knees in front of him. She glanced at me and shooed me with her hand, where he couldn't see her gesture.

I was smart enough to leave them alone.

Back in my room, I locked my door and slipped the chair back under the knob before crawling into the middle of my bed.

Maybe my mother is a tramp.

Or maybe it's the only way she knows how to save me.

But who's going to save her?

CHAPTER 4

At the end of third period, Mr. Sanchez's class, he stopped me from leaving. Again.

"I want you to see Ms. Green after school. I've already arranged it. She'll be expecting you in her classroom."

I shifted the heavy stack of books in my arms. "Why? I didn't do anything."

"You're not in trouble, if that's what's worrying you, Katherine."

"But—"

"Just be there. Understood?"

"Yes, sir."

"She'll give you a note explaining to your mother why you're late."

I turned, shuffled to the door and muttered, "Not like she'll notice."

"Did you say something?"

"No, sir." I blew out a breath, left the classroom, and stomped toward my next class.

I read once that people seek power. Only, they don't realize it's through the power they already possess that they seek it in the first place.

The last thing I feel is powerful. How could I, when everyone's always telling me what to do? Or forcing me to do things I wouldn't choose to do. Or don't want to.

Why can't everyone just leave me alone with my books?

Like me, Ms. Green is also a shade of bronze, though I'm a shade darker, what's called burnished. The first time I saw a statue made of bronze during a school trip, I recognized my shade right off. Read in the pamphlet that there was a word for it, and looked it up in the dictionary.

One day I'm going to straighten my hair the way Ms. Green does. I'll either wear it to my shoulders, like hers, or maybe a little longer. She's the prettiest teacher at my school. And that's not just *my* opinion.

I stood in the doorway of her classroom. She was writing math problems on the blackboard and didn't realize I was there. I watched her move with that special grace she has, until I knew I'd better speak up. "Ms. Green?"

She paused, looked at me over her shoulder and smiled. "Come in, Katherine. I'm almost finished. Take a seat at the desk across from mine."

Two books at the top of my stack crashed to the floor when I put the rest of them on the desktop. I put them back at the top, straightened the stack then sat.

"There. All done." Ms. Green wiped her fingers on a cloth, came around the front of her desk, and perched on the edge of it. "Mr. Sanchez said you figured out a math problem—an eighth grade problem—and told him it was easy."

I nodded and shrugged.

"He also said you have a fondness for geometry."

My whole body perked up, all the way to the ends of my hair. "Yes, ma'am. Everything in existence is a result of it. We just have to learn how to see it and use it."

"I wish I could get my students to understand that. They think it's a waste of time." She tilted her head and smiled. "And you're years younger than they are."

I felt my face flush with pleasure. And gratitude.

Ms. Green slid off her desk and moved my books to another desk. She grabbed a sheet of paper and a brand new sharpened pencil from her middle drawer.

"I want you to see if you can solve the three problems on the board."

She placed the paper and pencil on my desk.

"I'll give you a note, of course, but will your mother be upset at your being late? We should have checked with her first, but we were too eager to see if—"

"She won't … mind." I'd almost said *care*. That would have made Ms. Green ask questions I didn't want to answer.

"Well, then. Take as long as you need. If we go too late, I'll take you home and explain."

"It'll be okay. Can I start now?"

She smiled and nodded, took a seat at her desk, and started grading papers.

I glanced at the clock on the wall over her head then at the first question. Licked my lips and began scratching graphite against paper.

When I finished the last problem, I checked the clock again. It had taken me five minutes. I put my pencil down and cleared my throat.

Without looking up, Ms. Green said, "Question?"

"No, ma'am. I'm finished."

Ms. Green shot out of her chair like a rocket. She scooped up my paper and stood there checking my answers and how I got them. "We'll need to arrange another time. I want to give you another test."

My insides went all squiggly. "I was sure I got them right."

"You did, and it didn't take you any time at all."

"Isn't that good?"

"Very good." She smiled. "Aside from geometry, what else interests you? Have you thought about what you'd like to do when you grow up?"

"I like to read about genetics. And medicine. Diseases interest me."

"Do you understand what you read?"

"Most of the time."

"You want to be a doctor?"

I shrugged. "I think so."

"I'd like you to stay after school again tomorrow. Would it help if I call your mother?"

"I'll tell her." *Will not.*

"I promise not to keep you more than, say, thirty minutes?"

"Okay. Should I do anything before then?"

"Just show up like you did today. Now, let me write a quick note about today for your mother. And I think," she winked, "it's better to add a sentence or two about tomorrow as well. Don't you agree?"

"Yes, ma'am."

I stuck the note inside the top book and lifted the stack into my arms.

"Do you always carry so many books?"

"Yes, ma'am."

"No book sack?"

"I'm used to it. Okay if I go now?"

"Of course. See you tomorrow."

My feelings bounced back and forth between being pleased with myself and worried my mother would find out. Or that *he* would, and that he'd take it out on me or my mother. Maybe both of us.

When I reached Mr. Johnson's store, I stood behind the person buying chips, beer, soda, and cigarettes. Soon as the man left, I smiled at Mr. Johnson.

"Not buying today, Miss Katherine?"

I shook my head. "Just a new paper bag, please. Mine got messed up. What's the chance of rain?"

"I don't ache as much today." He slid a small, flattened paper bag from under the counter and into the top book, on top of Ms. Green's note.

Three customers lined up behind me, so I said goodbye and started for apartment four-oh-five.

The elevator wasn't working. Again. Or someone was holding it open on a floor. Again. My arms were getting sore. Sighing, I went to the door for the stairs and managed to open it with the tips of my fingers of one hand then my foot. Took in the biggest breath I could and started up the steps through the graffiti-scarred walls as fast as I could go, which wasn't that fast. One wrong step and my books or I could land in one of the many puddles or piles of you-know-what.

Running out of air, I pushed through the door on the fourth floor and leaned against the wall, gulping in air that smelled only slightly better.

By now, my arms shook pretty bad. I got the apartment door open and used my backside to close it as quietly as I could. Mom's bedroom door was open. They were at it again—I recognized the squeak of mattress springs. I needed to get to my room, but I also needed something to eat. As quietly as possible, I put my books on the table and made a sandwich, which I put on top my book stack and started for my bedroom.

It's not that I wanted to look into Mom's room, it was more that I wanted to check to see if I could get past the door without them knowing I was there. Let them see my closed door later and figure out I was home. And leave me alone.

When I was a foot or so from passing in front of the door, I heard *him* say, "Ride me. Yeah. Ride me, bitch. Faster." Then I heard a hand slapped hard against skin. Then again. If he was beating my mom while doing *that* to her …

I had to check. I paused in front of the open doorway, mouth open, eyes wide. His eyes were closed, but not my mama's. Even from her face in profile, it seemed to me she wasn't enjoying it as much as he was, if at all. I cringed when he slapped her bottom. Wanted to cry when he twisted her nipples so hard she winced. Between bounces, she glanced at me and jerked her head toward my bedroom.

My feet moved as fast as I could will them to. All the while, I was terrified I'd drop one or more books or my sandwich.

On my bed, door closed and locked, chair back under the knob, I sat next to my books spilled across my mattress.

I'd forgotten to get something to drink.

Again.

CHAPTER 5

I won't bore you with what was on the test Ms. Green gave me the next day, but I admit I was pleased when she told me they were advanced problems. They were easy for me. Fun. Especially the geometry ones.

Ms. Green stared at my graded paper for a moment then raised her eyes to meet mine. "You did so well. Your classes must be so dull for you."

I shrugged then nodded.

Ms. Green reached for a folder on her desk, opened it and shook her head. "You did better than most of my students when I gave them the same test. And, yet, your recent grade point average doesn't match what you're capable of. In fact, it's far below what it should be." She fixed her soft brown eyes on me. "Is there a reason for this? I mean," she gestured toward my test paper, "you breezed through this."

"I guess I'm sometimes distracted."

"Want to tell me more about that?"

I put my head down and chewed my bottom lip. The last thing I wanted to do was disappoint her, but I couldn't tell her—*not her*—what was bothering me. Ms. Green liked me. I didn't want that to change. Didn't want her to think less of me.

"I think, Katherine, that I should speak with your mother. I'll send you home with a note, asking her to come here so we can talk. Is four a good time for her? Does she need to come later?"

I shook my head, which I kept down. I didn't want to look her in the eyes when I lied to her.

She pressed on. "Maybe during the lunch break or before school starts."

"There's no good time, Ms. Green."

She didn't say anything for a while. Head still lowered, I began to fidget. I looked up, but only because I heard her pen scratching on paper.

"You can go now. Give this note to your mother."

"Yes, ma'am." Without looking at her, I took the note, scooped up my books and left without either of us saying another word.

All my joy was gone.

The only relief I had was knowing my mother would never see that note either.

***

Sometimes there are good moments in my life. Not often, but sometimes. Like, I was able to use the elevator when I got back to my building. Like, *he* wasn't there when I entered the apartment.

My mother sat at the small kitchen table, one hand pressing the phone receiver to an ear, while the other hand held a cigarette burning down in her fingers. The ash attached was over an inch long. Why didn't she flick it off or something? The saucer was full, but that never bothered her before.

She glared at me as she listened to the person who was telling her whatever it was she obviously didn't like. I ran through a mental list of my day. I'd done nothing to earn the look she gave me.

I went to my room and dropped my books onto my bed. Left the door open. Sat on my bed, listening, not hearing anything, until she slammed the receiver onto the phone base hanging on the wall. Then her footsteps coming toward my room.

Her body filled half the doorway as she leaned against the door jamb, arms crossed. No smile for me. No, Glad you made it home safely. No, How was your day?

"So, you the brightest little thing that *Ms. Green* ever seen."

What was I supposed to say?

"Answer me, missy."

Butterflies of dread competed with the thrill of Ms. Green's compliment. "I don't know, Mama. Was that Ms. Green? Is that what she said?"

"And what about all them notes you never give me?"

"I didn't want to bother you."

"So you let that Ms. Green bother me instead. You damn lucky Buster gone when she call. You damn lucky he didn't pick up that call from that prissy teacher of yours."

"She's not actually my teacher. She's eighth grade."

"Then what the hell she bothering you for?"

"You won't tell *him*, will you?" I waited, eyes pleading with her.

She stared at me for several seconds, puckering and un-puckering her lips. "No reason to bother him with that nonsense."

I let out a breath and my shoulders down from around my ears. "Thank you, Mama."

"Get somethin' to eat. And stay in your room. Hurry it up. Buster not in the best mood today." She rubbed her ribs and walked away.

This time I remembered to grab a cola to go with my sandwich and a glass of water for later.

This time he made it past my door during the middle of the night.

CHAPTER 6

How does a singularity expand or multiply itself? Mirror imaging. At some point, close to the center, is overlap, where it's possible to perceive both. But, at that point, which is which? And does it matter? The original can break the mirror and remain intact. But both are of the one.

No need to look in a clear segment of the cracked bathroom mirror over the sink to know my eyes are swollen from not going back to sleep after *he* finished with me. From crying until I got up to take my bath at four thirty-eight. Don't want to see what I look like. Just want to remember who I am, on my own. Or, at least, who I was. But I feel *her* disappearing so look anyway. Make sure I'm still there.

After *he* left me, I lay still for awhile then got up and shut my door. Didn't matter if I locked it anymore, but there was still enough of my *selfness* left inside me that I locked it anyway.

Anything that feels solid does so due to magnetic repulsion. Repulsion keeps atoms from merging.

My repulsion for *him* has gone way past Pluto. Way past Andromeda, even.

I washed and washed myself down there, trying to get clean. Crying as quietly as I could, while I watched the red coming from me thin out in the water and spiral down the drain.

All that soap and scrubbing, and I still felt dirty.

He touched me everywhere before he put his finger where he'd put it before. Then he put it in that other place down there.

If I could kill him, I would. Set me free. Set my mama free. Only, she'd find another one just like him, or worse. Maybe she'd wait a week to replace him. Or a few days, like she did for *him*.

I want to escape from here in the worst way. But I'm stuck.

Quiet as a caterpillar, I left the bathroom and started for my room. Buster's snores stopped me. Infuriated me. I tip-toed into the kitchen and wrapped my hand around the handle of the biggest knife we had. Hoped it was big enough. Sharp enough. That I was strong enough.

Halfway to Mama's bedroom, I stopped. There'd be consequences if I succeeded in killing him. There'd be worse ones if I didn't. He'd grab that knife and … The mental images caused me to break out in a sweat. I put the knife back and got dressed.

Can't get out of here fast enough this morning. Can't move fast, either. Walking strange, like a duck, maybe. Does my mama hurt like this every time?

Extra toilet paper wadded in my underwear, sandwiches in the new small brown paper bag, arms straining from all the books, I left earlier than usual. It'll take me longer to make it to school since I'm moving so slow.

Early-morning darkness wrapped around me. Even small as I am, it doesn't hide me. Nothing can. No one will. I'm stained, and I wonder if everyone who looks at me will see it too. Like a neon light flashing over my head:

Dirty girl.

More feelings than I know what to do with flutter like moths inside my lit-up brain. I'm furious with myself for not at least wounding him in his genitals or cutting *IT* off. And his offensive finger. I'm angry because I'm too small to defend myself against him. Oddly, these things also heap humiliation on top of what I already feel.

Dirty girl.

Weak girl.

Scaredy-cat.

Whose only weapon are words *he* can't even understand, so they're wasted on him.

I don't want to speak the language of abuse, but there are some determined to teach it to me.

Not a test I want to pass.

Or take.

CHAPTER 7

Trips to the bathroom before every class. Have to change the wadded toilet paper every hour. The bleeding is slowing. Finally.

In Mr. Sanchez's class, I shift in the hard wooden chair attached to my desk for about the hundredth time. Feel the tears straining against my eyelids. I. Will. Not. Cry.

Mr. Sanchez called on me. I kept my head down and shook it.

Please leave me alone.

He said, "I know you know this, Katherine."

I dropped my forehead to my arms folded on my desk.

"Are you feeling bad, Katherine?"

I nodded a few times.

Feeling bad.

Feeling pain.

Feeling icky where I shouldn't.

Feeling a scream stuck in my throat, pushing against my teeth to get out past my lips.

Mr. Sanchez left me alone after that.

Or so I thought.

Five minutes till three, if the clock's right. Last class of the day. At three the bell will ring. I'm already shaking.

Every kid in my class is ready for that loud jangle to split the silence or still the teacher's voice. I'm so tired from working as hard as I did to act as normal as I could all day. But, I don't want to go home.

My teacher's talking but I'm not listening. Couldn't hear much more than the ache all day long, inside and out. Ms. Antoine stopped talking mid-sentence. Classmates' heads turned to look at the door, so I turned mine too. Ms. Green was standing inside the room, to the left of the door.

She held up a hand. "Sorry to disturb."

"You need me for something?" Ms. Antoine asked her.

"Waiting to see Katherine Barnes."

All heads swiveled to look at me. I nearly choked on my saliva from swallowing so hard. I folded my hands together and stared at my fingers. Last thing I want is more tests. Don't even want compliments.

Don't want attention.

From anyone.

Just let me disappear.

I flinched when the bell screamed.

Ms. Green walked to my desk. "Let's get your books and go to my classroom."

She took half, the heavier ones.

I needed to go to the bathroom, but I'd wait till she'd said whatever.

In her classroom, Ms. Green motioned for me to sit at a desk. I did. She closed the door and sat in the desk next to me. Almost made me smile to see her do that. There's something funny about an adult squeezing into a child-size desk. But the corners of my lips have forgotten how to tilt up.

"Mr. Sanchez said you weren't feeling well today."

"Yes, ma'am."

"Did you see the school nurse?"

"No, ma'am."

"She's still here. Would you like me to go with you?"

"No, ma'am. I need to go on home."

"I understand. You'd rather let your mother take care of you."

My chin nearly touched my chest. I nodded once. *Liar, liar. Pants on fire.*

"Did your mother tell you I spoke with her?"

Nod.

"Did she say anything about what we discussed?"

I gave a shrug followed by a nod.

"Let's go. I'm taking you home."

I jerked my head up. "No. I mean, you don't need to do that."

"Need and want are two different things, Katherine. I'll help you carry your books to my car. I'm not letting you walk home while you don't feel well."

If you imagine I was silent all the way, you're right. So was Ms. Green. I peeked at her once. Wished I could read her thoughts. Because her expression was like a blank mask with a whole lot of something going on under it.

She also must have looked up where I lived. She didn't ask for directions even once.

Ms. Green eased her car into a slot and turned off the engine. I thought she wanted to talk to me some more, but she didn't. Instead, she grabbed half my books and started to get out.

"I can go the rest of the way by myself," I said.

"I want to talk to your mother."

"I don't think she's home."

"Let's find out."

The tremors started deep inside me and worked their way to my muscles and skin. Sweat sprouted all over my body. One look at her face told me there was no point in trying to change her mind.

At least the elevator worked. Subtract at least that much from my humiliation. Nothing could subtract anything from my fear.

Ms. Green knocked on the door. Like a visitor. No one came to the door, but we could hear voices from the other side. Ms. Green knocked harder and longer.

He flung the door open. Half. Naked. His *flagpole* pressed against the fabric of his too-tight, not-so-white underwear.

Just let me die. Right here. Right now.

At the dead silence that lingered several seconds, my mother got up from the sofa. One arm tried and failed to cover her breasts, while, with her other hand, she adjusted her panties. "What goin' on, Buster?"

"Little Katie brought me a present." He looked Ms. Green up and down, licked his lips. "Unh-huh. You a fine piece." He licked his lips again and cackled in that disgusting way of his.

I gagged.

Ms. Green snapped her spine straight and her chin out. "I'd like to speak to Mrs. Barnes."

"Ask me real nice."

Ms. Green stared him down and said, "Mrs. Barnes? May I speak with you? Please."

Mama said, "Just let me get my robe."

He looked back over his shoulder and said, "Stay where you at." Returning his ugly face to Ms. Green he said, "She busy now. Takin' care of me."

"Katherine isn't feeling well. She needs her mother to look after her."

He finally looked at me. "Well, now. Maybe Little Katie got a fever or something. Maybe I need to use my special thermometer and check it."

I ducked behind Ms. Green.

Ms. Green reached around and held onto my arm. "Maybe the best thing, since you and her mother are otherwise *occupied*, is for Katherine to come home with me tonight."

He stepped out and grabbed me. Most of my books fell from my arms. Holding onto me, he kicked my books into the apartment. "She ain't goin' nowhere but where I tell her."

"Mister—whoever you are, it's inappropriate for Katherine to go in there with the two of you doing what you're doing right out in the open."

He shoved me inside. I fell over my books and onto the filthy linoleum. "Not like she ain't used to it." He sneered and stroked his sweaty bare chest. "Girl gotta learn sometime, even one young as her."

"This is unacceptable behavior."

He slammed the door in Ms. Green's face. I bolted for my room.

CHAPTER 8

"Knock, knock."

"Who's there?"

"Gettin."

"Gettin' who?"

"Gettin' you outta here."

A social worker, accompanied by Ms. Green and an armed policeman, showed up at the apartment. I was both terrified and relieved to see them, having been kept prisoner in my room for a week.

During those seven days, when *he* passed out after *doing my mother*—his words for it—or after inhaling a lot of beers, or both, my mother would sneak a sandwich and a cola or water to me. She'd also stand watch while I ran to the bathroom to do my business. And that was only when he was snoring loud enough to rattle window panes.

What I don't know is what she did when he came to my room each night. Nor do I ever, EVER, want to tell anyone what he did to me during that time. Or what he made me do to him.

Ms. Green found me in my room, curled in a ball on my bed, covers pulled over my head.

"Katherine, get your things together. You're leaving this hellhole."

She started gathering my books scattered across the floor, scattered when he'd flung them off my bed when he came in the prior night for one of his, what he called, playtimes.

"Do you have a suitcase?"

"No, ma'am."

Ms. Green looked around my room. "We need something to put your things in."

Mr. Johnston was right. Those giant plastic trash bags *are* good for something besides keeping everything but your feet dry in the rain.

I shoved clothes and stuff into that bag faster than I'd ever moved before, not that I had much to shove. Ms. Green stayed to help me, both of us cringing from time to time, at the raised voices and vulgar things being said by *him* in the other room.

"The items you placed on your bed, is that everything?" Ms. Green asked.

"Everything I want to take with me."

She wrinkled her nose. "It's not my intention to be rude, but your room smells like someone's been sick in it. More than once."

I stuffed a shirt into the plastic bag. "Sorry. That was me. But I stopped noticing the odor. Read once that's called olfactory desensitization."

She stared at me with an unreadable expression for about two heartbeats then said, "You continually surprise me."

I tried to smile, failed, and looked around to see if I'd missed anything.

"Not a day passed," Ms. Green said, "that I wasn't worried out of my mind about you. Even though I pushed heaven and h—everyone— to get the paperwork done, it felt like forever. Everything had to be legal, you understand."

"Yes, ma'am. Thank you."

Ms. Green tried to hug me. Much as I wanted her to, I'd been touched too much lately.

She pulled her arms back. Her eyes watered up. "Katherine, do you need to see a doctor?"

"No, ma'am. I'll be okay. I just need some sleep."

"And food, if how you look is … Well, nevermind that for now." She hefted my bag into her arms and went out of my room ahead of me.

I loaded my books into my arms and left my room without a glance back. What was there for me to look at? No gazing back longingly for me, like in some of the novels I'd read. They could set my room on fire, as far as I cared, starting with the bed.

As soon as I entered the living room, my mother started wailing and reaching for me. "Not my baby. Don't take my baby."

He was sitting in his filthy underwear, cross-armed on the sofa, with the policeman standing no more than two feet away. The policeman wore a scowl that would've made me pee my pants, had it been aimed at me.

Ms. Green put herself in front of me. "Katherine cannot stay here."

Hands fisted on her hips, my mama said, "Katherine Eris Barnes. You tell this *Ms. Thing* that you don't wanna leave yo' mama."

"Try to take care of yourself, Mama." Against my will, my eyes slid to where *he* was. The look he gave me. Made me shiver through and through.

Ms. Green gently propelled me toward the door.

"Katherine Eris Barnes," Mama screamed, "you get yo' damn scrawny ass back here."

Mama shouted other things, but they're not fit to repeat. My face burned at the names she called Ms. Green, who kept her head high and proud.

I waited for tears to come when I heard the door close behind me, but I was dry as the packed, grass-less ground in front of the building.

Our single-file parade headed for the elevator—social worker, me, Ms. Green, policeman.

I kept my eyes open as the elevator door slid shut. Didn't know where I was going, but it had to be better than where I'd been.

CHAPTER 9

Mama stood, arms folded, outside the school entrance the following Wednesday. One side of her face was swollen. There were scratches on her hands and arms. I was pretty sure her legs were scratched, but they were covered by pants I'd never seen before.

"Mama, you look beat up."

"I'm fine. You look okay, baby. You been treated okay?"

"Yes, ma'am."

She grabbed my shoulder and walked me, fast, to the right, past the buses. A taxi waited at the exit end of the curved driveway. I peeked inside. The meter was running.

"You came in a taxi?"

"And we leavin' in it."

"Are you taking me to my foster home?"

"Get in, Katherine. We talk about it later." She took hold of my arms, put her face close to mine and said in a lowered voice, "Probably best you don't say nothin' 'bout nothin' till we get where we goin'. You follow me?" She tilted her head toward the driver.

"I understand. Where're we going, Mama?"

"Someplace better."

Mama opened the back door and I slid in, struggling to keep my books from falling. A small somewhat battered suitcase filled the space on the floorboard, where my feet should have gone. I started to ask her about it, but she shook her head. I clamped my mouth shut and wondered what was going on.

What seemed forever later, the taxi pulled up in front of the bus station. Mama got out so I could. Then she reached over and got the suitcase. The driver got out, opened the trunk, and pulled out a larger suitcase. Mama handed him a ten-dollar bill and told him to keep the change.

Once he was back in the taxi, I asked, "Mama, where'd you get that money?"

"There's a toilet on the bus, but let's go here, while we can."

"Where're you taking me?"

"Just tol' you. The bathroom."

I shifted my books to my left side. Mama sighed and took half of them as I took the smaller suitcase she handed to me, before following her inside. After the bathroom, we got something to eat and drink for right then, and a lot more somethings for on the bus.

As I finished off a ham sandwich, I asked, "Are you ever going to tell me where we're going?"

"Far enough so's no one can find us. Not that anybody gonna look."

"Don't we need tickets?"

Mama clutched her *new* used purse to her chest and said, "Already got 'em."

We'd picked plastic seats in a corner far from the front door. Mama's eyes watched every entrance. I caught her tension like a contagion. We sat there, looking like escapees from prison, until our bus was called.

We stood in line to hand over our suitcases. My heart thumped a little faster at the smell of the fuel and the rumble of the bus engine. Eagerness to follow other passengers into the open door at the front washed over me. I wondered where *they* were going. Wondered how many of them were also running away. And from what.

We settled into the last seat, near the toilet. My nose crinkled at the odor. I wanted to ask Mama if we could sit closer to the front, but she'd shrunk down in her seat by the window, eyes fixed just above the rim, watching everyone and everything. I don't think she took a real breath until the bus driver closed the door and pulled onto the street.

"Gonna be a long ride, Katherine. Might as well settle in."

"Can I sit by the window?"

Mama lifted me onto her lap, wrapped her arms around me, and rested her head against the back of mine. It took probably five minutes for me to relax into that alien position. I tried to remember the last time she'd shown me any affection but gave it up.

We stayed just as we were, and quiet, until we crossed out of Illinois into Wisconsin. I didn't want to break the spell we both seemed to be under, but I had a question inside me ready to burst like an over-stretched balloon.

"What happened, Mama?" She stiffened a moment, and I was sorry I'd asked.

"Nobody gonna steal my child from me. Enough been taken from both of us. Enough been given away. Enough." She rested back against the seat, arms tight around me.

I relaxed against her, my head tucked under her chin, and patted her hand. "Thank you, Mama."

"Happy birthday, baby."

I'd forgotten.

Her silent tears spilled onto my hair and scalp.

I didn't mind at all.

CHAPTER 10

At first I pointed and jabbered about what all I saw, but Mama wasn't as excited as I was, so I kept my thoughts to myself. Then a different thought came to me. "I don't have any clothes but what I have on."

"What you think is in them suitcases?"

"You went to my foster home to get them?"

"Didn't want to take nothin' from what was. Went to Goodwill and got us all new clothes and shoes."

Mouth hanging open, I looked at her, but she wouldn't look at me. "Where'd you get the money? You already cashed your check for this month."

She snickered. "Acted like I didn't know where Buster keep his cash. Acted like I didn't care. That gold chain he wear? Real gold. He stole it off someone. I stole it off him." She grinned at me. "Got a lot for it too."

I smiled back. "He's going to be mad as heck."

Her smile disappeared. "He owe me." She looked away. "He owe you too."

I went back to watching the world grow bigger outside our window. Watched the light change, the sunset blaze its rainbow pallet over fields, and the first stars come into view. Fell asleep in Mama's arms, but found myself in the seat next to her when the sun poked me awake.

We were on that bus nearly two days, and Mama still wouldn't tell me exactly where we were going. It wasn't that I minded traveling, especially as it was my first time, but I looked forward to getting off the bus.

Mama sat up straight. "We here."

I pressed my nose to the glass as we passed a large stone with words etched deep into it—*Welcome to Independence Point*. That wasn't the name of the town, though the thought of independence made me giddy. We'd landed at a place called Coeur d'Alene. That's in Idaho. The panhandle part, judging by the map inside the bus station.

I traced my finger around the outline of the state. "How'd you pick this place?"

"You ever play Pin the Tail on the Donkey?"

"No, ma'am."

"Hunh. Anyways, I shut my eyes, turned in a circle, stuck out my finger." She touched the town's name on the map. "That's where my finger went."

"We don't—didn't—have any maps at home."

"What's it matter where I found one?"

"What did *he* say when you told him you were leaving?"

"I told him nothin'. Child, yo' mama might not act like she got much sense, but I wasn't always like I been. Day they took you from me, I knew if I didn't do somethin', I'd lose you for good."

My chin quivered. "You wanted me?"

Mama leaned down and cupped my chin in her hand.

"Didn't know how much, till you was gone and I didn't know when I'd ever see you again." She stood up straight. "Buster backhanded me for cryin' like I did. Told me if I wanted somethin' to cry 'bout, he give it to me. Sonabitch did. I couldn't give him nothin' like what he give me, but I figured a way."

"What are we going to do here?"

"First, we find us a place to live. Even if we have to stay in a motel, we have enough to last awhile, till we get you into a school and me a job."

My eyebrows raised nearly to my hairline. "What can you do, Mama?"

"I figure on getting me a housekeepin' job."

My mouth hung open for about three seconds then I said, "*You're going to clean?*"

"Forget what been, Katherine. We got us a fresh start."

I followed Mama outside the terminal. She beamed at the blue sky dotted with clouds and said, "Whatever happen before this very second be forgotten."

I don't know whose memory I inherited, but it wasn't hers.

CHAPTER 11

"My name Sally Barnes. This my daughter. Katherine Eris Barnes. She eleven now. Smart, too. You test her. See if she ain't one of the smartest in this school. That lady out there don't believe me. Said I had to take it up with you."

The principal looked from my mother to me. I gave him an extra-bright smile. Because it was the first time Mama had ever bragged about me.

He shifted his stern expression to one of infinite patience. "Please, both of you, have a seat. Your daughter belongs in the fifth grade, Mrs. Barnes."

"She say she bored in them classes."

He fixed his eyes on me over his wire-frame glasses. "Katherine, is that how you feel?"

I nodded enthusiastically. "Yes, sir."

"And you believe that if we test you, we'll discover a reason to advance you to a higher grade? You believe your intelligence is high enough?"

"Plato said we all begin in ignorance. That we don't know what we don't know. Then we move into opinion, which is where some people get stuck, whether that's in the right opinion or the wrong one. If people can move past opinion, they enter into reason. Through preparation they move, or can move, into intelligence."

The principal stared at me but said nothing, so I kept going, believing he needed more convincing. "He also said there's no guarantee about this. That we have to achieve this fourth level on our own, what he called the level of heightened understanding. He didn't specifically label it wisdom, but that's what I'd call that state of mind and being. I'm not saying I'm wise, but one day I want to be."

Mama smiled at me then nodded once at him, and said, "Unh-huh. What'd I say?"

The principal's mouth hung open about a half inch as he stared at me from behind lenses that needed cleaning. He cleared his throat. "Yes. Well. I'll arrange for a variety of tests. Can you be here on Saturday?"

I looked at Mama.

"She be here. We both be here."

And that's how I ended up in an eighth grade class, with kids looking more grown up, because they were. There was one Native American kid in my class, but aside from him and me, everyone's faces were shades of white. Plus, I was the only kid whose clothes, though clean and neat, hadn't caught up with the latest fashions. So much for blending in.

Life was good for a while, calmer. My classes kept me interested. Classmates were polite, but not overly friendly. I think that's because I was more an anomaly than anything else. An unknown, for the most part, and they weren't as curious about me as I was about them.

Mama found us a furnished one-bedroom garage apartment to rent, about a half mile from my school and almost a mile from the resort where she got a job in housekeeping. The school bus picked me up, but Mama had to walk to work. That is, until the bus driver found out and let Mama ride in the front seat. In the afternoon, I'd get on the bus with the rest of the kids, but would be the last to get off. That's because he'd then drive to the resort to pick Mama up after her shift was over. Mama would sit in the first seat on the right side of the bus so they could look at each other and talk. And laugh. And flirt.

His name was Karl. Mama's boyfriend number one in the new place.

Karl didn't only like women his age. He liked them my age too.

Fists on hips, Mama said, "You a little liar. Karl got no interest in a little thing like you. Why you want to mess things up for me like that?"

"You're the one who left me alone with him while you walked to the store. Besides, you obviously don't know him all that well."

"Been with him a month. Long enough to know enough."

"You've known *me* longer."

"What you want me to do?"

"Get rid of him."

"He drive you to school and keep me from walkin' to work and back. What you want me to do about that?"

"You still have a lot of Buster's money left, don't you?"

"Hangin' onto it. Case somethin' come up."

"Something *has* come up, Mama. You'll walk to work and I'll walk to school, until you find a used car." I thought about what I'd said. "Do you drive?"

"Been awhile. Gonna have to get me a Idaho license." She glanced out the window. "Seem it be easier to do that, and drive, here than the city."

"I didn't know."

Mama sniffed. "Lot you don't know 'bout me."

"Maybe I know more than I should." I hung my head when she glared at me. We both knew what I meant.

"I still say you lyin' 'bout Karl."

"Either he goes or I get myself placed in a foster home again. But this time, I'll ask that they make it forever. And far away."

Mama dropped onto the sofa in our small living room. "Always somethin'. Life ever gonna treat me right?"

I sat in the chair next to the sofa and watched Mama think things through. The fact is, I didn't want to leave her. She needed me as much as I needed her. But I needed her to take care of me better than she had before, especially as she seemed about to repeat her same mistakes all over again.

"We're all we have, Mama. You see that, don't you?"

"We need a man with us. Keep us safe."

"That hasn't worked out so far."

"Just have to find a good man. That's all."

I shook my head. "No, we don't."

"I got needs. You don't understand. You too young."

"In case you forgot, my education about *that* is way ahead of most kids my age."

"Don't you sass me. I don't need yo' backtalk on top of all this."

"And I don't need Karl taking up where Buster left off."

Mama leaned forward, elbows on knees, her face in her hands. "Don't know what to tell him."

"Tell him you're sick down there or something."

Mama peeked at me from between her fingers then sat up straight and sighed. "Good as anything else, I suppose."

CHAPTER 12

Mama got rid of Karl that day, an Idaho license the next day, and a small used car within the week. She bought it from someone on staff at the resort. Late afternoons, when the weather was good, she drove us to one of the local beaches. Only, it wasn't a beach like Lake Michigan back in Chicago, just the sandy shore of one of the many lakes there, but way smaller.

The first time we got into the water, I said, "Does it feel any different to you to be 2,180 feet above sea level? It makes the bottom of my feet tingle whenever I think about being that high above other places."

Mama looked at me funny and shook her head. "The things you come up with."

"Does it?"

"Only thing feel different is all these trees everywhere. Lake where we come from, nothin' block the view."

"I like the forests surrounding us here. It's like being a baby bird in a huge nest, only green instead of brown."

"Leave it to you. C'mon. We gotta go to the store before we go home."

"Can't we stay a little longer?"

"Maybe next time."

I wrapped my towel around my waist the same as Mama did hers. We pulled into the parking space in front of the store. Mama started to get out. I said, "Don't you want to put your shirt back on?"

"Not till my suit dry."

"But—"

"People used to it here."

We were in the store about five minutes when I realized why Mama had left her shirt off. His name was Anthony.

Tall, attractive, I suppose. And stacking fruit into bins, retrieved from cardboard boxes on a wheelie cart.

Mama straightened her posture and smiled at him. "How you doin' today, Anthony?"

"Well, well, Sally. Nice to see you again. Who's this with you?"

Mama introduced me. I bit my lower lip and stood halfway behind her.

"She shy," Mama said.

Anthony made that sound people make when trying to suck something loose that's stuck between teeth. "Nothin' wrong with shy. Looks good on a woman."

Only Anthony wasn't looking at me or Mama's "shy." His attention was fixated on her breasts. I must have been looking elsewhere when she'd pulled her suit lower in the front. Another half inch and her nipples would be all the way out.

He picked up two honeydew melons, weighed them in his hands, talked to Mama's breasts. "I'd say these about right. Yes, ma'am. Nice and ripe." He raised his eyes to hers. "Sweet and juicy, too, from what I can see."

Mama giggled. I rolled my eyes so hard they hurt.

Anthony put the melons back in the box and shifted his attention from Mama's bosom to me. "You like hamburgers, Katherine?"

I shrugged. First time I'd had one was after we'd moved here. Mama would get the restaurant at the resort to make them up, along with fries, for our dinner. She alternated burgers and fries with grilled cheese and fries. Until she learned how to make spaghetti with meatballs, and until Karl had brought fried chicken home so often, we got sick of it. I could go a couple of years without wanting any again.

"What about hot fudge sundaes?" Anthony asked.

I looked at Mama. I couldn't remember ever having one, so didn't know if I liked them or not.

"Tell you what," he said, "how about I pick you lovely ladies up at six? I'll take you to this place where people on roller skates deliver your burgers to your car. You'd like that, wouldn't you?"

Mama answered for me. "She would. That's real nice of you, Anthony. Isn't that nice, Katherine?"

I shrugged then nodded since Mama was glaring at me.

Here we go again.

CHAPTER 13

One month later, I started sleeping on the sofa every night because Anthony took my spot in Mama's bed. At least he closed the door when they were alone in the bedroom. It almost didn't matter, considering how loud they got when they were *at it*.

Seconds after the bedroom door closed, and even in the middle of the night when they went at it again, I'd climb down the stairs and walk out far enough in the yard, until I couldn't hear them anymore. Then I'd sit and wait for them to get it over with. This wasn't a problem as long as the weather was nice. When it wasn't, it was fingers in my ears, pillows over my head, for usually an hour or more. I had bags under my eyes from lack of sleep.

How they carried on was annoying, but at least he left me alone. Plus, Mama went to bed smiling and woke up the same way every morning. It was such a change in her face and personality from when we'd lived in Chicago, I didn't want to complain. Okay, I wanted to, but I clamped my mouth shut whenever I thought about doing it.

Anthony was nice enough. He brought groceries home all the time. Even taught Mama how to cook. Sometimes I wondered if he stole them from the store because he brought so many. I didn't know how much they paid a person to stack fruit and vegetables, but my days of eating mostly sandwiches were over.

He also put an end to Mama's slovenly housekeeping. Before he moved in, if I didn't tidy and clean the apartment, it didn't get done. Mama said cleaning was all she did all day at work, so didn't have the energy for it at home. Anthony made it clear from the start that clean and orderly was the only way he'd stay.

One Saturday morning, after he'd been with us two months, Mama was mopping the floor. Anthony grabbed the mop from her and said, "This is the way I like it done." He demonstrated his technique for about twenty seconds then shoved the mop at Mama. "Do it the way I like it."

I'd stopped, polishing cloth in hand, to watch this exchange. Mama's expression was a mystery to me, but obviously not to Anthony.

He pulled Mama to him. "Do it right and I'll …" He whispered something in her ear.

Mama laughed and went after that floor with more energy than I'd seen her use in a long time. For cleaning, anyway. I stayed outside for two hours that night.

Anthony got off work at five-thirty on weekdays. Mama got off at four. Every day, at four thirty on the dot, he'd call and tell Mama what he wanted for dinner. One day we were outside washing the car. We had the radio on and were singing loud and dancing hard, so didn't hear the phone. Neither of us thought anything about missing his call.

"What you want for dinner?" she asked me.

"Spaghetti with meatballs." One of my favorites, but not one Anthony had ever requested. Until Anthony, it was really the only thing Mama knew how to cook well. I guess I owed him for getting Mama cooking in the kitchen.

Five forty-five, Anthony came stomping up the stairs. He opened the door with enough force that the doorknob dented the wall. "When I call, you answer."

"We were washing the car and didn't hear it ring," Mama said. "Dinner's ready. Why don't you wash up. I'll get you a beer."

Anthony stood in the doorway, nostrils flaring. He looked from Mama to me then stormed into the bathroom. I closed the only door in or out of our apartment and ran my fingers over the indention in the wall.

All through dinner, Anthony pouted like a baby. Didn't open his jaws to talk, not until a speck of sauce from the spaghetti I slurped into my mouth landed on the table.

Anthony put his fork down. "Katherine, get the sponge and wipe up your mess."

Mama cut into a meatball with her fork. "Let her finish eatin'. That sauce ain't botherin' nothin'."

"Now, Katherine."

I glanced at Mama, who tilted her head toward the kitchen. Sponge in hand, I wiped up the pinhead-size dot of sauce and sat down.

"Put the sponge back where it belongs."

I sighed, grabbed the sponge, and marched into the kitchen.

"Be sure to wash it with soap, rinse it well, and wring it dry. Then you can come back and finish."

Anthony watched me until I was back in my chair.

"Don't ever cook this again," he said. "Not until Katherine's able to eat it without making a mess."

Later that night, I lay in the dark, remembering something I'd read in my favorite book, which I'd forgotten under my mattress in Chicago:

Part of the beauty of a crystal is its mathematical order. Through the study of this structure, and other similar ones, we begin to grasp the cosmic order.

Anthony was all about order. And about giving them. I'd also read there's order in chaos.

So far, in my experience, I haven't seen a lot of beauty or order inside the chaos.

CHAPTER 14

I suppose Anthony saw us as too disorganized for his delicate sensibilities. He wrote up a task list and schedule for Mama and me, and taped it to the refrigerator.

I put my finger on the portion under my name, which he'd filled with tasks to be done between six and eight o'clock. "But I always do my homework at that time. Right after we eat. Chores when I get home, dinner, homework."

"You'll do it after your chores are done."

"I'm supposed to be in bed by nine. Bath at eight thirty, bed by nine. At least until I'm thirteen. Adequate sleep is necessary for someone my age." I didn't bother informing him that he and Mama were already costing me enough sleep.

"You'll do what's on there, until I say different."

He had Mama and me cleaning every day until he called at four thirty, and Mama had better answer that phone on the first ring. Not me. Mama. While she got dinner ready, I did all kinds of chores that had to be done just so, and completed by the time he walked in the door. He had more rules than I imagined could be thought up.

We woke when he wanted us to wake.

We cleaned the way he wanted things cleaned.

Mama cooked the foods he wanted to eat, and how and when he wanted to eat them.

We went to the beach when he took us, and Mama had to wear a shirt buttoned almost to the top over the very breasts she'd used to entice him to begin with. He said they were for his eyes and only his.

Mama had to shower with him and scrub his back. That word, *scrub*, is a euphemism, of course, for what they really got up to. There was never any hot water left for me by the time they got out. Even with that, they still kept me up at night.

It didn't take long before Mama stopped smiling.

Until *that* day.

When everything began to change again.

CHAPTER 15

My skin was hot. The sand was hotter. The water looked inviting. Not that I'd learned to swim yet, I just wanted to splash around a little and cool off. Plus, sitting with Grumpy was annoying me. "Mama, can I walk down the shore a ways."

Mama looked over at Anthony. He nodded once.

"Come with me, Mama."

She sought Anthony's approval again and got it.

I held her hand as we walked. Sometimes skipping as she strolled on the other side of me. It took a while, but Mama finally relaxed some. She was sweating, so unbuttoned her shirt but didn't take it off.

We were playing in the shallow water, splashing each other, and a bright yellow tennis ball landed between us. A furry red puppy wagged his tail as he caught the ball in his mouth. He stuck his rear in the air, wagging it and his tail in a fury, waiting for me to play with him. I grabbed the ball, still between his teeth, and let go as soon as he growled.

A deep voice said, "He won't bite. That growl doesn't mean a thing, except an invitation to play tug-of-war while the ball's still in his mouth."

Mama and I turned to face the man who'd spoken. He was friendly looking and wore a grin that made me grin right back, even though part of me didn't want to encourage him.

He said, "Give her the ball, Irish."

"That's his name?" I asked.

"For good reason, don't you think?" At my puzzled expression, he said, "He's an Irish setter."

Irish dropped the ball onto the sand and stuck his rear in the air again, tail going like a windshield wiper on high speed. He'd bared his teeth, but not in a mean way. I hadn't been around dogs before, so didn't know they could smile.

I tossed the ball and watched Irish bound into the water, snap up the ball then paddle and scamper back to me. I did this for I don't know how long, while Mama talked with the man. Only time I stopped was when Mama laughed. It was a sound she hadn't made in awhile and deserved a moment to be observed. Like something sacred.

The moment didn't last.

Anthony joined us, with our towels and things packed up. "It's time to go," he said. "Katherine, get out of the water."

Mama gestured to the dog's owner and said, "Anthony, this is—"

"I said it's time to go. Katherine, get out. Now."

We trudged to the car in silence. Halfway home, Mama said, "Katherine was having fun. You coulda let her be a few more minutes."

Anthony gripped the steering wheel. "You spoiled it for her."

"I didn't do nothin'."

"You unbuttoned your shirt while you talked to that man."

"I was hot."

"Yeah, and I saw for who."

"I unbuttoned it long time before he show up."

"How do you know him?"

"Don't know him. Was just bein' polite while Katherine played with his dog."

"Nothin' but a bitch in heat."

"Why you gotta be like that? I ain't give you no reason."

They argued all the way home, up the stairs, and after the door was closed. There wasn't a room they didn't shout at each other in. Then Mama told him she was tired of his bossy shit.

That's when Anthony revealed just how much of a fuse looking for a match he was.

That's when he backhanded her.

I expected her to cower and apologize, as she'd always done before, but she hit him back. And it wasn't any half-hearted slap either.

His fist smacked into her jaw and she went down. I ran at him, jumped on his back. Screamed and pulled his hair. Anthony scooped me around to the front of him. I kicked and howled as he hauled me to the sofa and threw me down. Gave me a smack across my face that made me go cross-eyed.

Mama ran at him like a yowling banshee. But he was bigger. Stronger. Tables and chairs got shoved out of place, toppled over. Fragile things crashed to the floor. Mama's face and clothes were spattered with her blood. She told him to get out. He slugged her abdomen. Hard. Then her jaw again, even harder.

Mama crumpled to the floor and didn't get up.

Anthony stood over her, puffing out breaths, fists balled and ready. He kicked her thigh with his foot and she didn't move or moan or anything.

"Clean up this mess, Katherine. When I come back, I want to see everything straightened up and shining."

As soon as I heard his car engine start, I ran to the window to make sure he left. I rushed to Mama and called and called her name, but she didn't answer me. I dialed nine-one-one.

"What is your emergency?"

"My mama's boyfriend just beat her bad. She's not moving. I can't get her to move or answer me or anything."

"Is your mother's boyfriend still in the house with you?"

"He left. But he said he's coming back."

"What's your name?"

"Katherine Barnes."

"Okay, Katherine. I'm going to stay on the line with you. Tell me your address so I can send an ambulance to help you and your mother."

The woman on the phone kept me busy checking vital signs as best I could and asking me questions like how old I was and what grade was I in—things like that—while I waited for help. The ambulance arrived about a minute after two policemen did.

I rode in the ambulance with Mama, more scared than I'd ever been in my life. More scared than when Buster had bothered me. The EMT tending to Mama handed me an ice pack for my face. I held Mama's limp hand and watched everything he did to her. Watched her eyelids. Willed them to open. They didn't.

The police followed us because they had more questions, and I was the only one who could answer them. They also took pictures of me and Mama. It took a lot of fussing and crying and explaining that

Mama was all I had and I wasn't going to leave her side, no matter what, and that I was sick and damn tired of people ordering me around. I figured using a curse word would let them know I meant business. The doctor tending Mama finally told everybody they were doing more harm than helping.

I had to use everything I knew to convince them to let me stay at the hospital rather than put me in a children's shelter. I didn't care if Mama was still unconscious, I Was Not Leaving Her.

And I was right to do that. Because I was the first person Mama saw when she opened her eyes three days later. I sobbed like a baby when the doctor told me Mama was going to be okay. No permanent damage, he told us.

The doctor must have called the police because they showed up to talk to Mama about an hour later. They'd had other officers go to the apartment the day *it* had happened, who'd arrested Anthony when he returned. They told us they had him "cooling off" in jail. Said they'd left him there until they knew if Mama wanted to press charges.

Maybe it was my still-swollen face, lips, and black eye. Or maybe it was her learning three days she'd never get back had gone by that caused her to say yes.

After everyone cleared the room, I climbed onto the bed and curled up next to Mama. She put her arm without the I.V. around me, and we lay there in silence for a while.

She sighed. "Guess I'm single again."

"We do all right when it's just us. Don't we, Mama?"

"Guess we'll have to."

Two days later, we returned to our apartment. Mama went from room to room, looking at the damage. She marched into the kitchen and ripped Anthony's schedule from the refrigerator. Ripped that poster into shreds and tossed the scraps into the garbage pail.

"Katherine, you straighten things up just enough." She said this as she walked toward the bedroom.

"Are you going to take a nap, Mama?"

"Been asleep too long as it is."

I started righting furniture and stopped when I heard her grunting and cursing. "What are you doing? The doctor said to take it easy for a few days."

"This *is* easy. Gettin' everything ever belong to Anthony outta here."

It sounded good to me.

Had it been winter, the blaze in the barrel out back, where we turned Anthony's clothes and other possessions into ash, would have been great to warm our hands by. Maybe even roast marshmallows. I'd read how people did that.

One day, maybe I'd even taste one.

CHAPTER 16

A few months later, while I was at school, Mama was in the county courtroom, testifying well enough to get Anthony sentenced to prison for five years. It seems it isn't only bad to do what he did to my mama, but also to me.

She picked me up after school that day. We went to the beach and ate spaghetti and meatballs from a plastic container, until our bellies bulged and we couldn't move.

A dog barked. We looked to our left. Irish and his owner were down the shoreline, playing with the tennis ball.

I glanced at Mama.

She watched him a moment then faced the water and said, "*Hmph.*"

I exhaled in relief. The man seemed nice enough and all, but I'd learned that's no guarantee about anything.

Maybe Mama was going to stay single, at least for a while.

Maybe I wasn't the only one getting an education.

***

The next day we had a history test. The day after that we got them back. I earned an A+. Even though I detest history, I can memorize well enough. That subject wasn't ever going to come close to being as thrilling as geometry or my health studies, but I wanted good grades. I had plans for my life, plans where grades mattered.

Abigail Wright sits to my left in history class. She's whiter than white, except for the freckles competing for space, and has red hair and green eyes. I heard her sniffling and peeked over at her. She ran a hand under her leaky nose and sniffed some more. I glanced at her score marked in red at the top of her test. She'd gotten a D-.

The bell rang. Lunchtime. I usually sat alone. So did Abigail. Seems some people get weird about red hair almost as much as some do about skin color. I got my tray and asked if I could sit with her, and did from that day on.

You can't sit at the same table, and next to someone during class, and not start talking. One thing led to the next, and soon I was helping Abigail with her studies. She didn't seem to mind at all that I was a couple years younger. Or that I didn't have breasts yet. Or my period. We had something that bridged that age and physical-differences gap: Friendship. My first ever.

It wasn't until she told me her father, also divorced from her mother and mostly out of her life, had been in and out of jail that I confessed that, as far as I knew, mine was still locked up. That brought us even closer together. She told me her mother goes in and out of relationships with men who abuse her, either with their fists, with their words, or both. Yet another way we bonded. I'd traveled this many miles to finally have a friend, one whose life was so like mine, I very nearly found it uncanny.

She lived on the next block from mine. But we usually visited and studied at my apartment, since it was less chaotic.

The one thing Abigail didn't seem to need to confess about her life was the one thing I didn't admit to her about mine. It wasn't that I wanted to keep a secret so important from her. It was that I was afraid she'd see me as tainted. Or just as awful, would pity me.

Abigail asked lots of questions about our history teacher, Mrs. Peterson, who was pregnant. I'd seen pregnant women, of course, but never so close that I could watch them expand over time right before my eyes. After class one day, I was talking with Mrs. Peterson when her baby stretched inside her. She had on a thin knit dress, and I clearly saw a foot stick out toward me. I was fascinated. She smiled at my response, but boy, did she blush.

I checked out the best book in the library about pregnancy, which caused the librarian to look at me askance. But only for a moment. She'd gotten used to the headier books I preferred to read.

Abigail and I poured over the pages. She frequently went even paler than usual over the facts and photographs, but I was intrigued. I also had a long list of questions to ask Mrs. Peterson on Monday.

Only, she wasn't there. Some tall, skinny man with dark curly hair and a thick black mustache stood behind her desk instead. My first substitute teacher ever. Mr. Stevens.

My hand shot up.

"Name, please."

"Katherine Barnes."

"Ah. The so-said prodigy. What's your question?"

"What's wrong with Mrs. Peterson?"

"I already stated it was a complication with her pregnancy."

"Yes, but, specifically, what kind of complication?"

"You wouldn't understand."

"I might."

He snorted and said, "Okay. It's pre-eclampsia. As I said, you won't understand."

I tilted my head to the left, as though that would help me recall facts better. "It *is* her first pregnancy, but what a shame. I noticed Friday that she was swollen. Since edema frequently occurs during pregnancy, I didn't think anything of it. And, perhaps what I took to be embarrassment actually indicated high blood pressure. I hope they began treatment in time, so she doesn't have seizures, or any organs begin to dysfunction. It could lead to death. I'm certain one of the first things they did was check protein levels in her urine. Then gave her aspirin and calcium, and any other medications she might need."

You could have heard an army of ants tromp across the room.

I glanced around. Classmates stared at me with their mouths hanging open. All except Abigail, who was grinning.

Mr. Stevens stared at me for a couple of seconds as well, though it seemed like a lot longer.

"Yes, well, that was informative. Perhaps a little more than the class needed to know, but informative."

My cheeks grew hot. I aimed my eyes at my closed history book centered on my desk.

Mr. Stevens droned on about a lot of long-dead people and events I didn't give a hoot about. I guess he realized how disinterested I was because he said my name loudly. I snapped to attention.

"Is it the subject or me you find less than enthralling?"

"Your presentation is fine, Mr. Stevens. It's the subject. I don't see how what happened all that time ago has anything to do with me right now."

He gave me a mini-lecture, which I pretended to listen to. But it was the last thing he said, just before the bell rang, that gnawed at me:

"Katherine, those who forget the past are doomed to repeat it."

I let him get away with that because he was partly right. But my experience with my mother, and Abigail's experience with hers, demonstrated what was wrong with his statement. A person's past may leave scars on their skin or bones, and they may remember every second of how the scars got there, but that's no guarantee the person won't repeat mistakes.

No need to forget the past in order to repeat it. Just a lack of will not to.

CHAPTER 17

As Mr. Stevens' comment stayed with me, I decided to check out the history section in the library. It was bigger than I thought it should be. That indicated there must be something to it. Otherwise, why would so many authors spend so much time getting degrees in history and writing so many books about it? Maybe some people felt about history the way I did about geometry and health.

Still, I found history books as dry as an old sponge. It wasn't until I moved a few feet to the right, to the Greek mythology section, that my interest got tweaked.

I thought Abigail's mama and mine caused problems. But they were nothing compared to Pandora, who opened a jar and released evil into the world. And the silly woman didn't put the lid back until the only thing left inside was Hope. What was she thinking? After all that mischief, why leave Hope bottled up?

Okay, so maybe it was a myth. But it was pretty obvious to me what the inventor of that story thought about women. Considering what I'd seen men do, the myth's author should have looked in the mirror. Or gotten out more. All he had to do was look around to see who caused most, if not all, of the world's troubles.

This didn't dissuade me from reading about Roman law. That bunch considered and treated women the same as children. Inferior to men. *Hunh*. Not in my experience, limited as it may be. I kept reading to see if any of those men ever woke up and got some sense.

Facts I read were intriguing but sometimes led to disappointment. Like Plato, for instance. I'd always admired him *so much*. But I came across something he said, that if I could bump into him in a public square, you can bet I'd set him straight about it. He said that "knowledge under compulsion obtains no hold on the mind." He was dead wrong. I'd gained knowledge under compulsion, and repulsion, from Buster, Karl, and Anthony, and it darn sure had a hold on my mind.

And what about that Saint Jerome? "Woman is the gate of the devil, the path of wickedness, the sting of the serpent, in a word, a perilous object." Dog poop! Buster, Karl, and Anthony had proven him wrong about that.

I told Abigail what Saint Jerome said. I expected her to agree with my opinion about the statement and him. You'll never guess what she said instead.

She got serious and whispered, "When I started having my periods, my grandmother told me tampons are the devil's fingers."

That made me stop breathing for a moment. I'd never thought to stick the label of Satan on Buster, but it fit. At least the other bozos in my mama's life had never gone as far as he'd dared.

Abigail tilted her head and stared at me. "What?"

Shrugging, I said, "Just pondering what your grandmother said."

My interest in this cultural stuff grew. I read about cultures that made women obedient to men. Made women walk behind them. Like I'd want to watch some guy's buttocks all the time. *Pul-lease.*

Women couldn't own property. How stupid is that? In some cultures, a widow couldn't remarry. I have to say, after a little over a decade with my mother, I sort of agreed with that one.

Then I read about this guy named Thomas Aquinas who said woman was "created to be man's helpmeet, but her unique role is in conception." What made all these guys so backward in their thinking?

Abigail has cramps with her period. She always looks like she's going to puke the first day. She holds her stomach and moans and tells me how much it hurts.

The first time she had a period after we became friends, I told her, "I don't ever want mine."

"You have to have them if you want a baby."

"I know. But still …"

"Besides, it's practice."

"For what?"

"Having a baby hurts like a thousand times more." In response to my expression of disbelief, she added, "My mom told me. She said I hurt her so bad it nearly killed her."

"I knew there were contractions, but I never associated that level of pain with them."

"Didn't your mom ever tell you about when you were born?"

"Everything I know about that comes from books."

"Your mother *never* talks about this stuff?"

I shook my head.

"My mom talks about it all the time. Never lets me forget it."

No way would I tell Abigail that my mama was the last person I wanted to discuss any of this with. Not after all I'd witnessed her doing with Buster.

As for that Aquinas guy, let him conceive and have contractions just once, and I bet he'd change his opinion. He wouldn't be so eager to make women go through that, like a baby-machine or something. That is, if he had any sense.

One thing was crystal clear to me.

Men weren't better than women, just cagier. They'd made sure they got the better deal.

And hung onto it.

CHAPTER 18

Surely there had to be civilizations where women were in charge, and I was determined to find out what and where they were. Maybe even live there one day.

I read about the Mosuo in China. Men handled the political roles, but women were the head of the house, over their extended family that lived with them. Property was inherited through the matriarchal lines, and women made the business decisions. Children were raised with their mothers, which made me wonder where the fathers lived. Children also took their mothers' last names, rather than their fathers'. That didn't concern me either way.

My mama was the head of our house by default, though who knew how long that might last. Put a man in her bed, and she abdicated that role, and common sense, in a heartbeat. And although she was improving—because she had to—I couldn't exactly see her making any major business decisions. I still had to help her with our money and budget.

The ways of the Mosuo sounded terrific. Until I got to the part about their free-love sexuality stuff. Send Buster to them for a week. They'd change their minds in a hurry. That or kill him.

There was a slight semblance of this way of life among the Akans in the Gold and Ivory Coast areas, but that was mostly about inheritance. And men still ran pretty much everything else.

The Bribri in Costa Rica and northern Panama seemed to split their roles. Some things were for women only, like determining which clan children belonged to, inheritance—again, and some sacred ceremony where only women prepared a cacao drink they used. Bribri men were the shamans who touched the dead—they can keep that one, sang the funeral songs, and prepared funeral foods. I couldn't help notice they didn't put men in charge of anything to do with the living. Guess they figured out that one a long time ago. Less harm caused that way.

Still, everything I read about these groups said they thrived. I guess with years and years of practice, those women believed in themselves. But it didn't make me want to go to any of these places, as I'd hoped. If I were interested in anthropology, maybe. But I'm not. I've already had to study human nature way more than I would have liked.

At least there were a few places on the planet that understood women and men were equal, but not nearly enough of them. Made me wonder why women had put up with this nonsense for so long, passing it down from generation to generation.

Made me wonder what the world would be like if the tables were turned.

And whether there was a way for me to accomplish this.

Two quotes I'd read in my favorite, left-behind book came to mind. The first was by J. J. Van der Leeuw. "The real mystery of life is not a problem to be solved, it is a reality to be experienced."

The other was attributed as a motto of Mary, Queen of Scots. "In my end is my beginning."

A flash of insight came to me. I knew what I wanted to do with my life. Had to do with it.

I'd make men pay for their sins in a way that would really get their attention.

I just had to figure out precisely what that way was.

CHAPTER 19

Mama managed to stay single longer than I thought she could or would. She didn't seem too bothered by this, which, I admit, surprised me. One day, while she was out and I was home, I figured out why. I found *it* under her mattress when I put clean sheets on her bed. I say *her bed* because after she got back from the hospital when Anthony beat her, she said it was time I slept on the sofa so that we sort of had our own rooms. I think this had more to do with *it* than anything else. I'd seen enough of Buster's to figure out what *it* was and where *it* went.

As soon as I turned the hideous thing on, I dropped it. Held my breath when I picked it up, shut it off, and stuck it back where I'd found it. The nasty thing sent shudders all through me, even while I washed my hands three times with hot water and soap.

But I still didn't understand why she needed it. Nor was I going to tell her I knew what she kept hidden under her mattress. At least now I understood where the buzzing I'd heard at night came from. I'd thought it was an insect trapped inside.

I'd gotten my period three months after I'd turned twelve. And my breasts. And hips. And attention I didn't want from boys. Abigail didn't share my feelings about that. She couldn't wait to start dating and did. Fifteen and dating. If I ever decide to date, it'll be when I'm ninety and the man is too old to bother me about sexual things.

However, I listened intently as Abigail described her dates to me. Information is information. Knowledge is power and all that. But I still didn't tell her about my experiences, no matter how much she insisted she enjoyed what she called doing stuff without going all the way.

Abigail and I were closer than ever, which is why I let her convince me to use tampons. She said if I didn't, she'd never go to the beach with me again. Sure enough, the next time we went to the beach, I started. I wasn't expecting it, and the only thing Abigail had with her was—you guessed it.

It was a production for her to instruct me as to how to insert it. I thought I did a good job of getting it where it belonged, even though it felt funny when I walked. The darn thing expanded seconds after the water reached over my waist. My eyes nearly bulged out of their sockets. I wanted to go home. Abigail had more than one with her and insisted I go through the entire humiliating experience all over again. Thank goodness I learn fast.

Then things changed somewhat. Abigail, being a couple of years older than me, and way more interested in sex, got serious with a senior. She got married right after we graduated. I was her maid of honor. At first, I was afraid I might lose my only friend, but that didn't happen. Abigail regaled me with the intimate details of the physical side of their relationship. She almost made me curious enough to find out for myself what it was like, when it was with someone you wanted to do it with.

Almost.

Since I was fifteen, and even though I was eager to further my education, I decided to wait a year before going to college. Besides, I needed money. That meant applying for scholarships, grants, and such, and waiting for approval. I got a job as a check-out clerk at the same store where Anthony had worked. I also learned that he hadn't behaved in prison, so had his time inside extended. That was a huge relief. The last thing I wanted was for him to show up one day, looking to get his old job back. Or looking for Mama and me.

I received a full scholarship, though decided to find a way to supplement the funds as best I could. Equally satisfying was that I'd been accepted at Stanford for my undergraduate degree in molecular biology. That meant I had to leave Mama in Idaho, but I was close enough to visit her during semester breaks, without travel costing too much.

I'd taken an entrance exam provided for students who wished to accelerate their studies, so as not to have to start from scratch. I aced it and started with the second-year courses.

With all the changes involved, surprisingly, the one that rocked me the most, initially, was my introduction to computers. I had to teach myself, at warp speed, how to type, as well as how to not lose any of my documents or blow the darn thing up by hitting the wrong key.

And there was Heather, my dorm roommate. All five-foot-nine buxom-blond inches of her. Because she was all of nineteen and I was seventeen, she believed she was superior or supposed to boss me somewhat. It was also a case of extrovert meets introvert, the latter being me. I decided not to complain about how much she talked or how often she had friends coming in and out of our room, for one reason: she had a phone installed and let me use it without having to pay for my calls to Mama and Abigail.

Neither of us had to worry about borrowing each other's clothes or shoes, not that she, obviously well off, would want to adorn her gorgeous self with my bargain-store pickings, no matter how nice they were. And although I'd developed some curves, nothing of hers would have fit my petite five-foot-two form.

There was another factor in her favor. Heather wasn't in the least curious about my life before Stanford, or at all, which was a relief. Ask me no questions, I'll tell you no lies.

The Thanksgiving holiday approached during the first semester of my relished foray into the world of molecular biology. I decided to use this break to comb through the shelves of books on this topic in the library so I could be as informed as possible. I waited until Heather was out socializing before I called Mama and disappointed her.

"It's okay, Katherine. If you need to stay there for the holiday, I understand."

"I'm sorry, Mama. It'll be our first Thanksgiving apart. But I've already arranged to be home with you during December break. No way will I miss Christmas at home. I won't let you spend it alone, and we'll have more time."

"Still, if you can't make it then either, that's okay."

"I'll be there."

"But if you can't, if there's something else you want to do, or if you have to study ..."

"Mama, you don't sound like you're feeling well. You're usually so energized when we talk. Are you okay?"

"Just tired. Gotta lot of overtime goin' on."

Mama changed the subject and ended the call not long after.

***

I'd found a student with a car, who'd be driving near enough to Coeur d'Alene to drop me off for Christmas break. The day before we left, I called Mama every hour, until eleven o'clock that night, and never got an answer. She knew I was arriving the next day, so I figured she was busy with preparations, and had probably been invited to a Christmas party. That, or the resort needed her help with holiday festivities. She had mentioned working overtime.

I started to call her at the resort, but we'd always said calls interrupting her at work were for emergencies only. Better to just show up than scare her half to death. She could tell me all about whatever she was up to, once I got there. I'd even help out at the resort for no pay if it meant spending more time together.

I missed her so much, I seriously considered sitting in her lap with my arms around her neck, as we'd done on the bus trip to our new life in Idaho. And cuddled like that, we'd gab and gab until the wee hours of the night.

The image was so delicious it took hours before I fell asleep.

CHAPTER 20

I told my ride, "The white two-story with green shutters, there on the right. Just pull up in front of the house. Right here is perfect." I grabbed the overnight bag, bought at Goodwill, from the backseat. "I'll be waiting here at the time and day we agreed. If you think you'll run late, you have my number."

"Call me if anything comes up for you," he said.

I'd had him drop me off in front of the landlord's house. I shouldn't have been embarrassed about the garage apartment, but I was. Let him, and others he might tell, believe I sprouted forth from a middle-class family. What business was it of anyone's what the truth was. During the drive, I'd listened to Marcus talk about his family's magnificent horses he'd ride while visiting his folks, the skiing time on the slopes they planned on getting in, and all the other things people with money do for the holidays. I got creative with my own stories—I lied.

I pretended to walk toward the front door of Mr. Hopkins' house until Marcus disappeared around the next corner. Mama's car was parked in front of the garage apartment. I was disappointed her nose wasn't pressed to the front window, eagerly watching for my arrival. Or flying down the stairs to welcome me home—we'd just spent our longest time apart. Two reasons for that not happening came to mind: she was either in the bathroom or in the kitchen, making sure the spaghetti sauce and meatballs didn't burn.

Only, that's exactly what I smelled when I opened the ground-level door to the wooden stairwell.

CHAPTER 21

I started to knock then decided it was best to let Mama stay in the kitchen and attempt to salvage our burnt dinner.

My key didn't work. She hadn't mentioned anything about changing the lock, or why she might need to. I pounded on the door and shouted for her. I placed my fists on my hips and affixed a false disapproving expression on my face. When she opened that door, I'd pretend to fuss at her for burning my favorite meal, which I figured happened in her excitement—meals tended to burn when Mama's mind was full. Then I'd wrap her in a bear hug, see what I could do to repair the sauce, and then wrap her in a bunch of bear hugs.

She didn't come to the door.

The odor grew worse.

I pounded again and shouted some more.

Nothing.

I dashed down the stairs and ran straight to Mr. Hopkins' back door. I pounded and pounded, but he didn't answer. Then I realized the garage door was open and his car was gone. I ran back to the apartment, and only because I was feeling temporarily insane, did I pound on our door and shout for Mama again.

I'd always resented the cheap, hollow door Mr. Hopkins had used, but now I was grateful. I left my overnight bag by the door and hurried down the stairs. I slipped and slid down several steps, ignored the pain, and rushed to Mama's trunk to get the tire iron. It was a fight to get the key into the lock, because of how uncontrollably my hands shook. I grabbed the tire iron and rushed back up the stairs.

I beat the door with the tool until I created a big enough hole, close enough to the knob, to reach in and unlock it. I picked up a few splinters and cuts on my arm but didn't care, because smoke poured through the hole and began to fill the stairwell.

Coughing like crazy, I flew to the living room windows and threw each one of them open all the way. Rushed to the kitchen. Turned the stove off. Stuck the smoking pot of blackened sauce in the sink. I opened the window above the sink to let the smoke out, waving at it with a dishcloth, all the while choking. Had Mama fallen asleep in the tub again? Had the smoke gotten to her?

I wet the dishcloth and held it over my nose and mouth. Smoke stung my eyes and made them leak. The bathroom door was open, the tub empty. That window got thrown open, as well.

The same was done in the bedroom. Certain I'd find her in there, unconscious from smoke inhalation, I looked around. No sign of her. But something had happened in that room. The bed was shoved to the side and positioned at an angle. The lamp lay in fragments on the floor. The smashed nightstand the small lamp belonged on was across the room. Items from Mama's dresser were either tipped on their sides or on the floor.

My mouth and throat went dry. My pulse raced even faster.

I returned to the living room and looked around. Most of the smoke had cleared. Furniture and furnishings were scattered and broken in there as well.

"Mama?"

A response came in the form of a moan. I dropped to all fours and raked my eyes around the room.

She lay sprawled on the floor, between the dining table and the back wall. I stumbled trying to get to my feet but finally made it to her, believing I could drag her outside, into fresh, cold air that would revive her.

That's when what had started out as a bad dream became my worst nightmare.

Mama's face was battered beyond recognition. The shattered ulna of her right arm protruded from broken skin. Her skirt was puddled around her waist. Her ripped panties were bunched into a tiny clump a yard or so away. Blood smeared her thighs. Other odors mingled with the acrid smell of the smoke and burned sauce. I vomited, wiped my face with the dishcloth and turned back to Mama.

Her eyes were closed. I knew enough to understand that meant she was still alive.

I fell to my knees at her side, grabbed her shoulder. She thrashed, as though fighting her assailant away.

Stunned, I let go of her. "Mama, it's me. It's Katherine. Who did this to you?"

Mama seemed beyond comprehension. I was losing her and didn't know what to do. "No! Don't do this. I'll get help. Hang on, Mama."

I stumbled to the phone and placed the call. Like before, the person who answered wanted me to stay on the phone, but I hung up and returned to sit by Mama. To talk to her. To convince her to stay with me.

"You've healed before. I'll help you. I'll contact my advisor and tell her I need to skip a semester or two. Longer, if I have to. I'm already a year ahead. My grades are too good for them to balk. I'll stay with you. So you see, you have to stay with me."

Mama's swollen eyelids fluttered open into slits. What I could see of her eyes met mine then she went still. A breath, her last one, left her. Her gaze stayed fixed on me but unseeing.

"No, Mama. No." I attempted CPR, but the first time I pressed on her chest, broken ribs snapped even more beneath my hands. I ran to the door. Where the hell was the ambulance? Where were the police?

I returned to Mama and collapsed beside her, my throat so constricted I couldn't breathe. Then screams, followed by wounded wails, ripped from my throat. Sounds I had no idea I could make. Sounds nature intended as a call for help, so others came running to the person's aid. No one came.

Ignoring streaming tears, I gently raised Mama's shoulders and held her against me and rocked back and forth. "You can't leave me like this, Mama. No ma'am, you cannot leave me. It's Christmas. Your present is in my bag. We have plans, and you leaving me isn't one of them. We have so much catching up to do. I'll go to the store and get more stuff for sauce and meatballs. I'll cook. It'll all be fine, Mama. Do you hear me?"

Mama didn't answer.

Mama didn't come back to me.

I don't know how long I stayed like that, clinging to her, soaking her with my tears, but I finally, gently, put her back on the floor. I stroked her face and kissed her forehead. And talked to her. Again, for I don't know how long. Time had stopped. Everything had stopped. Except the pain and hollow sensation that overwhelmed me like a dark, ravenous shadow.

A siren sounded, faint at first, then grew louder as it approached. Enough common sense came back to me, to realize our apartment was about to become a crime scene. Forensics would comb through every inch of the place. I found Mama's vibrator under the mattress and stuck it at the bottom of my bag.

Then I returned to Mama, held her hand with the fewest broken fingers, talked to her, wept so hard it choked me. And waited. Wondering who the hell had done this to her.

I was furious with myself for not knowing what to do to help her, certain there had to have been something I could have done to keep her alive.

Words of Buckminster Fuller came to me. "The wave is not the water. The water merely told us about the wave moving by."

I'd been hit by a wave, the undertow too much to bear.

And I was drowning.

***

Abigail had a spare room, so I stayed with her while the police went through the apartment for forensic purposes. Then it would have to be professionally cleaned, and Mr. Hopkins would have to install a new door. I'd debated about whether or not to keep the apartment, and decided I would, at least for a while. It was only $250 a month. I made that, and more, writing papers for students.

I insisted on knowing the results of the autopsy:

Death a result of intracerebral hemorrhage due to physical trauma.

No surprise about that conclusion.

But they should have added, Death also caused by unskilled daughter who doesn't know as much as she thinks she does.

What was a surprise were the drugs in her system. Marijuana, cocaine, amphetamines. Mama hadn't been high on life, as I'd thought.

The other surprise discovery, my second, was the presence of semen in her vagina. And elsewhere.

The police questioned me. "Who was your mother in a relationship with?"

"She didn't tell me she was seeing anyone, much less in a relationship."

"So, you'd say you and your mother weren't close."

"I thought we were."

"When'd you last speak to her?"

"Two days before I came home. I called repeatedly the day before I left, but she didn't answer."

"And she didn't say anything about a boyfriend? Didn't mention company joining you two for Christmas dinner or anything?"

"Nothing at all. Only that she would fix spaghetti and meatballs. She knows it's my favorite."

And that's when the interview had to stop for almost a half hour.

Once I regained my composure, I explained about Mama's history of choosing abusive men. "It's as though they have radar tuned to the same frequency. Or a heightened sense of smell that allows them to sniff each other out in a crowd."

"She'd had a number of such relationships, all abusive?"

"I thought she'd gotten better about that. She let me believe she preferred being single."

"What about the drugs? Had she always been a user?"

"I don't know anything about them." It was obvious they didn't believe me. "I swear on her life that I had no idea."

"What about you?"

"What about me?"

"You use?"

"I have too much respect for the human body to go anywhere near that poison. I've never taken as much as a sip of anything alcoholic either. I've seen what these chemicals do to people's faculties and organs. I have a good mind and big plans. I'm not about to fry or overstimulate or alter my brain in any way. Is that clear enough for you? *I didn't know she was using anything.* And she didn't tell me, because she knew how I would have reacted."

They bothered me for another hour then let me go. The next day, they contacted me to say Mama's body could be released. The forensic coroner had finished with her.

Finished with her. They'd forget about her soon. I wanted to envy them that luxury.

I had no idea what I was supposed to do. Or how I'd pay for it. With Abigail and her husband's help, funds from my own account, and a couple hundred dollars contributed by Mr. Hopkins, we managed a Potter's field-type burial, even though that service was typically reserved for unknown or indigent individuals. It was a pitiful turnout at the grave, with only me, Abigail, her husband, Mr. Hopkins, and two employees from the resort who stayed for the prayer then left.

I checked with the detective working the investigation every day, including the day after the funeral, to see if they had a suspect. They'd interviewed Mr. Hopkins and nearby neighbors to see if anyone had seen or heard anything—no one had. Exasperation in his voice, he informed me that combing through the numerous fingerprints found there would take a while.

"What do you mean by 'numerous fingerprints'?"

"Not quite Grand Central Station. But she weren't no recluse either. Look, Miss Barnes, we'll contact you if we have anything to report."

"Don't you mean when?"

"Sure. That's what I meant. Got another call coming in." He hung up.

What had Mama been up to?

CHAPTER 22

Plautus said, "Nothing is more wretched than the mind of a man conscious of guilt." He nailed that one.

I wallowed in "if only's." If only I hadn't received the full scholarship to Stanford. If only I hadn't had such lofty goals. If only I'd gotten a job and stayed with Mama. If only I'd found a community college closer to home. If only I'd convinced Mama to move near my school. There were more. There always are.

The one "if only" I couldn't beat myself up about was my attempt to get Mama to recognize her poor choices in men. Because I *had* tried. Often. I was the one who persuaded her that she didn't need a man. Or thought I had. That she needed to focus on herself and her life.

But that's not where she came from. She believed she needed a man in order to feel or be complete, though I think *feel* is the word that fits best. She didn't believe in herself. Didn't feel about herself the way she craved, so looked to men to give her that feeling, as though it could never come from within. A fallacy, of course. Self-esteem has always been an inside job. How often had I told that to her, especially after I'd left home, hoping it would sink in?

I could say it was because she was raised in an abusive home, so didn't know any better. The truth is, she never talked about her parents, had no photos of them, and I never met them, so have no concept of what her environment or formative years included. If she had siblings or other relatives, that was news to me. But, as the saying goes, that dog don't hunt. Look at the environment I was raised in. Perhaps some people repeat what they learned, while others, like me, run like hell to avoid it.

The only reason I could fathom for believing in myself was that my mother had taught me the opposite, by virtue of her behaviors and their consequences. What I find remarkable is how often people will move away from a bad smell in a hurry, but choose to linger in a bad relationship. Especially women.

This led me to further research, which led me into deeper guilt. Why hadn't I thought to look into this matter sooner? I could have approached Mama with facts rather than the childish edicts of, "It's him or me" and "You need to think better of yourself".

One fact stared me in the face, one so simplistic, I missed it: Mama didn't do better, because Mama didn't believe she could do better. Her "deserve" quotient was nearly on empty, if not running on fumes. She'd been willing to change, once, for my sake, but couldn't change for her own.

At the library, I looked up different reasons cited for why some women stay in such relationships.

There was fear, as in being threatened by the partner, if the woman tried to leave. I'd never heard any explicit remarks such as these from any of Mama's men. That didn't mean they weren't uttered, but perhaps they were implicit. Being so young, I may have missed that.

There was the belief that abuse was normal. I'd once read that, frequently, what we call normal is often just usual. Since I didn't know anything about Mama's family, and as she had no girlfriends whose conversations I could overhear, I had no idea what Mama believed about this. Maybe she was an eternal optimist, in her own way, and believed she'd one day find the magic formula to get the louse in her life to act right.

Leopards and spots, Mama. Leopards and spots.

If Mama was afraid of being judged by others, for repeatedly getting into abusive relationships, perhaps that was one reason she didn't seek friends or engender close ties with anyone. There was no one around to hold up a mirror, who wasn't me, that is, so she couldn't see what her life really looked like.

Avoidance goes only so far, Mama. Eventually, the beast devours you.

Verbal abuse had come with the territory, at least once the first blush of any new relationship Mama got into wore off. Perhaps she'd experienced the same while growing up, so believed any attention a man paid to her was the pathway to love and acceptance. Better negative attention than none at all. This theory had numerous, obvious flaws. If she were still alive, I'd point them out to her. Maybe make a list and tape it where she could read it every day, until her mind absorbed each one.

None of Mama's men had been especially popular. Buster did have a rep in the hood, or so he liked to proclaim. No one would have thought her crazy had she complained about mistreatment. She might have been ignored, but would have been believed.

We didn't have religion, so she didn't feel forced to stay in a bad marriage or to marry again. I'd managed to be born in wedlock, and there were no other pregnancies, at least that I knew about. That nixed Mama feeling compelled to keep the "family" together.

I read that some people stay because they don't trust the police or any similar authority to help them. Mama never even tried to ask for help from any of these people.

Nor could I buy the lack of money reason. Because, back in Chicago, Mama had everything the government could provide and turned over her welfare funds to every man she invited into our lives. She could have chosen to stay single and keep her money or find a man who worked for a living.

Then, of course, she got her first job after we moved and, with my budgetary influence, became independent, or so I believed. It may have been a meager existence, but it was a result of her efforts, for the most part.

The report said some women believed they had nowhere to go. Of course, someone finally realized there was a need for shelters, but Mama never indicated any desire to go to one with me. Only after I'd been taken by the social worker, had she found the strength to remove us from Buster hell and into our new life in Idaho.

This information answered some of my questions and left me with others. Like, how do women fall into such a trap, and so easily?

One way is what I came to refer to as the first-blush syndrome. That scenario usually plays out this way: The man dresses nice and acts nice, perhaps even respectful, on a first date or dates, like Anthony did. He reads the woman's self-esteem issues accurately—he's well practiced—and does or says whatever will get her into bed. Then the veil of illusion is yanked off. She's in the throes of an oxytocin high, bonded to the man through chemicals released during sex, and in a love relationship all by herself and doesn't know it. Only it isn't love at all. Love was never displayed by any man Mama got involved with, not even my father. As for Mama's example of it …

My best guess is that some women are so desperate for love and acceptance, or financial security, they approach dates like interviews for jobs as lifetime maids and secretaries, who'll lure men with sex, or promises of it. Since Mama's culinary and housekeeping skills were pretty much nil, and she never went for men who had extra money to spend, at least, not on her, I have to stick with the love and acceptance aspect and leave the rest out.

My research led me into the dark world of narcissistic personality disorder. Nasty stuff goes on there. Men with this disorder woo the woman, get her feeling secure and cherished, then abuse her, usually verbally, berating her until she feels utterly worthless and unable to do anything right. If she stands up for herself, he goes after her in all manner of despicable ways. If she gives in, he despises her. Either way, the abuse never stops. Until she gets as far away from his tentacles as possible, somewhere he can't reach her.

Like Idaho.

Only, there is no such place. They, or variations of them, exist everywhere.

This left the question of why, even if a woman escapes, does she continue to pick losers who will abuse her?

I had a number of assumptions and presumptions about that. But there were two things I was certain of: I'd never follow in my mother's footsteps when it came to men, and I'd make them pay for their treatment of women.

They'd gotten off too easy for too long.

CHAPTER 23

Abigail sat hunched over in the stuffed chair, her feet propped on the matching ottoman. She dipped the small brush into the bottle of bright tropical-orange polish then stroked the color onto the large toenail of her right foot. "You're being too hard on yourself," she said. "Even if you'd glued yourself to your mother's side, she'd have found a way to get involved with some man who'd treat her just like all the others."

"I could have stopped her."

"She was a grown woman. It was her choice. Whatever you're telling yourself about being able to do anything about that, stop it. Look at how I handled it with my mother. I got out of there as soon as I could. I don't bother her, she doesn't bother me. We stay out of each other's way and business, and we're both happier."

"At least you have the luxury of having a mother you can choose to ignore. Anytime you change your mind, or she does, you're only fifteen minutes or a phone call apart." I sniffled and said, "It's not fair. I'm only seventeen, and motherless. *And*, it took a lawyer, whom I'll be paying in installments for another year, to prove to the state that I don't need a legal guardian because of my age. If it hadn't been for my dean at Stanford vouching for me … It's not what I imagined for my life."

Abigail stuck the brush back in the bottle. "I'm sorry, K. I'm trying to get you to realize you didn't do this to her. You're not responsible for what happened. Any of it. And don't make it sound like you're alone in the world. You've got me. Always."

"Thanks, but that doesn't make the feeling go away, no matter how many times I, you, or others say it." I stood up and removed my keys from my jeans pocket.

"You're leaving? Why don't you stay? At least have dinner with us."

"Thanks, but I'm going home."

"Are you positive you don't want to spend tomorrow here? I hate your spending Christmas alone."

"I refuse to spoil everyone's fun. No way can I feign a celebratory mood."

"If you change your mind ..."

I gave her a weak smile. "Thanks, but don't wait for that to happen."

"Still sleeping on the sofa?"

"I can't bring myself to sleep in her bed."

"Guess the next step will be letting the apartment go. You'll return to school soon, anyway. Then, I suppose, I'll never see you."

"I haven't decided about the apartment, but we'll see each other and stay in constant contact. I'll let myself out. Don't want you to mess up your toes."

"Call me anytime you need to talk."

"I'm starting to feel talked out."

I kissed Abigail's cheek, pulled her front door closed behind me, and got into Mama's car. A quick stop at the store for a stack of TV dinners then back to the apartment.

The professional cleaners had done a good job. Still, it took a few days after Mama's funeral for me to go back there for as much as a few minutes.

It became necessary to return to the apartment sooner than I'd liked. I had to get away from the sex I tried to not listen to between Abigail and her Hubby-Buns. My tearful, morose presence cramped their newlywed style. Although they protested when I announced my departure, it was nothing more than courtesy expressed to a wounded friend, and we all knew it but were too polite to admit it.

I turned the oven on, punched holes in the cellophane as directed, and popped a chicken dinner into the oven. Tonight, I'd heat up the turkey selection. It was, after all, Christmas Eve. I'd do the same for lunch tomorrow. Normal families had turkey and dressing and cranberry sauce for their Christmas meal. Who knew?

My edification about holiday protocol and tradition, enforced by Abigail, came from politely suffering through programs provided by smiling hosts and hostesses showing how Christmas should be done.

Lavish dinners and decorations, deliriously happy family and friends seated around a table appointed with candles, a tablecloth, holly twigs with ornaments, seasonal dinnerware and linen napkins folded just so or secured with ornate napkin holders. It was all a foreign language and culture to me.

Abigail pleaded with me to help her pick out a tree and then decorate it. First time for everything, I suppose. I also suppose that under different circumstances, these activities, which felt frivolous and expensive to me, would have put me in a jolly, holly, Christmas mood, as thrust upon listeners by one of those songs playing incessantly on the radio. Abigail sang along to all of them. I didn't know the words to even one.

Christmas movies played on every channel. I forced myself to watch them. Not because that had been a tradition in my home. I watched them because it hadn't been.

I sobbed and blubbered through each movie, interspersed with occasional strings of obscenities, in an effort to diffuse some of the turmoil clamoring inside me.

When I used the last tissue in the apartment, I grabbed a notebook and pen, sat on the sofa and began a list. It wasn't a long list. But Buster's name was at the top, followed by Karl, which was followed by Anthony. Fourth on the list was a thick, dark question mark, added in case whoever had murdered my mother was someone other than one of them. As far as I knew, Anthony might have escaped from prison or arranged for a friend to go after Mama. A few other names came to mind, so I wrote them down as well.

Innocent or guilty of my mother's demise, they needed to pay.

CHAPTER 24

The police had no clue as to who had killed Mama. I felt helpless in this regard. I'd never choose to pursue a degree in criminology, but I could pursue one that would never leave me feeling as helpless as I had when I'd found Mama in the condition she'd been in.

I decided to keep the apartment. Mr. Hopkins had every right to ask me not to, but he told me as long as I paid the rent, it was mine. Said a good tenant, even an absent one, was good to find. All I had to do, he told me, was give him a month's notice if I changed my mind. At least one of his reasons for agreeing was out of compassion. I know this because every several seconds as we spoke, he'd pat me on the arm then wipe his eyes and blow his nose. So far, he's the singular being of the male species I can tolerate without any suppressed animosity.

I kept Mama's car and drove it back to Stanford, though it took my attorney, who wasn't too attached to strict adherence to legal details, to get the title transferred to my name.

A mechanic friend of Hubby-Buns checked Mama's car, making sure it was in good condition for the drive back. He put on two new tires to replace the baldest ones, and did all of this for no charge. Said it was a Christmas gift, since we'd gone to the same school. However, I suspected Abigail convinced Hubby-Buns to arrange it. Especially because I didn't remember the mechanic from school or anywhere else. Why would I? He was years older.

After I said a tearful see-you-soon to Abigail, I returned to school, determined to attain my goal, and in record time.

I've always known how to apply myself, so persuaded my advisor to approve my escalated curriculum. I completed my undergraduate degree and zipped through to my Ph.D., in as few years as possible, as valedictorian, and at twenty-one, the youngest on stage.

Months later came the MCAT test required to apply to medical school. I aced the test. Because of my perfect score and credentials, I was accepted. This led to another full scholarship at Stanford.

How could I help but wonder what Mama would have thought of this. She would have been proud of me, of course. Yet, deep down, I knew she would have also nagged me about dating, or rather, my lack of it. I was asked out. Often. And my answer remained the same. Eventually, the invites ceased, which left me content with my studies and my life.

As Stobaeus said, "The world is single and it came into being from the center outwards." It would remain as such for me. I was determined to stay single, as much as I was determined about anything else.

All the while, the seed of my ultimate goal germinated in the appropriate part of my brain.

CHAPTER 25

I began to relax once I entered medical school. I read the books, attended the classes I wanted to attend, and, as always, aced exams. This thoroughly pissed off my roommate. Jealousy personified.

Jenni had to be one of the most studious people I'd ever come across but still couldn't keep up with me. She called my approach lazy. I called it logical. Why should I sweat or strain or strive when I didn't need to? It wasn't as though I didn't apply myself as needed. But I also applied myself through hours in the library, reading about women's history, mathematics, and advances in molecular genetics.

For amusement, I engaged in long gab-chats with Abigail, the only person I considered a true friend. Abigail didn't judge me or my brain. She asked how medical school was going and laughed when I told her it was easy. That's called being loved and appreciated for who you are. And, it was reciprocal.

Abigail was like my alter-ego, enthralled with being a wife and queen of her home. So far, Hubby-Buns was disproving my assumptions about *all* men. However, even that could be a matter of time. Still, they'd been happy longer than I'd expected. Abigail said it was great sex that kept them in that state. I resigned myself to taking her word about that.

Major first-year exams are scheduled for tomorrow, in embryology and pathophysiology. I spent the early part of the evening at the library, and returned to my dorm room just before nine. I'd been looking forward to a quiet remainder of my evening and was disappointed.

Jenni had squeezed her study group into our small shared space. I gathered my favorite loungewear and toiletries as the group discussed disease states and gametes and the like. Their conversation ceased as I made my way to the bathroom for a shower. Stopped yet again when I was done in the bathroom and crossed to my side of the room. Their eyes stayed fixed on me when I curled up in bed, put headphones on, opened and began to read a book that had nothing to do with the upcoming exams.

It wasn't my intention to disrupt them with my silent lack of involvement with their cramming but that was the result. They questioned each other for another hour then disbanded for the night. Who can cram when someone who gets all A's is taking it easy no more than two yards away?

Jenni slammed her books shut, picked them up and banged them down on the corner of her desk. Walked to the side of my bed, fists on hips. "You annoy the hell out of me."

I removed my headphones. "What now?"

"You go to labs, but skip most of the lectures. I'm stuffing my brain with data, and you're acting like these exams are no big deal."

"You need to mind your own business." I recalled Abigail's tearful frustration in history class, sighed and closed my book. "Would you like me to help you study?"

Apparently not.

Jenni huffed at me, mumbled crude words and rude suggestions under her breath, and then stayed up most of the night ingesting more facts.

She woke a puffy-eyed mess in the morning. I was well rested.

I turned in my embryology exam after twenty minutes. My instructor looked at me askance then said I was dismissed. Curious as to how Jenni did, I occupied a seat in the hallway and waited, watched the clock, watched the classroom door. No one exited until the hour was over.

Jenni was one of the last people out. She glanced my way, sniffed, stuck her nose in the air and departed.

It was the same for the pathophysiology exam.

Jenni isn't speaking to me.

CHAPTER 26

Dean Broward sat at his polished desk, wire-frame glasses perched too near the end of his nose, making certain I couldn't miss his scowl. He waited for me to speak.

"Sir, this memo you sent ... I don't understand why I'm under investigation."

"You've been accused of cheating."

I strained to stay composed. "By whom?"

He waved my question away. "Your professors confirmed that you attend labs but miss their lectures."

Hmm ... Where had I heard *that* before? "I assure you, sir, I don't cheat. Nor do I need to."

"Yours is a challenging curriculum."

"Yes, sir."

"How, then, do you explain receiving perfect scores?"

"I believe I know who complained."

"Miss Barnes, that's the least of your concerns."

"Sir, I know there are some who are jealous of my accomplishments and abilities. If they spent more time minding what's theirs to mind, perhaps they'd do better."

"I don't appreciate your attitude."

"What evidence do you have that indicates I *may* have cheated?"

He shook his head. "The evidence is obvious."

"No, sir. It isn't. It's supposition driven by envy. I retain information better than many. And I hardly think I should be penalized or judged because of it."

Dean Broward glared at me, and as he did this, my mind flashed back to the first time Mama and I met the principal in Coeur d'Alene. "Test me."

"What?"

"Test me, sir. Test me in every subject we've covered, as well as those we haven't, any included in the first two years. I'll pass those exams as well. I've read all the books, and as I just said, I retain information. Let me prove that my grades are a result of my aptitude."

He studied me for a moment then sighed. "All right, Miss Barnes, you've made your case."

"Does this mean you believe me?"

"You'd have to be a fool to suggest the opportunity to prove yourself in such a manner." He pushed his glasses to the bridge of his nose, picked up his pen and aimed it at me. "However, from this moment on, you are to attend every scheduled class. I *will* verify that you follow through."

"Yes, sir. I will. Thank you, sir."

"You could lose your scholarship over this."

"I won't miss another class."

"Medicine isn't solely about what's in published tomes. We must be willing to apply what we learn. Sometimes what we have to learn is the spirit of collaboration. This means interacting with others, engaging in mutual pursuits to discover answers. It's a part of gaining experience so that, as physicians or specialists, we're more well-rounded. Unless, that is, you intend to spend your life in the solitary pursuit of research."

"I understand, sir."

"You're dismissed. Go." He waved his hand. "Go retain something."

I wondered how disappointed Jenni would be when she discovered I was still her roommate and going nowhere but up.

CHAPTER 27

His monotone voice sounded more like a lazy insect only slightly interested in arriving at his destination. "Osteoblasts create new bone and repair old ones through the extraction of calcium from blood, as well as present a bone matrix. Osteocytes maintain and repair bone substance and strength. Osteoclasts dissolve and reassemble old bone matrix material into the blood."

Sort of like, What goes around comes around, I mused as the professor rambled. It was a huge yawn for me to sit through that lecture about information I've known since I was nine. Who hired this guy or gave him tenure?

The only thing that kept me from nodding off was to sketch the cells in my notebook, all the while noting their geometry and fractal-like qualities. Simultaneously, I amused myself by recalling someone's likening these three bone cell types to Hindu deities.

There was Brahma, the Creator, which matched to osteoblasts. Vishnu, the Preserver, had been likened to osteocytes, or, rather, the other way around. That left Shiva, the Destroyer, to align with osteoclasts.

I watched the clock as the ancient professor droned on. Finally, my last class of the semester was over. Spring break had officially started. I elected to spend it at the apartment in Coeur d'Alene, which I'd decided to keep for an undetermined time. Easier to stay there, despite how emotionally wrenching it was, rather than listen to Abigail and Hubby-Buns do the deed each and every night. And morning. And on his lunch breaks.

The last time I'd visited Coeur d'Alene, it was with enough money in my account to redecorate, with Abigail's help, as decor was not an area of expertise for me. In a gesture of generosity and compassion, and prior to my visit, Mr. Hopkins had painted the previously off-white walls a shade of pale apricot.

An area rug now covers the place on the floor where Mama died. As though that makes a difference. The memory is seared into my brain. But Abigail insisted, and her point was a valid one. Although, I never step on that part of the rug or allow anyone else to.

Silly, perhaps. Or not.

With great anticipation, I headed north, eager to spend time with Abigail. She was equally excited about seeing me, especially as she had some kind of surprise for me.

Back in her car, after we'd finished eating an early dinner out my first full day there, I said, "Okay, enough. What's this big surprise?"

Abigail grinned and cranked the engine of her Toyota. "You'll see."

"You know how I feel about surprises. Few have ever been favorable."

"You'll appreciate this one. Put yourself in my capable hands. I know what's needed to get you out of this blue funk."

"I'm not in a blue funk."

"Trust me, you are."

"I suppose if anyone has a right to be in a funk—not that I agree with you—it's me."

"Yeah, but you've taken up residence there, and it's time to move on."

I let Abigail blather on about more domestic matters than I cared to hear, and didn't even question when she got onto the highway and traveled west. That is, until she kept going.

"Where are you taking us?"

"Spokane."

"I'd have been happy to go to the beach. What's in Spokane?"

"You'll see."

"Please stop saying that and just tell me."

Abigail let out a frustrated sigh. "I'm taking you to a WAM meeting. And before you ask, the letters stand for Women's Advancement Movement."

I looked at her askance. "Are you saying I need to advance in some way?"

"Oh, honey, in every way. But we'll start with this."

"What do you know about this group?"

"The name says it all—advancement for women. What else do we need to know?"

I didn't ask any more questions. I knew Abigail wouldn't or couldn't answer them to my satisfaction. She was bent on surprising me. Let her have her fun. After all, it was a meeting. And that meant it had a beginning and an end.

It was the middle that concerned me.

CHAPTER 28

We parked along the street in a mostly commercial area. Then walked back to a two-story Victorian house in pristine condition, its landscaped yard completed by a white picket fence. Up the steps we went, onto the veranda appointed with ferns and white wicker furniture. In the foyer were two women seated at a table draped with a tablecloth.

Abigail dropped an envelope into a basket positioned in front of the first woman, and said, "That's a contribution from both of us." She smiled at me. "My treat."

We moved to the next woman who handed us blank name labels and pens. We wrote our names on the adhesive labels and applied them to our blouses before entering a large room with chairs arranged in rows. A podium was centered in the bay segment at the end of the room, which I took to have been, once upon a time, a formal parlor. I followed Abigail to vacant chairs in the front row and waited.

As had Abigail, I'd assumed that a women's advancement movement was established by women devoted to crashing through glass ceilings in professional fields protected vigorously by men. My assumption was only partially correct.

At the scheduled starting time, a woman went to the podium, introduced herself as Emily Saunders, and called the meeting to order. As she spoke, her piercing blue eyes, set against ivory skin and jet-black hair that had to be dyed that shade, made eye contact with the twenty or so women in attendance. She made a few announcements then turned the podium over to women who wished to give their testimonials.

I sat riveted as several women told their stories, all the while fighting back tears. I didn't know whether I was grateful to Abigail or ready to wring her neck.

After four women spoke, Emily called a refreshment break. Abigail went to the restroom. I corralled Emily by the cookies.

She glanced quickly at my name tag. "What do you think so far, Katherine?"

"I have questions."

"Please, ask away."

"When did you start this group?"

"It's a movement."

"Same question."

"I didn't start it. Our founder is Patricia Hill, and our inception happened six years ago."

I looked around at the women in the room. "Is she here tonight?"

"Oh no. We're a satellite, so she wouldn't be here for our meetings. Headquarters is elsewhere. However, she strives to make annual appearances at each state's main satellite group, which is becoming more difficult now that we're expanding."

"Did Patricia start these meetings because she was abused? Or was her motivation compassion for women who had been?"

"It's probably best if you wait to hear her tell her story, but you may appreciate knowing she started with herself and three women."

"And relies on donations, I see."

"We always attach more value to something we pay for, hence the donations. But Patricia is wealthy and contributed substantially to initially fund our operations. She still contributes a great deal."

"How nice for her."

Emily stared at me in silence for several moments then said, "How her wealth came to her is part of her story. She's quite candid about it. She's quite candid, period." She took a bite of a sugar cookie, licked the crumbs from her lips and added, "At the very first meeting, one of those three women was still healing from chemical burns received during a domestic confrontation. Another young woman—a teen, really—was someone Patricia found living in a cardboard box behind a dumpster in an alley. She'd run away from home after being sexually abused by an uncle. No one believed her. No one protected her. His assaults didn't cease, so she ran, preferring to be homeless rather than helpless."

I didn't say anything, but Emily couldn't help but notice my breaths had quickened and that I'd looked away.

"After one year, Patricia had three hundred members. That number has catapulted to over three million members, with, roughly, ten to twenty groups in each state. She's started to expand into several countries, as well, though her goal is to have at least ten groups in every country. Ambitious, for sure, but a worthy pursuit."

Emily tilted her head and kept her unblinking eyes fixed on me. "Members are from every social, economic, and political background. I admit, though, not every member was personally abused. Some are related to or friends with women who have been. They join to help others. However, despite how long I've been involved, despite my own experiences that motivated me to get involved, I still find it stunning to realize how many women have been abused in the various forms. Do you also find it stunning, Katherine?"

I nodded.

"The thing about abused women is that they often feel alone, isolated, as though no one will understand their pain, fear, and humiliation."

"I've read enough about this to grasp what it is they feel."

She fixed her blue eyes on me. "Only read about it?"

I didn't answer, but neither did I look away this time.

"You're welcome to continue to attend our meetings." She smiled. "That is, should you wish to expand your research."

"Thanks, but I'm on spring break. I'm in medical school at Stanford."

Emily's smile stretched wide. "Then you're in luck. WAM headquarters are near your campus. Follow me."

I followed her to where she'd tucked her purse away in a kitchen cabinet. She extracted a folded sheet of paper, unfolded it and handed it to me. "Here's the location, date, and time of the next meeting. Even if you go only once, at least do it so you can meet Patricia and hear her story. She tells it at the start of each meeting for the benefit of new attendees. If you decide to go, tell her I sent you with my greetings."

I thanked her as I folded the paper and dropped it into my purse.

The last thing I was inclined to do was form some sisterhood type of relationship, much less get up and spill my guts at such a meeting.

I'd never shared the details of my experiences with anyone, not even Abigail. I wasn't about to start now.

I'd been on break a little over twenty-four hours and already it would be a relief to return to school. A relief to escape back to even the boring lectures.

Anything but wallow in this topic.

CHAPTER 29

I glanced at the three-ring binder filled with recipes Abigail had handwritten and forced on me before I returned to Stanford. The likelihood I'd ever use even one recipe was close to nil. No cooking allowed in the dorms would be my excuse if she asked, which she might, because Abigail was in town. She'd called and told me she'd driven in, gotten a room at a motel downtown, and would pick me up in thirty minutes for dinner and what she called a night on the town, whatever that meant.

I freshened up and changed clothes in the bathroom, brushed my straightened hair, and dabbed on some lip gloss.

Jenni looked up as I grabbed my purse and headed for the door. "You're going out? Let me guess. You worked on and finished your paper while you slept."

I paused with my hand on the doorknob. "I can think of no reason why the activities of my life should concern you."

"Geez. It was just a comment. No reason to get all clenched up about it. It's just unusual—make that extraordinary—for you to go out on a Friday night."

"Your point being?"

"You barely talk to me anymore, not even to insult me."

"You're the one who slings insults, and always first." I turned the knob. "I know it was you who accused me of cheating."

Jenni turned radish-red. "I would never do that." She fastened a sneer on her face. "You think too much of yourself."

"And, yet, your beta-adrenoceptors have exerted a dilator response on the basal tone of your facial cutaneous venous plexus."

Her snide expression collapsed into one of disdain. "You really think you're something special, don't you?"

"I don't think about it. However, it's apparent you do."

"Leave me the hell alone."

"I intend to, and would have done so several seconds earlier had you not interfered."

"You're such a bitch."

"Talking to your reflection again?"

I made it out of the room before the book she flung at me hit the door as I closed it behind me. Another demonstration of a penchant toward violence from her and I'd request a roommate change.

Abigail was fifteen minutes late. "Sorry, K. Buckle up. I'm starving."

"Did you decide where you want to eat?"

"I asked someone to recommend a nice place. My treat."

"You look fabulous. Not at all like someone who drove in today."

"Actually, I got in last night."

"I didn't know. I suppose you had your reasons for not telling me. You must have slept well. You look rested."

A small smile played on her lips. "There's an art to relaxing."

"And you have the art?"

"Oh yeah."

"Maybe you can share it with me."

"I intend to."

CHAPTER 30

I rested back in the passenger seat and sighed with contentment. "That steak was huge. We should go somewhere and walk it off."

"Forget walking it off. We're going to dance it off."

"You know I don't dance."

"I know you know how. I taught you."

"That was in your living room. No chance of humiliating myself there."

Abigail drove a few blocks then turned into a parking lot, which caused me to sit up straight. "This is a motel."

"It's where I'm staying."

"Oh. Okay. I can live with dancing in your room."

"Don't be silly. They have a lounge."

Abigail drove to the back of the motel and parked in a slot several spaces down from a back entrance. She pointed. "We'll go in through that door."

We entered the hallway. Abigail pointed to the first room on the left. "That's my room."

"I really don't want to go to the lounge."

"Loosen up, K. I need this." She looked back and grinned at me. "So do you. More than you know." She slowed her steps, wrapped an arm around my waist and said, "C'mon, K. Let's have at least one drink and see how you feel. Do this for me, okay?"

"If I want to leave after one drink, you'll do it?"

"Sure. But you'll change your mind. Trust me."

The music boomed and hurt my ears. People packed every square inch on the dance floor, every small table and booth, passageway, and around the bar.

Abigail shouted over the cacophony, "Follow me."

I squeezed through people as I trailed her to the bar. We found about eight inches of unoccupied space and stopped.

"What do you want?" Abigail screamed next to my ear.

"Orange juice."

"With vodka, right?"

"You know I don't drink."

"One little shot won't do anything."

"Abigail."

"All right."

Either the juice was off or the bartender ignored her. "My drink isn't right. I think there's alcohol in it."

"Relax, K."

"I'm not into these kinds of places."

"I am."

"Obviously. Are you looking for someone?"

"Why?"

"You keep looking around the room."

"Just checking out the scenery." She looked at me and rolled her eyes. "Honestly, K, you're the most uptight person I know. But I can fix that."

"In this environment? Good luck."

"I've got something better than luck." She fished around in her small purse and pulled out a small medicine bottle, no label.

"What's that?"

"Mood elevator. One pill in your drink will do the trick."

"My mood doesn't need elevating. Neither does yours."

"Honey, trust me, you have no idea what you need."

"I don't do drugs, or alcohol, and you know why."

"You sound like a broken record. *I don't do this. I don't do that.*"

Abigail plunked a pill into her drink, stirred and sipped. "See? Nothing to it." She dropped a pill into mine and gave the straw a few swirls.

"I'm not drinking that."

She puckered her lips into a pout. "You don't trust me. You're going to ruin my fun. After all these years of loyal friendship and …"

Abigail kept going until I couldn't stand it anymore. "All right. I'll sip on it." That seemed to appease her.

I'd sipped about an inch of the beverage in the tall, narrow glass when Abigail began to jump up and down in place, waving a hand in the air. At first I thought she was happy about the music then followed where her eyes were focused. Two men fought their way through the throng.

"You know them?" I asked.

"I met them here last night."

"And told them you were coming back tonight."

"I told them *we* would be here tonight."

My spine stiffened. I grabbed her arm. "How could you do this? First of all, you're happily married to Hubby-Buns. Second of all, I don't date."

"I never got that about you. I mean, what's the big deal?"

"I have my reasons. One of them being that men are disgusting."

She faced me and grabbed my arm, hard. "Don't you dare embarrass me, Katherine Barnes. I need a break from routine, and I want my best friend to enjoy it with me. Now act like a normal person for once. Can you please do that much?"

The insult crushed me. Getting it from Jenni was one thing. Getting it from Abigail was quite another.

The alcohol and, I suppose, the pill, whatever it was, were starting to take effect. I'd show her just how normal I could act. All I had to do was copy her antics.

What could possibly be difficult about that?

Easy-peasy, right?

CHAPTER 31

Abigail cheek-kissed the two men when they finally reached us. She rested her hand on the upper arm of the man with blond hair. "This is Jared. He's my dance partner tonight."

He rubbed Abigail's bottom. "Baby, we are gonna *dance* until we can't move."

She giggled and slapped his arm playfully then pointed to the other man, tall, brunette, with brown eyes focused on me a little too intently.

"This is your date, Katherine. His name's Clyde. I figured since both your names start with a hard sound, you should be together."

Jared snickered.

Clyde raised my hand and kissed the back of it. "I'm pleased to meet you, Katherine. Don't you look delicious this evening." He pulled a business card from his jacket pocket, handed it to me, and said, "In case we discover we like each other enough to get together again." He winked.

Pretend, I reminded myself. I dropped his card into my purse and attempted a giggle like Abigail's but hiccuped instead. To cover my ineptness, I plastered a grin on my face.

This wasn't as difficult as I'd imagined.

What a question—can I be normal? I can normal your derrière off, Abigail Wright.

On the dance floor, we gyrated under strobe lights that made me dizzy. Abigail let Jared grope her. She groped him in return. I decided to ignore them. That was mostly because Clyde was acting like a gentleman, making it easy for me to let the other two act stupid. Still, I wondered when this night was going to end. A person can pretend only so much and for only so long.

After six more songs, Clyde asked if I was thirsty. I nodded and asked him to get me an orange juice. He took my elbow and guided me to the bar.

It had to be bad juice or an inferior product because it tasted as bad—make that worse—than the one Abigail had gotten for me.

Clyde and I stayed at the bar until we finished our drinks then returned to the dance floor. I forgot about time. I forgot about school. Forgot that I detested everything about this environment and these people. Actually, it was more that I no longer cared. Nor could I recall why I'd objected before.

Abigail tapped me on the shoulder and motioned for me to follow her. Arms waving in the air to the music, and with Clyde's hands on my waist, I did.

The lounge doors closed behind the four of us, but the bass thumping through the door and walls like a heartbeat followed us.

"What's going on?" I asked. "Are we calling it a night?"

Abigail and Jared had their arms around each other. She said, "These nice men are going to walk us to my room."

It made sense to me. Abigail was in no condition to drive me back to my dorm. Spending the night with her was the logical thing to do.

We walked, though Abigail and I mostly staggered, along a couple of hallways. She pulled her key from her purse. Jared took it and opened the door.

I turned to tell Clyde goodbye, but Abigail pulled me into the room.

She turned on the radio and began to sway to the music. Jared clutched her to him, hands squeezing her backside, and they danced like that for several seconds. Then Abigail laughed and pushed him onto the king-size bed.

I watched, transfixed, as Abigail began to dance and remove her jewelry. She kicked off her shoes and kept going, dancing, removing one article of clothing at a time, until she was down to her bra, panties, garters and stockings. She always wore pantyhose. What was going on?

That question and others were in my mouth but couldn't make it past my lips. Confusion set in. I wanted to get out of there but my body ignored orders from my brain.

Abigail looked at me, winked and said, "Consider this an early birthday present. Enjoy it, K. Once you get into it, you'll see what you've been missing." She pushed Jared onto his back and straddled him, began to unbutton his shirt. He unhooked her bra and played with her breasts.

This was all wrong and I couldn't pinpoint why.

The room began to spin.

Clyde slipped his arm around my waist and led me to the bed. He slid my blouse over my head, unhooked my bra and tossed it to the floor. His fingers trailed over and around my nipples. He smiled and said, "Let's see how long it takes for chocolate to melt."

CHAPTER 32

Half-awake and eyes closed, I diagnosed that I must have been in an accident and my head had split open. I was sure of it, based on the pain level. I must have lain undiscovered for a long time because my tongue felt glued to my palate. I opened my eyes into slits and moaned as a streak of sunlight coming from a gap in drapes covering a window to my left hit me in the face. I slammed my eyes shut, moaned again, and wondered which hospital I'd been taken to.

Each second I lay there, another portion of my body made its condition known to me. Heaviness across my chest. Sore and sticky between my legs. Nipples and breasts, achy and tender. Something was wrong with me, but at least I was where hospital staff would take care of me. I called for anyone who might hear me but all that came out was a hoarse whisper.

I forced my eyes open. The ceiling, the drapes, the dresser and mirror across from me—all wrong. I had no clue where I was. The weight on my chest shifted. Looking down, I saw it was an arm. Hairy. Muscular.

Although it hurt, I turned my head to the left. A naked man lay snoring face-down on the bed, the back of his head to me. Panic flooded through me. In my attempt to slide from under his arm, he woke, faced me and pulled me closer. Screams came fast but faint. Despite the pain it caused, I kicked at him and beat him with my fists.

"Hey. Hey. Relax, baby. Did you wake from a bad dream? After last night, you should be purring like a kitten."

I struggled away from him and staggered to my feet.

The man propped himself up on an elbow and raked his eyes over me. "Come back to bed." He threw the covers off and stroked his erection. "I'm even better when I'm sober."

"Who are you?"

"The man who turned you on last night. Well, one of them." He studied me for a moment then grinned. "You *are* hungover. It's Clyde, baby. Now come here and give me some more of that brown sugar." He licked his lips and waggled his tongue.

My hand flew to my chest and I felt skin. I stepped back, onto something—my jeans. I grabbed them, turned, and slid them on. Holding my head I searched for the rest of my clothes. "Where am I?"

He gave me a sleazy leer and said, "No-Tell Motel." At my horrified expression, he added, "Abigail's room? Remember?"

"I don't remember anything."

He snorted. "Don't tell me you're one of *those?*"

I found my bra and put it on. "I have no idea what you mean." Found my blouse and slipped it over my head.

"One of those women who play it wild then fake amnesia."

"I'm not faking anything." I found my shoes and slid them on. "You said this is Abigail's room. Where is she?"

He shrugged. "No idea. Maybe she and Jared went to get coffee or something."

"Who's Jared?"

"Now you're really stretching it."

"I'm not stretching anything."

"That's right. You left the stretching to me." Clyde sat up in bed. His erection gave no indication of diminishing anytime soon. "Look, baby—"

"Don't call me that!"

"All right, *Katherine.* Keep your tits cool."

"You're revolting." I found my purse between the dresser and the wall.

"That's not what you thought last night."

"I told you, I don't remember anything about last night."

"Then come back to bed so I can give you something you *will* remember."

I glanced at the bathroom, desperate to use it for a number of reasons, but I was more desperate to get away. As quickly as I could manage, I moved toward the door.

"When you recover," Clyde said, "call me."

"Rot in hell." I slammed the door behind me, exited the hallway door and buckled over from searing head pain as sunlight blasted me full-on. One thing I did recall was that Abigail had parked here at the back, just not where exactly. Up and down, I scanned the rows of cars parked next to the building and at the fence line opposite this back entrance. Abigail's car was probably there, but I was in no condition to recognize it.

Body throbbing everywhere, I walked around to the front of the motel and entered the lobby, where I asked the person tending the reception desk to call a taxi for me. The clock on the wall behind the desk showed the time was 11:32. I panicked, again, when I thought I'd missed my morning classes. Then I remembered it was Saturday.

I waited inside, to the right of the double doors, out of the harsh light, and fought back tears brought on by Abigail's egregious betrayal.

CHAPTER 33

Thankfully, Jenni was absent from the dorm room. I grabbed clean pajamas, swallowed a few analgesics and two glasses of water, and stood sobbing in the shower until the water ran cold.

I caught the reflection of the upper half of my body in the mirror. There were bruises on my breasts. I checked to make sure Jenni was still out then rushed to the full-length mirror. There were bruises and finger marks everywhere.

Jenni found me curled in the fetal position in bed when she returned sometime in the afternoon.

"So, the prodigal student decided to return."

I pulled the covers over my head. "Not now."

"You've never stayed out all night before. First time for everything, I suppose. So, where did you sleep? Or, is it more like with whom?"

Lying was the only option. "My best friend was in town. I stayed with her so we could gab until the wee hours."

"That's disappointing, and, sadly, probably true. I'd hoped you'd regale me with tales of wanton lust fulfilled rather than something that dull."

"Sorry to disappoint you."

"I doubt that."

"Please tell me you're going out again, and that you're leaving soon."

"As it happens, I am. I need a sweater because *I'm* going to be out late. Only I plan to have a better time than you did."

"Good for you. And when you get back, please don't tell me anything about it."

"You're such a smartass, emphasis on ass."

"I'm very near copying you and throwing hard objects in your direction."

Jenni slammed the door right after calling me a bitch.

The phone woke me at 4:47.

"Hey, K. That was some fun we had last night. Although, Clyde said you don't remember any of it, or you're pretending you don't, and that you left in a tizzy."

"Abigail—"

"Believe me. You had a good time. I was there, remember?"

"I vaguely remember who was there but that's all."

"Damn. The whole point was for you to enjoy yourself *and* remember it. Guess I should have given you half a pill since it was your first time and all."

"Abigail—"

"Definitely should've given you just half."

"Speaking of the pills, where did you get them?"

"Jared gave them to me. I told him you were kind of on the uptight side, being a virgin and all. He said one pill in alcohol would loosen you up. Then he laughed like hell at his own joke."

I rubbed my forehead, as though that might erase the several types of pain erupting inside. "You drugged me. I can't believe you did that. To me."

"You wouldn't have relaxed if I hadn't."

"I wasn't relaxed. I was chemically altered."

"Whatever. I know you had at least one orgasm. As for me, I lost count of mine."

"I don't believe you."

"No way would I lie about that. One for you—maybe more, and who knows how many for me."

"That's not what I mean."

"Anyway, Jared and I brought coffee and breakfast back to the room. Needed some fuel for round two. Or was it round five? Anyway, we were *all* disappointed you weren't there." She laughed. "But we didn't let it affect us for long. One man is good. Two's even better. They left a few minutes ago. That Clyde is a stud. You should call him again. Go out with him a few times to get more experience then invite Jared to join you. You won't regret the attention they give you. Plus, it's way past time for you to broaden your horizons."

The ache in my head had improved slightly before the call, but Abigail's revelations about the evening, and herself, caused it to throb again. "I can't believe you set me up."

"What set-up? I test-drove each of them, and the pills, the night before. I wasn't going to pick someone unskilled for my best friend. Or for me, for that matter."

"I'm covered with bruises."

Abigail laughed. "Those aren't bruises. They're passion marks. You know, hickeys. Remember? I used to get them all the time and would tell you how they got there."

"My nipples are sore."

"That was Jared. I told him to go easy but he was excited."

My stomach lurched. "I'm sore elsewhere."

"That's the cost of being a virgin, K. Clyde didn't mind, not like some men would. But they all love it tight. You're lucky I found him."

I cupped my forehead in my hand. "You don't understand what you did to me."

"I did you a favor. A big one. And I'd think you'd express a bit more gratitude."

"The last thing I am is grateful. You had no right to use me that way." I lambasted her for another five minutes, ignoring her attempts to interject her opinions. The effort exhausted me and I stopped speaking.

"I don't get you," she said.

"Then let me help you. I was sexually assaulted and abused as a young child. Forget my giving you details. It isn't important that you know them. What is, is that you, of all people, did this to me. I thought you loved me." I would have yelled and ranted, but my head was pounding.

"You never said anything. Why didn't you ever tell me any of this?"

"I never wanted to tell anyone. It's all too humiliating and painful. In fact, you're the first person I've spilled my story to, and the only reason I did was so you'd understand what you've done. So you see, the last thing I wanted or needed was a sexual escapade. You did me no favor. In fact, quite the reverse. You've compounded my shame by degrading me in such a manner."

"Geez, K, I'm sorry. But it's your fault for not ever saying anything." She paused, waited for me to speak then said, "Look, I'm only here for one more night. Let me buy you dinner. I can fill you in on the details."

"I don't think so."

"C'mon, don't be like that."

"You deliberately drugged me. You arranged for two men—two complete strangers—to engage sexually with me, without my permission, and watched me closely enough to claim I had an orgasm. And *you* think the problem is *my* attitude?"

"Really, K, I can't believe you're so upset."

"I'm not upset, Abigail, I'm devastated. The expanse between those two emotions is so vast that I seriously doubt you could comprehend it."

"We're still best friends. Aren't we?"

I hesitated a moment then said, "I'll have to get back to you about that," and placed the receiver back in the cradle.

A different kind of friend would have asked the looming question, What about your precious Hubby-Buns? But I didn't care. That was her problem. And his. Let them figure it out.

I had too many emotions roiling inside me to deal with anyone else's stuff.

As I thought about what she'd revealed to me, and imagined the scenario in my mind, I broke into a sweat. I barely made it to the bathroom in time as my stomach began to express what I felt in a tangible manner.

CHAPTER 34

I woke mid-morning on Sunday, feeling almost myself again, physically, that is. Jenni's bed remained undisturbed, and I wondered if it was her feeble attempt to compete with me about staying out all night as well as grade-wise.

After a steaming shower, two cups of tea, three glasses of water, and sunglasses affixed to the bridge of my nose, I made my way to the cafeteria for a late and light breakfast. It was obscenely nice weather out, when it should be dismal, like my mood.

Feeling somewhat revived, I went to the library to look up cures for hangovers. More of the same of whatever you ingested or hydrating were the top contenders as remedies. I chose hydrating.

It was easy to stay in my room the remainder of the day. In bed. Downing a glass of water every hour I was awake. The sole intrusion happened when Jenni dropped by with several of her friends to get something she needed.

According to Johannes Kepler, "Nature uses as little as possible of anything." I felt justified using as little physical, emotional, and mental energy as possible.

I forced myself to sleep, anything to avoid facing what had occurred.

And what I'd lost.

During the first lecture on Monday morning, as I dug around in my purse for a pen, I found and extracted the folded paper Emily Saunders had given to me what seemed a lifetime ago. I opened it. The next WAM meeting was scheduled for Wednesday evening. Feeling like an abused woman, I decided to attend. What would be the harm in seeing what Patricia Hill had to say, I wondered.

WAM's facility turned out to be a multi-storied structure designed by an architect who believed the more turquoise glass the better. Stunning in design, it was positioned near the front of, I estimated, about fifty or so landscaped acres that included groves of trees.

A couple hundred women occupied seats in WAM's auditorium. I sat in the end seat on the last row in the middle section, in case a silent exit was needed or desired, and watched women dressed in suits, jeans, long skirts, and so on, position themselves closer to the stage.

After ten minutes or so, a tall woman with blond hair fixed into a chignon, and dressed in a tailored pantsuit, crossed the stage. She stopped behind the podium. The audience erupted in applause and cheers. The woman raised her hands to quiet them.

"My husband cheated on me repeatedly. Each time I attempted to discuss this with him, he became verbally abusive. Salt in the wound, you might say, though he didn't restrict his abuse solely to words.

"Most of you won't be surprised to hear that I stayed with him. I doubt many of you here would ask why. We all have our whys for staying in an abusive relationship. Our boundaries erode. Our self-esteem plummets. And we think that if we can just find the magic formula, we can make our world right again. That with that formula, we'll be able to fix what's broken in our partner, all the while failing to recognize that the brokenness we should be more concerned about is within us. It is, after all, the only one we can fix.

"One of the greatest shocks is to realize they didn't break us. They did, however, reveal we were already broken. Once we recognize this fact, we can begin to heal ourselves. Although, sometimes we do need support from those who understand us and our situation. But, often, it takes something specific to wake us up, to get us to move out of that degrading environment, no matter how afraid we are.

"I became pregnant. It was a high-risk pregnancy. I lost my baby. And not once did my husband demonstrate any care, concern, or even a moment's grief over the loss of our child. Was this the final straw that moved me out of that relationship?"

Most of the women yelled, "No!"

She pointed at the audience. "That's right. I stayed with him, even though his infidelity and abuse continued. I stayed where I was, as though one of my shoes had been nailed to the floor. I spun in circles but went nowhere. I stayed because I'd given up on myself. Then he did something that did wake me up. He had sex with my best friend."

Boos issued forth from the audience. So far, I was relating only minimally to the woman's story.

"Did I pack up and leave?"

Attendees who knew the routine shouted, "No."

"No. But some switch inside me flipped, a switch I'd never known existed. I decided to take revenge."

I sat up straight in my seat, ears twitching in anticipation.

"Please understand that revenge is not what I recommend, but I will always be truthful with you about my experience. Would you like to know what I did?"

When the women yelled the affirmative, I joined them.

"I set up a video camera in our bedroom, disguised, of course. Then I seduced my husband's best friend. Got him to come to my house when my husband was away on one of his supposed overnight business trips. I pulled out all the stops, as the saying goes. I wanted that recording to be as raunchy as I could make it."

What an unappealing method, I thought.

"My husband was home the next night. I put on the same sleazy outfit I'd worn for his friend and convinced him that I was willing to engage in sex games. I lured him to the bedroom, got him naked then handcuffed him to the bed. His *antenna* stood at ready attention."

All but I laughed. I cringed at the image of Clyde's "antenna," and Buster's. My stomach did a flip-flop.

"While my husband anticipated getting his jollies, I played the tape. To say he was furious would be an understatement. What I never asked him, and didn't care to ask, was which one infuriated him more—the tape or that he wasn't going to get from me what he'd expected?

"Neither did he expect what came next. I took the same belt he'd used on me and lashed him good. The fool didn't beg me to stop. Instead, he cursed at me. Called me every vile name in the dictionary.

"He screamed at me the entire time I packed my things. Threatened me over and over. But that didn't stop me from finally leaving him. And before you ask, I took the tape and destroyed it. And before you ask, I have no idea who eventually freed him from the cuffs or when. Nor did I care.

"It would have humiliated him to admit I'd beaten him, literally and figuratively, and for me to state all he'd done to me for public record, so no charges were filed. Nor did he contest the divorce. In his relief to be rid of me—and I think a bit of fear as to what I might do to him next—and his being an extremely wealthy man, he turned over half of everything, as mandated by California law, and with barely a whimper. I used some of that money to start this group and expand it around the country, as well as across the pond."

She stretched her arms out wide and said loudly into the microphone, "Ladies, welcome to WAM. My name is Patricia Hill, and like you, I'm a survivor."

I was on my feet, cheering and whooping with the rest of them. Perhaps our stories weren't the same, but she'd said two words that resonated in every cell of my being.

Survivor.

That's what I am.

She'd also said revenge.

I didn't care for her particular strategy, but the word tasted sweet in my mouth.

CHAPTER 35

What followed Patricia's testimonial was general housekeeping matters for the organization, and that was followed by several testimonials. I waited for at least one woman to tell a story similar to my childhood one but waited in vain. Later, I mentally gave myself a head slap. Why would they? They were sharing what had happened to them as women in relationships. I'd never been in one. Patricia had said they'd entered their relationships already broken. At the very least, we had that in common.

After the meeting ended, I waited until after the women who'd rushed to crowd around Patricia disappeared, before approaching her.

She glanced at my name tag and extended her hand. "Hello, Katherine. I haven't seen your face before. First time to a meeting?"

"I attended one in Spokane recently. Emily Saunders says hello."

"I'd ask how you liked it, but you're here. Do you plan to become a member?"

"What's involved?"

"Each of us contributes to making the organization better and more effective. But the most significant thing we do is support each other. We don't have set dues but do request monthly contributions, based on what each woman believes she can contribute. Some women who are better off financially contribute for those who are struggling. You see, some of the women who find their way to us are still in shelters. We help them in numerous ways, such as image makeovers when needed for a job or to help them feel better about themselves, skills training, and job placement. Do any of these appeal to you? Any chance you're in need of employment?"

I shook my head. "I'm in med school—Stanford—and I have financial means. Nothing like yours or some of the others, but enough."

"What drew you to the Spokane meeting?"

"I went with a friend."

Patricia began to gather her papers. "Want to tell me what brought you to a second meeting?"

I shrugged. "Basic curiosity. Emily recommended I hear your story."

She studied my face with her piercing gray eyes then patted my arm. "That explains it then. Walk me out?"

I stayed with her as she locked up and let her do the talking. We parted in the parking lot as we went to our separate cars.

Patricia exuded composure. She was kind. Maternal. Three things that registered as a deep thirst in me that craved quenching.

If I decided to attend another meeting, my sole reason would be to spend time with her.

CHAPTER 36

For the next four weeks, I attended every lecture and lab, applied my focus to my studies as needed, and always found a reason during free times in the evenings and on weekends to be at WAM headquarters. I made myself resourceful and useful by filing, making photocopies, stapling whatever, answering the phone at times, anything that would cause them to allow me to hang around.

As for Abigail, I'd neither called her nor received a call from her, which suited me. It hurt to lose touch with her but was also a relief. Nor did I know if it was even possible to remain friends. The only thing I was certain about was that I could never trust her again. When trust is gone, what's the point?

Also curious—and which turned out to be a true favor—was her getting me to a WAM meeting in the first place. She hadn't known I'd been abused, nor had she been a victim of such treatment. I surmised it was another attempt on her part to "fix" me.

Saturday of the fourth week, I finished filing the last folder. Patricia and I were the only ones left.

"You put in a long day, Katherine. Let me treat you to a late lunch." She checked her watch. "Make that an early dinner."

"I can pay for myself."

"No doubt, but I'd enjoy the company. And as I invited you—"

"Okay. But the next time's on me or at least we split the tab."

"Deal. Let's lock up this place. One car or two?"

"Two is probably best."

I followed Patricia's Lexus to a quaint café with outdoor seating in a back courtyard. A soft breeze rustled through leafy trees that formed a canopy overhead. She asked that we be seated at a back table, near the fountain.

Patricia scanned the menu. "I think I'll have a champagne cocktail to start. What about you?"

"Water's fine."

"You don't drink?"

"No."

"Will it upset you if I have one?"

I glanced at her then back at my menu. "No." I felt her eyes watching me.

The waiter took our orders and disappeared. We sat in companionable silence until he delivered a cup of coffee for Patricia and a cup of tea for me.

Patricia blew on the steaming liquid in her cup, sipped then said, "Do your parents live here as well?"

Emotions sprung forth from a well deep within. My eyes filled, my throat constricted. I shook my head and managed to say, "No father. My mother died."

"I'm sorry. How long has she been gone."

I cleared my throat. "Feels like forever."

"And yet, it still feels like yesterday at times, doesn't it?"

"So often, it takes my breath away." Then the unexpected happened—I burst into tears followed by sobs I couldn't stop. The waiter avoided any banter, put our plates down, and beat it out of there.

Patricia rested a cool hand on my arm. "How long have you held these emotions in?"

I searched for a tissue in my purse and came up empty. Patricia dug one from her purse and handed it to me. I pressed the tissue to my eyes then blew my nose.

"Katherine, some women come to us eager to vent about what's happened to them. Some are reticent. Perhaps reserved is a more appropriate word. I think we both know which one you are."

I nodded and blew my nose again as more tears spilled onto my face.

Patricia handed me a fresh tissue. "One of our members—Brenda Schwartz—provides pro bono services as a therapist. Technically, she's a psychiatrist, which means she can assist you, if you'll let her."

My head snapped up. "You think something's wrong with me?"

"I think you're in great pain, pain you've internalized for so long, you don't know how to get beyond it. If you don't deal with it in a productive manner, it can have long-term detrimental effects on you psychologically, mentally, emotionally, even physically."

She took my hand and waited for me to look at her. With my other hand, I dried eyes that refused to stop leaking.

"What do you say, Katherine? You've found every excuse to be near me for weeks but have yet to open up. I can offer support, but Brenda can offer more. She can offer a path that helps you heal and returns your power to you. I promise that you won't be the first WAM member to turn to her. Will you let me arrange an appointment for you? How's next Saturday morning?"

My eyes met hers. Hers pleaded for me to take action. Mine pleaded as well, but I couldn't pinpoint what for. "Okay."

"Good." She patted my hand. "Let's eat. Even with your lovely complexion, I can see you're pale."

I loved my mother. She'd shown me care in the only ways she knew how. This was a level of concern and compassion I'd never known and had always craved.

Patricia handed me another tissue, which I used immediately.

Finally composed, I started to eat, though mostly toyed with my food. Patricia ate with a heartier appetite, but I could feel her watching me.

CHAPTER 37

To say it was awkward to sit across from Brenda Schwartz is an understatement. Most people would have seen the plump, silver-haired woman with gentle green eyes, and felt as though they were visiting with their kindly grandmother. As I'd never had a grandmother, kindly or otherwise, or had engaged the services of someone in Brenda's profession, I was anything but comforted by her demeanor and soothing voice.

"Are you comfortable, Katherine?"

I ceased shifting around on the plush, cushioned sofa. "Yes, thank you."

"I don't doubt your word. However, you look anything but. Is it the setting? Perhaps me? Or is it the idea of confiding in someone you don't know?"

I shrugged. "The latter, I suppose."

"Some people find it easier to speak about personal matters with a stranger who will never reveal to anyone what's said. I hope that in time, you'll come to see this as your very own sanctuary."

"Thank you, Dr. Schwartz."

"Please, call me Brenda. Maybe a cup of tea will help."

"My stomach is a little off. Guess I'm more anxious about this than I thought."

"Peppermint it is."

She switched on an electric kettle positioned on the credenza behind her desk and dropped a tea bag into each of two mugs. "Do you take sugar? I have honey, if you prefer."

"Just the tea is fine."

A few silent minutes later, she handed a mug to me and sat on the opposite end of the sofa. I took one sip, felt my stomach revolt, and warmed my hands cupped around the mug.

"Whenever you're ready, Katherine. Or would you prefer I ask questions?"

What is it about these WAM women? The floodgates opened. I sobbed and used half a box of tissues while pouring out the most significant low points of my life. Only, I didn't give details. Rather, I listed them like bulleted agenda items, using two words or less. I left out the most recent one involving Abigail's perfidy.

Brenda put her mug down and slid closer to me. She rested a hand gently on my arm. I leaned against her and wept as though I'd stored tears for decades as opposed to having shed a good measure of them exactly a week ago. In fact, I'd become extraordinarily sensitive recently and didn't care for it.

She patted me and said, "That's it, dear. Get it all out. Tears are cleansing."

I sniffed, hiccuped, and said between sobs, "Lacrimation inspired by emotions involving the limbic system contain protein-based hormones such as prolactin, adrenocorticotropic, and Leu-enkephalin. The parasympathetic aspect of the autonomic nervous system controls the lacrimal glands via the neurotransmitter acetylcholine through the nicotinic and muscarinic receptors."

Brenda paused her patting then said, "And it feels good to release those chemicals, doesn't it?"

"'Behold the sea … And, in my mathematic ebb and flow, giving a hint of that which changes not.'"

"Where's that from?"

"A poem by Ralph Waldo Emerson."

"What brought that to mind?"

"Lately, I'm inexplicably releasing an ocean of salt water. Drops of what will never change."

"You're right that our past can never change. But we can change how we allow it to influence us. Are you willing to do that?"

"I suppose I'll have to. The last thing I want to become is a frequent weeper."

"Shall we start down that road now? Together?"

I sat up, blew my nose and nodded. "I prefer to go sequentially."

"Whatever feels right to you."

"It may take more than one session."

Her lips formed a small smile. "Yes, it may, and I'm here for you."

That set me off again. This time, however, I regained control within a minute or so.

All this time, I'd imagined I'd coped quite well with my emotions. I had no idea I could feel the level of sadness and rage that spewed from me.

I didn't make it past age twelve in the time we had left, and I departed feeling like a soggy strand of spaghetti.

Yet, surprisingly, I looked forward to the next session. And to the day when I'd feel cleansed.

That shouldn't take more than a century or two.

CHAPTER 38

Still on my knees, I pressed the handle down on the toilet. Wobbly-legged, I went to the lavatory and rinsed my mouth, splashed my face with cold water, brushed my teeth, and then returned to my side of the dorm room.

Jenni kept her head lowered over her textbook as I passed her at her desk. "If you give that virus to me, I'm going to be seriously pissed off. In fact, none of us appreciate that you've come to class three days with it. If you think you'll affect your competition by making us all sick, forget it."

"I have no competition. Therefore, I have no need to affect or infect, as it were, anyone."

She slammed her book closed. "Always so damn smug." Jenni scooped up her books and said, "I'm getting out of here, as far away from you as possible."

"You know what they say about letting the door hit you."

I understood their fears. I was advanced enough in my studies and grasp of the information to pass the upcoming exam no matter how I felt. They were not.

However, I did not appreciate this intruder into my system. Some small infectious agent had chosen my living cells in which to replicate, using me as its host organism. How long had it waited inside me as a virion, an independent particle looking for a buffet, before penetrating my cells and well-being?

I grabbed my notebook and pen and began to sketch the DNA or RNA genetic material encapsulated in the capsid protein coat surrounded by lipids.

What kind of virus causes a person to vomit upon waking, feel better as the day progresses, only to expel the stomach's contents again the next morning?

I literally felt the blood drain from my face.

No.

Please, no.

I checked my calendar. Nine weeks since I'd last menstruated.

In a quaking flash, I was out of my pajamas, into street clothes, and out the door. I jogged to the elevator and pushed the button repeatedly. Too slow. I took the stairs, shoved open the door that led to fresh air and sunlight that failed to refresh or warm me, and speed-walked the several blocks to the large chain drugstore.

My hands trembled as I read the backs of each box, finally selecting one. The man at the register said nothing, but one of his eyebrows arched when he looked at my purchase and gave a quick glance at me.

I jogged to the dorm, into my bathroom, and tore open the box. Read the instructions—it took three times to focus. Did what was required. And waited. And checked the results.

Oh God.

Like all vertebrates in existence, we spin into our lives in the womb as a spiral. The spiral's *eye* represents its center of gravity from which it seeks and finds its balance. Balance in motion.

As a child blissfully alone at home for an hour, I'd filled the kitchen sink with water then removed the plug and watched the water begin its spiral down the drain. I'd dropped a toothpick I'd gotten from the school cafeteria into the water and stared mesmerized as the speed of the toothpick's motion changed but its orientation remained unchanged. It pointed in the same direction at all times, just as the planets stay true to their axes.

Jakob Bernoulli referred to this as the "change without change".

Only, this was one huge change, and a reality that knocked me off balance.

For several moments, I didn't know in which direction of orientation *I* should point.

Then I did.

CHAPTER 39

After screaming into my pillow for a half hour, and a good cry about being twenty-two, pregnant, and alone, I picked up the phone to call Abigail for two specific reasons: To ream her for being an integral contributor to my condition and to get Clyde's full name, if she even knew it, so I could look him up and tell him what he'd done. I dialed her area code and the first three digits of her number then remembered he'd given me his card.

I dumped the contents of my purse onto my bed. The forgotten card was there. Clyde Morgan, Insurance Agent. What a farce.

His office phone number was listed, so I returned to my bed, where my phone was, dialed his number, and waited to be connected.

"Clyde Morgan speaking."

"This is Katherine. Do you remember me?"

He altered his professional tone to one I'm sure he imagined to be suggestive. "Maybe you could give me a few hints."

"We met about six weeks ago, in what you called a No-Tell Motel. You, Jared, and Abigail. Does that trigger your memory?"

"Oh, yeah. Melt-in-your-mouth chocolate girl. You melted in my mouth a few times. So you finally called. I thought maybe you'd lost my card. Baby, say the word. I'm ready and willing to—"

"Ding-ding-ding. You just said the magic word. Ten points for Clyde."

"Whatever the magic word is, I'm ready to say it again so you open up to me."

"Open up to this—I'm pregnant."

Clyde went silent for a millisecond then barked, "What the hell does that have to do with me?"

"Everything. It's yours, and I want to know what you're going to do about it."

"I'll tell you what I'm going to do—nothing. It isn't mine. No way in hell am I going to let you stick this on me."

"You're the only one who's ever—"

"Don't give me that crap. Imagine my surprise when, after all your friend's carrying on about you being a virgin, there was no cherry to pop. As a gentleman, I kept your secret."

"Buster."

"Lose my card, bitch, and the brat. And if you even think about calling my wife, you'll regret it."

He slammed the phone down. I cradled the receiver to my chest until the annoying sound the phone company uses reminded me to hang up.

Buster had done more damage than I'd realized.

There was only one thing to do.

I called Abigail.

CHAPTER 40

"I swear," Abigail said, "I didn't think it could happen the first time. Well, it was three times, actually. Clyde's a fast recharger." She sighed loudly into the phone. "What are you going to do?"

I shook my head at the enormity of Abigail's ignorance about physiology. Then another awful thought occurred to me. "You're certain Jared didn't—"

"I'm certain. He fingered you while he went down on you, but that's all. We'd agreed ahead of time who was going to do who."

I was past caring about her grammar. "I can't tell you how disgusting hearing this is to me."

"It's all a matter of perspective. And you didn't answer my question."

"If I abort my child, will I be able to live with myself? That's an answer that remains unknown until the moment after it's done, when it's too late to change my mind. If I surrender my child for adoption, how will it feel to wonder how she or he is doing or how much she or he might resent me? And if I keep my child, how will it affect completing school and my career?"

"You keep calling it 'my child'. How can you make the right decision if you keep doing that?"

"I don't know what to do."

"Whatever you decide, I'll help you in whatever way I can."

"That's generous, considering it was you who—"

"You don't need to rub it in. I never meant for *this* to happen."

"I'll get back to you once I know what I'm going to do."

"Hey, K. I'd really appreciate it if you don't tell you-know-who how you got this way."

"Lucky for you, that's the last thing I'd want to do. Hubby-Buns will remain in his bubble of ignorant bliss."

Right until the moment it pops.

What I did was schedule an appointment with Dean Broward.

He lowered his glasses to almost the tip of his nose. "I'd heard you've been unwell. Virus all gone?"

"The effects linger."

"It must be one heck of a strain."

"That's an understatement, sir."

"How can I help you?"

"I thought perhaps, with your influence, I might be tested separately. I'd like to take my boards early."

"School too dull for you?"

I shifted forward in the chair. "It isn't that, sir, but I am eager to move further along and at a faster pace. As fast as can be arranged."

"I'm sorry, Miss Barnes. That's not possible." He held up a hand when I started to interrupt. "There are protocols, and protocols must be followed. How advanced you may be can't alter this. Anything else?"

"No, sir."

That was that. I thanked him and left. As I walked back to the dorm, I considered my options.

I still had no clue as to which decision I should make.

CHAPTER 41

My test-tube crashed to the floor and splintered. Fortunately, it was still empty, so it was only a matter of cleaning up glass shards. Jenni and several others snickered.

I'd dropped the tube as a result of a cramp. My initial thought was food poisoning. My second was that I was about to miscarry.

I grabbed my purse, walked to the professor's desk, and explained I wasn't feeling well. He excused me from the class and I left with one hand resting protectively over my relatively still-flat abdomen.

The infirmary should have been my destination, but I wasn't ready to face that. Fear of word getting out, especially to Jenni, prevented me. Besides, it was only the one cramp, and that could have been caused by something completely unrelated.

It was at the halfway point between the building and my dorm that I realized, whatever it took, I'd keep my child. Plans began to form in my mind about how I might reduce my classes and get a part-time job so I could afford a sitter. I made a mental note to find out what Stanford's arrangements were for students with children. Perhaps they'd provide housing and sitter care. No way would I subject my child to Jenni and her snide comments. No reason to be concerned about that, I reminded myself. I was nearly a hundred percent certain it was against policy for me to live in the dorm with a child.

These thoughts had a liberating effect. I was going to be a mother. Mother to a daughter who'd be protected and cherished. It would be another six to eight weeks before an ultrasound could confirm gender, about the same time I should feel the first flutter.

My baby had to be a girl.

Had to be.

I changed course and headed for the library to look up girls' names on the computer. After an hour or so, I'd decided on her first and middle names—Caitlin, which is Gaelic for pure, like Katherine, but this time I'd keep her that way, and Deirdre, also Gaelic, which means raging. Caitlin Deirdre Barnes. Pure and strong. And protected.

Alone in my room, I gently rubbed my abdomen and said, "You'll be looked after better than I was, Caitlin. I'll never subject you to a life like mine. We'll live in a clean home, in a nice neighborhood, where our sheets are washed twice a week, perhaps more often, and in a top-of-the-line washing machine. You'll have the best food money can buy. Peanut butter and bologna will never be your sustenance out of necessity. I'll be financially set, so you'll attend the best schools, wear clothes from department stores and boutiques, and never need to lock your bedroom door at night."

I continued my one-sided conversation until Jenni returned.

"If how you look is any indication," Jenni said, "you must be feeling better."

I beamed a smile at her. "I am."

She plunked her books onto her desk. "Leave it to you to cover your embarrassment about dropping a tube by pretending you're still ill. I have news for you—you're human. Like the rest of us. So get over yourself."

I laughed and lay back down.

Hours later, Jenni said, "If you don't stop that damn humming, I'm going to throttle you."

Mama had never sung to me, at least, not that I could recall. It would be different for Caitlin. But I'd have to learn lullabies, rather than limiting my efforts to humming my own awkward compositions.

Hand draped over my growing spiral daughter, I drifted into sleep.

CHAPTER 42

Realizing I likely needed assistance with my decision to be a mother, and being basically on my own, I revealed my condition to Patricia, which was a good move on my part, though I left out the grotesque details of how I got into my condition. Nor did she or others at WAM pry.

After the next meeting, she introduced me to some of the top members, including physicists, research scientists, an anthropologist, and several physicians, one of whom—Agatha Simpson—became my OB/GYN. Women from every profession rallied around me. The biggest surprise was when I learned WAM had a laboratory, restricted to certain members qualified to use it. I hid my disappointment, when I asked Patricia how soon I could see it and when I could use it, and she responded, "Perhaps one day. We'll see."

It was after nine in the evening, and we sat companionably on the plush sofa in her tastefully appointed office, something we'd done every night for the last week since I'd revealed my impending blessed event, as she'd called it. I accepted a cup of tea from her and said, "I'm amazed at the level of intensity about this organization these professional women have."

"They're devoted to our revolution."

That was new information. "What revolution?"

Patricia smiled and winked. "I hope that in our lifetime—and if I have anything to do with it, it will be—women will rule the world. We're preparing for that day."

I grinned. "I like the sound of that."

"Here's something else you may like. There's no point in your continuing to volunteer your services here."

My smile faded. "You can't mean ... I thought you—"

"What I'm trying to say is that starting retroactively, you'll be paid for your services, which I hope you'll continue up to your delivery and long after. Considering your field of study, you'll fit right in, that is, unless you decide to enter a different field once you're legally an M.D. However, any lab time will have to wait until after you've stopped breastfeeding, which I hope you'll do. We'll find something engaging for you to do until then. No exposure to chemicals for you and the little one."

"You're thinking far ahead, further than I have."

Patricia carefully placed her cup into her saucer. "What I never say during my introduction, and only a select few know, is that my pregnancy wasn't just complicated, it ended my ability to have another child. So you see, my interest in you and your child is personally motivated. I may be presuming when I shouldn't, but I already consider myself auntie to your little one."

I beamed at her. "I'm delighted you feel that way. Caitlin will grow up surrounded by the best-of-the-best women. What mother could ask more?"

"Good. That's settled. Are the crackers and tea helping the morning sickness?"

"Yes. Although, my roommate thinks I've developed a weird eating habit."

"She hasn't guessed?"

"As the saying goes, not the sharpest tool in the shed."

"Agatha told me you're around seven weeks."

I nodded, beamed, and patted my abdomen.

"More than likely, you have a while before you begin to show. When that happens, the pretense will be over."

"I'll deal with it then. The longer I can go without enduring my roommate's comments the better."

Patricia stood and stretched. "Time to go home and for you to get some rest."

We walked together to our cars. Patricia kissed me on the cheek and said, "Auntie Patricia. I love the sound of that."

Wearing a silly grin, I got into my car and cranked the engine. It would be a while before Caitlin called me Mommy.

I loved the sound of *that*.

CHAPTER 43

The dorm parking lot was full, which I should have expected, considering the time. I drove around in the lot for several minutes, hoping someone would pull out, but no one did. That meant finding a place on one of the nearby streets. It had happened before, especially now that I was staying later at WAM, and would require finding a space possibly as far as a few streets over. That was fine with me. The walk would be good for me and for Caitlin.

I found a spot three streets away, locked my car, and started on my trek, all the while talking in my mind to what was, I hoped, my developing daughter.

A tall, reed-thin man turned the corner and came toward me on the sidewalk. I pressed my purse into my side and looked straight ahead.

When he was two feet away, he said, "How's it goin'?"

I nodded but said nothing and kept walking.

"What? You too stuck up to say hi?"

I increased my speed.

"Bitch, I'm talking to you."

My quickened steps sped to a jog and I hurried around the corner. I paused, looked back, and saw I was alone. He'd obviously gone into one of the houses or maybe one of the parked cars. I slowed my steps, patted my abdomen, and said, "Caitlin, I'll have a great deal to explain to you one day."

In the event my path crossed with another man who had an attitude, I drew my keyring from my pocket and placed two keys between my fingers. I muttered to myself about the audacity of the man to spoil a beautiful evening such as this one. Well, he could forget it. No way would I allow him to control my mood.

A gorgeous, thick-trunked oak tree I loved was coming up on the right. Moonlight kissed the leaves, bathing them in a blue-white shimmer. I'd take Caitlin to gardens and museums and zoos. We'd explore the world, using all our senses, and I'd experience everything fresh and new and pristine through her innocent eyes and budding awareness.

As I started to pass the tree, I entertained myself with these and other musings about all we'd see and do together.

And is why I didn't see or hear him leap at me from behind the tree. My keys flew from my hand. His hand, smelling of nicotine and urine, clamped over my mouth as he dragged me to the side of the house. He may have been thin but he was all muscle.

No lights were on in the house, which meant the occupants were asleep or away. Still, as soon as the opportunity presented itself, I'd scream like a banshee and get someone's attention.

The moment he loosened his grip, I bit his hand and opened my mouth to yell. He anticipated me, spun me around, and sent his fist into my solar plexus. Gasping for air, I staggered back and collapsed to the ground.

"Snotty college bitch. You and all the others who think you're too good for me."

He unzipped his pants and started toward me. I froze, just as I had each time Buster had come into my room.

A light went on in a window in the house next door. This was my chance. I opened my mouth again to scream. He straddled me and slammed his fist into my jaw. Hard.

Hard enough to cause me to lose consciousness.

"Observe due measure, for right timing is in all things the most important factor." So said the Greek poet Hesiod.

That quote came to me as I lay dazed on the ground. I came fully back to consciousness and opened my eyes, spotted the full moon above me and to the right in the ebony sky, and felt tears stream into and around my ears. I was alone, naked from the waist down, though my breasts were exposed.

Pain radiated in my face and chest. And lower.

I pulled my torn shirt together in the front—my bra had been ripped in half. I let it dangle where it was, rolled over and got onto my hands and knees.

In the ambient light from the lit window next door, I spotted a dark lump to my right and crawled to where my jeans lay crumpled in a patch of dirt and thought, Grass never grows in shade.

My panties were a yard or so away. I slid my underwear on followed by my jeans. Where my shoes were was anyone's guess. I located my purse at the base of the oak tree and checked inside. My assailant hadn't robbed me. Not of money, that is. I stepped on something hard—my keys.

I staggered to the front door of the house where the light had come on at whatever time that had been—I had no watch and no sense of how long I'd been unconscious. The house had one of those two-door set-ups—a screen door and a regular one. I pressed the yellow-illuminated doorbell button. When no one came, I pressed the button until the porch light clicked on.

An older man's voice called out, "Who is it?"

"My name is Katherine. I've been attacked and I need help."

He opened the front door, leaving the screen door latched. His eyes raked over me. He frowned and said, "I'll call the police."

"No!"

He gave me a quizzical look. "Young lady, you need an ambulance."

"I need you to call a friend for me. Please." I gave him Patricia's name and number. "Ask her to get here as quickly as she can."

"Want to wait inside while I call and till she gets here? Maybe clean up some?"

"No. Thank you. If you don't mind, I'll sit on your steps."

"I don't mind."

He left the regular door open, I suppose to keep an eye on me through the screen door. I took a seat on the top step, doubled over and with my hands on my abdomen.

And pleaded silently for Patricia to hurry as the cramps grew worse and the pain in my back more severe.

Stay with me, Caitlin. Please, baby girl, stay with me.

CHAPTER 44

In what seemed an eternity later, a car pulled up curbside. Agatha Simpson, my WAM OB/GYN, threw open the passenger-side door of Patricia's car and flew to where I sat weeping and moaning.

"Oh, my dear. This assault *was* as bad as the caller indicated, wasn't it?"

I nodded and continued to cry, only now, loudly.

The old man came to the screen door. "She needs a doctor."

Agatha looked at him and said, "As it happens, I am her doctor. Thank you for contacting us." She turned back to me. "Can you walk?"

"I think so."

She wrapped her arm around my waist and helped me to my feet. "Oh no."

I looked at where her eyes were aimed. My blood had stained the top step and the one below it. Agatha clutched me to her as we went down the steps and into the back seat. She slid in next to me. "Patricia, we need to get Katherine to a hospital, stat."

"No," I said. "You have a fully equipped facility at headquarters."

"If you insist. But I have to warn you that you may be miscarrying."

"I was raped. I don't want anyone but you two to know. Let's go. Now."

Patricia put the car in gear and started forward at speed. She glanced at me in the rearview mirror. "You need to file a police report so they can catch and prosecute the bastard who did this."

I doubled over in pain. When I could breathe again I said, "No police. Just get me to headquarters."

Patricia glanced at me again in the mirror. "You're not going to let the bastard get away with this, are you?"

I met her reflected eyes. "No. But he'll have to wait."

***

A summary of what followed the few days after the attack is enough, or at least, all the detail I care to give. Agatha contacted Dean Broward to tell him I would be out a few to several days for medical reasons, and refused to give specifics when he asked. She performed a dilation and curettace, in common lingo, a D&C, to clean the remaining placental tissue from my womb. I received several pints of blood and I.V. fluids, and remained in a facility bed for forty-eight hours.

Once I was strong enough, emotionally as well as physically, we buried Caitlin on the grounds, in a small ornamental chest Patricia picked out. We planted a California laurel sapling atop her tiny grave. Patricia assured me the young tree could grow to a height of sixty feet.

"A family tree of sorts," I said as I patted soil into place at its base, which she, Agatha, and I watered with our tears and water from the watering can we'd brought with us.

As for people at Stanford, I told Jenni and any fellow student who asked, that the reason for my absence was personal and to mind their business. I told Dean Broward it was female problems, which caused him to drop the topic. I presume he got word to my instructors because none of them inquired, merely said it was good to have me back.

One evening a week later, I sat in Patricia's office with her and Agatha, each of us sipping tea in silence.

Patricia placed her cup and saucer on the coffee table. "It's time, Katherine."

"For what?"

"What are we going to do about the man who did this? I can't stand the idea of him getting away with what he did to you and God knows how many other women."

"I have a plan," I said. Both women sat straighter and waited. "I want to hire a private detective, a female for obvious reasons."

Agatha and Patricia looked at each other. Agatha said, "One of our local members happens to be a P.I."

"Good. How do I contact her?"

Patricia went to her phone, keyed in several numbers, and said, "Is it convenient for you to come to my office now? Perfect. See you in a few." She returned to her seat. "It won't take long for her to get here."

I leaned forward. "She's that close by?"

Again, Patricia and Agatha looked at each other. Agatha smiled. "Her office is here. We—meaning us and some of our members—tend to need her services fairly often."

There was a knock at the door, which was then opened by a petite woman with blue-green eyes and flaming red hair cut in a bob.

Patricia smiled at her. "Close the door, please."

She did and walked over to where we sat, altering her gaze between Patricia and me. "What's up?"

Patricia said, "Connie Hunter, this is Katherine Barnes."

Connie strode to where I sat, extended her hand, which I stood to shake.

"Katherine was raped about a week ago."

Connie faced Patricia. "Sonofabitch."

"Which caused her to miscarry."

Connie looked at me. "Son of a friggin' bitch!"

My eyes met hers and I said, "For all intents and purposes, he murdered my daughter."

She pulled me into a bear hug, let me go almost as quickly, and plopped onto the sofa next to me. "Let me guess. The police aren't getting anywhere."

Agatha leaned forward. "We didn't involve the police. It was Katherine's preference."

Connie fixed her eyes on me. "Why not?"

"I prefer to handle this in-house, so to speak."

Connie grinned and slapped me on the thigh. "A woman after my own heart. Okay, where'd it happen?"

"On Stewart Street. However, I first saw him on Arthur Street. Are you familiar with the area?"

"No place in this town I haven't driven through, walked the streets of, or even crawled in the dirt on my belly. Give me details."

I did, from first seeing him to the last thing I remembered.

"What's he look like?"

"Tall. I'd say six feet, maybe an inch or so taller. Sharp features. Late twenties or early thirties at most. Reed-thin but muscular. He was strong."

"Maybe. Could've been an adrenaline rush or some other chemical in his system. Keep going."

"His hair on the sides and back was short and dark. Longer on top and dyed white or platinum blond."

"Anything else?"

"He wore an earring in his left lobe. A small silver sword. It dangled, about an inch in total length, from lobe to point."

Connie sat forward. "Here's my take. He lives in the area. Possibly on Arthur. If not there, not far."

"I wondered the same," I said.

She nodded and gave me a quick smile. "I give myself a ninety-percent chance of being right about that. He knew the area too well. Knew how to cut through yards to get to that tree pretty damn fast and in the dark. The other option is that he's a repeat rapist, and that's one of his preferred areas. But even the police would have found him if that were the case. Someone would've reported his ass. I go with the first option." She fixed her gaze on me. "Something must have triggered him."

"He didn't like my not speaking to him when spoken to."

"Nah. Too easy. Not that his why matters." She nodded. "That street, and immediate area, is the go-to for me."

Patricia nodded. "It's a start."

Connie leaped up. "Which is what I'm going to do now. I keep my Jeep packed and ready for spontaneous surveillance."

"Would you like me to go with you?" I asked.

"Nah. I surveil better alone. It may take a few days for me to locate him. Then I want to track his habits. What do you want me to do once I find him?"

"Contact me, through Patricia, if you have to. I'm in school at Stanford. Let me give you my number at the dorm. Although, I prefer you not leave a message on my machine other than to call you. My roommate is the last person I want knowing my business."

Connie extracted a business card from her pocket and handed it to me. "That's my home phone, which I either forward to my office here or my car phone. You can reach me 24/7, unless I'm out of my car or between points and it's inconvenient to pick up. If I don't answer, leave a message." She withdrew a small notebook and pen from a pocket in her jean jacket. "Give me your number."

My name and number tucked away, Connie hugged each of us, marched to the door and said, "You'll be hearing from me."

Jenni, thankfully, was in the shower when Connie called two days later and before my first class on Friday. That presented the opportunity for us to discuss plans—hers and mine. Some of the latter, I kept to myself.

My last class was a lab. It was easy enough to slip a scalpel into one of the long pockets of my lab coat then into my purse.

Two hours before Connie was to pick me up, my phone rang. At first I feared she was calling to cancel. When I heard Abigail's voice instead, I was both relieved and troubled.

Mixed feelings bubbled to the surface. On the one hand, all I'd been through—well, nearly all—was a direct result of her actions. On the other hand, hearing the voice of my oldest friend pulled at my emotions.

I decided to be polite. "How are you?"

"Kinda nervous about calling."

"Understandable."

"You remember that woman we met at that meeting that time, the one who ran it?"

"Emily Saunders."

"That's the one. She contacted me to go to another one of those meetings. I told her to take my name off the list. I went that time thinking it would be about the feminist movement, you know?"

"I've been going to the ones here."

"Why?"

"You know why. Besides, the women here are good company."

"Whatever floats your boat. You know, K, I thought I'd hear from you before now. You said you'd let me know what you decided about, you know, the *problem*."

A sigh escaped me, a result of having to cover this ground again. Grateful Jenni was out of the room, I said, "The problem, as you call it, no longer exists."

"*What* a *relief.* Did you go to the clinic alone?"

"I didn't go to a clinic."

"Geez, K, I know you know your stuff, but it's dangerous to do it yourself. You could ruin something."

I drew in a deep breath, exhaled, and explained, needing only five tissues to get through it. I stopped talking and waited for Abigail to speak.

"Look, it sucks that it happened. Still, he did you a favor. Now you don't have to worry about the decision. He also saved you the cost."

"Are you genuinely this dim and insensitive?"

"What's *that* supposed to mean?"

I cupped my forehead in my hand. "You don't get it, do you?"

"I get that you're not tied down with a kid. I get that you're still walking around. What's the big deal? So it was rough sex. You back off a day or two then go back to the regular ways for a while."

"My study group starts in ten minutes. I need to go."

"Oh. All right. Call soon, okay?"

"Sure."

Abigail and I live in different worlds.

G. W. von Leibnitz said, "The world is not a machine. Everything in it is force, life, thought." With the exception of Mr. Hopkins, at least according to my limited experience of him, men were all about force. Abigail had life but she was clueless about anything truly significant.

She was also my touchstone regarding my past.

It was a quandary I didn't appreciate.

CHAPTER 45

Headlights of a beat-up, double-parked car I didn't recognize flashed at me. Good thing Connie had told me what to look for. I slid onto the passenger seat. "Where's the Jeep?"

"One, I don't want my vehicle recognized. Two, we needed a trunk."

"What about people seeing your Jeep in the area every day and night before now?"

"Only the first night. After that I used a different car during the day and a different one at night. Besides, I parked a few streets away and kept in the shadows on Arthur while watching for the bastard."

"And your hair?"

"Wigs and caps I got. We'll need these as well." She handed a plastic cap to me. "Looks like you need one of these too." She pulled a bobby pin from her hair.

I twisted my hair into a knot, pinned it in place, and covered it with the plastic cap, positioning the elastic so that no hair could fall out.

Connie handed me a regular brimmed cap, slapped one onto her head, put the car in gear and started driving. "Still positive you want to follow through with this? If not, now's the moment to back out."

"No way. However, as I told you, you don't have to do more than point out the house and drop me off."

"I said I'm all in."

"Thanks. I mean that more than you know."

"Believe me. I know." She opened the glove box and handed me a lint roller encased in a plastic bag. "Run this over you everywhere while we ride, even on the bottom of your shoes. I've already done my thing with it."

Task completed, I bagged the roller and put it back in the glove box. Between us was a small paper bag with its top folded down an inch or so, which sent me into a momentary flashback to my Cabrini-Green days. "This bag contains what I asked for?"

"Yep."

"Any problem getting it?"

"I'm not called Crafty Connie for nothing."

As she drove toward Arthur Street, we reviewed our strategy.

I started trembling as we passed the oak tree. "That's where it happened."

"I know. I also know you're shaking. That's not good."

"It's from rage, not fear."

"Oh. Well. That's different then. This is me, keeping my mouth shut."

Connie turned left off of Stewart Street, drove slowly on Arthur, and pointed to the fifth house on the left. "That's our target's house. Eric Clarkson."

"Not that his name matters."

"I hear you. But I like to be thorough."

Connie turned right at the corner and parked in the first available curbside spot. She turned off the engine and said, "We stick to the plan. All the way. We only deviate if absolutely necessary."

"Right."

"Don't forget your stuff." She handed me the small paper bag.

I opened the bag and saw a wax paper-wrapped square. "What's this?"

"Ham sandwich. I needed cover, just in case."

"Since you didn't ask Agatha for these items, I presume she would object to our project."

Connie shrugged. "Probably not. But you didn't say to involve anyone else."

"You *are* good."

"Before you touch anything, we need to put these on." She pulled two pairs of purple nitrile gloves from her jean jacket and handed a pair to me. "I've got extras if we need them."

I put the gloves on then handed the sandwich to her, which she tossed into the back seat.

"What about your fingerprints on the bottle and syringe?" I asked.

She stared at me. Her eyebrows disappeared under the lowered brim of her cap. "Seriously?"

"Sorry." Carefully, I removed the protective cap from the syringe and poked the needle into the foil top of the bottle containing *botulinum* toxin. When the syringe was full, capped, and tucked into one of my pockets, I said, "Ready?"

"You bet your ass."

I reached for the door handle. Connie grabbed my arm and said, "Wait."

She turned off the interior lights. "Now. And remember what I said about closing the door quietly."

"Won't we be seen?"

"One, did you notice the streetlights for most of Arthur are out?"

"You?"

"You bet your ass. Two, we keep to the dark areas. Just follow what I do." She started forward then stopped. "Remember, no names."

Keeping in the shadows as much as possible, we walked back to the corner and crossed the street, edging our way forward as near to shrubs and trees as possible. We turned into *his* yard and crept along the side of the small wood-frame house, avoiding the long tire-worn driveway that was missing most of its crushed shells. Even in the dark I could see that the driveway extended to a covered area yards from the back of the house. A small car of indistinguishable make was parked underneath.

His TV blared beyond the closed windows. Connie halted, placed a finger to her lips then peeked into the living room window. She motioned for me to follow her to the back of the house.

Positioned in front of the back door, she whispered, "He's slouched in his ratty chair in front of the TV."

"Are we going to knock or something to get him to open the door?"

She slid a small case from an inside jacket pocket. "Top student in lock-picking class. Silent as a cat. My instructor said I was friggin' scary."

"I'm glad you're on my team."

"Friggin' A."

"Why the altered version of that word?"

"Patricia allows certain obscenities—the milder ones—but not that one. No one in WAM says it twice."

"I'll remember that, not that I ever use it."

Connie grabbed the knob with her left hand. "Time me."

CHAPTER 46

Connie had the lock open, without making a sound, in under a minute—I counted the seconds. She put the small case away and checked the kitchen through the window, nodded, and eased the door open, leaving it ajar once we were both inside. To say the kitchen was fit for a pig would be accurate on all counts.

She lifted something from her belt.

"What is *that*?" I whispered.

"Stun gun. We want him immobilized, right?"

"You bet your ass."

She grinned and winked. "Stay here."

"That's not the plan."

"It's my plan. It's easier if I sneak up on him and zap him. Then you come in. In the meantime, if something goes wonky, you're close enough to the back door to get the hell out."

"What about you? No way will I leave you with him."

"I can handle it. I've incapacitated bigger guys than him." She withdrew the car key from her pocket and held it toward me. "Just in case."

"Keep it, in case you need to get away. I'm close enough to my dorm to run."

Connie nodded, pocketed the key, and said, "This shouldn't take long. Stay out of sight."

She got down on her hands and knees and started forward slowly. I moved as close as I could to the doorway and listened. I heard what I assumed was the stun gun, and then a gurgle followed by a *whump*, which I took to mean he'd hit the floor.

"Ready when you are," Connie called out.

I made my way through the cluttered dining room, into the equally sty-like living room. "Roll him onto his stomach."

As Connie did that, I extracted the syringe and uncapped it. "Lift his shirt and pull the waistline of his pants down about three inches."

She followed my directions. "Damn. Does this guy ever wash?"

"Fortunately, I was unconscious so remained unaware of his lack of hygiene." I knelt beside him, felt for the correct entry point, made certain the syringe was ready to go, and said, "Just a little prick."

Connie snickered.

I capped the syringe and slipped it into my pocket. "Roll him over."

Connie rolled him onto his back then pulled from one of her many jacket pockets, a small roll of duct tape. She ripped off a piece big enough to cover his mouth then bound his wrists and his ankles.

He looked from Connie to me, terror clear in his eyes.

"Remember me?" I asked.

He shook his head.

Connie said, "Wrong answer, ass-wipe. Oh yeah, that's not a practice you follow."

I waved my hand in front of his face. "I'm the, quote, snotty college bitch, end quote, you raped a couple of weeks ago. Around the corner, behind the large oak tree. Remember now?"

His eyes widened. Panic set in when he realized he was mostly paralyzed. His muffled squeals were pathetic. I felt no pity.

Connie got to her feet. "I'll pull the car to the back of the house. Then we'll load lard-ass."

Once alone with him, an idea came to me. I removed his earring and tucked it far down into my front jeans pocket.

He kept his eyes aimed at me. His expression shifted from panic to pleading to fury and back more times than I cared to count.

"So many emotions occur in such a moment," I said. "Fear, disbelief, terror, panic about being helpless and out of control. Concern about what's going to happen to you." I placed my face inches from his. "Just as I detest what you did to me, you're not going to like what I do to you."

The soft crunch of driveway shells on the dark side of the window drew my attention.

Within seconds, Connie stood at his head. "Heave-ho."

"What about the TV and lights?"

"Leave them on. Let people think he's here."

CHAPTER 47

Connie had backed the car in, stopping even with the rear wall of the house. She'd also left the trunk open to make it easy to dump him in.

"Get in the car," she said. "And remember how to close the door."

As gently as possible, Connie closed the trunk then got in behind the wheel. The headlights stayed off as we turned left out of the driveway, and were turned on once we turned right onto the street where we'd parked.

"How far is this place?" I asked.

"Far enough. Remote enough. We'll be there in about a half hour. I timed it from here."

"You really do like to be thorough."

We glanced at each other and said simultaneously, "You bet your ass."

We laughed for several nervous moments then made the remainder of the drive in silence, broken solely by occasional feeble *thumps* from the trunk.

Connie turned off a two-lane blacktop road onto a one-lane dirt road, which seemed to wind for miles, but was no more than a mile and a half—I asked. She pulled into a clearing and turned the engine off.

We hauled him out of the car, which he didn't make easy, and placed him on the ground several yards away. "You have a good flashlight?" I asked.

"Always." She retrieved it from the backseat. "I don't know why you need a light to dump him here."

"I need it for the second part of my plan."

"Which is?"

"Help me pull his pants down."

"Uh-oh."

I faced her. "You're welcome to wait in the car for this part. Just don't try to stop me."

"I wouldn't dream of it. It's just, this is a party favor I didn't expect."

Together, we got his pants and odoriferous underwear down to his knees. His attempts to thrash his arms annoyed me. "Raise his arms over his head and sit on his hands. If you're squeamish, face the other direction." I removed the covered scalpel from my jacket pocket and sat on his legs.

"Whoa. You're going to go Cosa Nostra on his ass, aren't you?"

"Do you know what the translation of those two words is?"

"No."

"Our thing." I put the flashlight on and aimed it in his eyes. "Appropriate, don't you think, *Eric*? You forced me to receive your *thing*, you disgusting excuse for a human being. In the process, you killed my unborn daughter. You ripped her from my womb. As far as I'm concerned, this is the only appropriate penalty for someone like you. And there are so many like you. Far too many."

I handed the flashlight to Connie. "Look away anytime you want or need to, but hold the light steady."

"Not that I blame you one bit, but you really hate this guy."

"I hate all men, every last disgusting waste-of-space one of them."

"What about the father of your child?"

"He was nothing more than another unwelcome, uninvited sperm donor."

"Shit. Another rape?"

"In more ways than you know, and by more than one person."

"I guess that explains the animosity."

"More than you can imagine. I need a plastic bag."

Connie fished one from one of her many pockets and I placed it over his genitals to protect my clothing from blood spurts. Eric began to urinate into the bag. I let him finish then emptied it and placed the bag back into place.

I didn't dawdle during my surgical removal of his genitalia, nor did I particularly hurry. It was surprisingly easy, or perhaps not so surprisingly, to ignore his muffled screams that became sobs that slipped into whimpers and moans then silence as I sliced through his shriveled, offending parts.

We hid him in thick brush and covered him as thoroughly as we could, leaving him to die, which I estimated wouldn't take too long, just long enough for him to consider his deeds, if he even used his remaining time in such a productive manner before shock set in and death followed. I did the same with his genitals but in a separate place yards away from him.

Connie held out her hand. "Give me the gloves and the bag. I'll get rid of them." She put the bloodied items into a fresh plastic bag and handed me a clean pair of gloves. "Just in case."

As we made our way back onto the two-lane, Connie said, "Well, that was different." She glanced at me. "Do you feel avenged?"

"I'm just getting started."

"You know, you're kind of on the scary side yourself."

"No woman ever needs to be afraid of me. Even those who betray me."

She gave a quick glance at me then returned her focus to the road. "Is that meant as a warning for me?"

I faced her. "No. I'm indebted to you. I didn't tell you what I'd planned, nor did you attempt to stop me."

"Yeah, well, I considered it one for the team. Including me."

I faced her. "You too?"

She nodded. "I was nineteen. Bastard got off 'cause he had a rich daddy who paid for a new building on campus in exchange for the college police and dean dropping charges. Called me a trollop who'd seduced sonny-boy, adding, 'and God knows how many others.' Who the hell says trollop anymore? There was one major flaw in his logic."

"Which was?"

"I like women."

"Did you tell them that?"

"What would have been the point? That fact would've meant as little to them as the truth did."

"You're right. I'm sorry you went through that."

Connie shrugged. "I recovered. Made me stronger. And it confirmed what I already knew about my preference. Ready to get back to the dorm?"

"Take me to headquarters first. There's something I want to do."

***

Connie walked with me to the laurel sapling. I dug into my pocket and removed the tiny silver sword. I found the just-right twig on a small branch and secured the earring to it.

Connie whistled. "I'm slipping. Didn't even notice it was missing."

"I suppose you could say I'm developing a level of craftiness myself."

"That's an understatement. What now?"

I caressed the slender trunk down to its base and rested my hand on the soil. "Caitlin, my precious girl, that's one bastard down, an unknown number left to go."

"Friggin' A."

I stood and backed up.

Connie wrapped her arm around my waist. "What about the scalpel? You want me to get rid of it for you?"

I shook my head. "I'm going to clean it and put it back in the lab where I took it from, minus its cardboard cap."

"Like I said, crafty. Who knows when they'll find him? And they damn sure won't think to look in a Stanford lab for the weapon."

"Friggin' A."

I drank in a deep breath, held it several seconds and exhaled. Head tilted back, I looked at the stars. "What a glorious night."

CHAPTER 48

It was nearly midnight when I crawled into bed. I'd been careful not to wake Jenni as I returned to my room, which was a wasted effort. Her bed was empty, as was the bathroom. I took a quick shower, got into my pajamas and into bed. I slept better than I had in months—a full twelve hours.

Patricia always provided trays of sandwiches and cookies on weekends, for those who worked or needed to be in the company of those they trusted. This made it easy for me to skip getting something to eat on campus and arrive at headquarters sooner.

"Sorry I'm late," I told her as I scrambled to put my purse up and get to work.

"No need to apologize."

I scarfed down one of the small, triangular crust-less sandwiches then two more.

Patricia chuckled. "Glad to see your appetite is returning."

"Definitely."

"Help me get something from my office."

I nodded, grabbed a couple of ginger cookies, which I ate as I followed her. Once in her office, rather than retrieving anything, she closed the door. "Sorry about the fib," she said. "I preferred that our conversation be private."

"Okay."

She gestured toward the sofa. "Let's sit."

I lowered myself onto one end of the sofa.

Patricia sat in her favorite cushy chair across from me. "Day before yesterday, Connie said she thought she'd located your assailant. Has she gotten back to you with anything new?"

"Yes."

She shifted forward. "And?"

"He's been dealt with."

Her eyebrows shot up. "Mind if I ask how?"

I looked away. "He'll never again bother another woman." I faced her and looked directly into her eyes. "Not in this life or the next."

Patricia went completely still. For a moment I was terrified about what she might say or do.

"So," she said, "problem solved."

"Problem solved."

"Do you mind sharing the details?"

"Will they offend you? Because if so, I'd rather keep our relationship intact."

She crossed her heart and held up her hand, palm facing me. "Our sisterhood is our bond."

Patricia let me speak without interruption. When I finished giving her every minute detail, she smiled and said, "Wham!"

I grinned at her. "You said it."

We were silent for two milliseconds then began to laugh.

And we continued to laugh.

Until we cried.

CHAPTER 49

I scooted back on Brenda's sofa, a mug of tea in hand. Nose inches above the steam, I inhaled the minty aroma.

This time, rather than taking a seat on the other end of the sofa, Brenda occupied the plush chair next to where I sat, which was positioned at a ninety-degree angle to the sofa. She sipped her tea. I sipped mine and waited.

"Katherine, one thing WAM women do is protect each others' secrets." She rested her mug atop a coaster on the small table next to her. "Only in the most extraordinary circumstances will any of us ever mention anything to anyone in the organization, and this occurs solely between or among a few select women at the top level. Do you understand what I'm trying to say?"

"Only partially."

"I hesitate because I don't want to disrupt your and another WAM member's relationship."

Every muscle in my body tensed. "Where's this going?"

"Only as far as you choose. Patricia gave me no specifics, you understand, but she did suggest that you might have something significant you need to talk about. Something you may need to deal with for the purposes of healing. Any idea what that might be?"

I looked away and stayed silent.

"I hope you won't be angry with her for mentioning even that much to me."

"I'm not. She's looking out for me."

Brenda exhaled a sigh of relief. "Thank goodness."

I wrapped my hands around the mug and leaned forward. "I would like to talk to you, but I need to know your oath of doctor-patient confidentiality is sacrosanct."

"It is."

"Even if the topic broaches the legal arena?"

"Even then. I assure you it won't be the first time."

154

The pile of sopping, wadded tissues on the cushion next to me grew as I told her about the rape and the loss of Caitlin. My eyes were dry as a bleached bone when I told her about what I'd done to Eric. I omitted any mention of Connie.

"Katherine, people who wound others are themselves wounded. Violence often begets violence and becomes a vicious vortex of self-entrapment."

"I don't care about *their* wounds," I shouted. "I care about *our* wombs, ours and our daughters'."

"Please don't take my statement as a personal affront. I assure you it wasn't meant that way."

"Now that you know what I'm capable of, do you find me repugnant?"

Brenda stared at a point on the far wall then said, "Not at all." In a voice that sounded as though she'd mentally left the room, she added, "Most of us have no idea what we're capable of until we're forced to find out."

I left my question unasked. "I'm relieved. Surely you see that I couldn't trust the establishment to right the injustice. Even if they'd locked him away for the remainder of his life, which we both know they wouldn't, it wouldn't have been punishment enough."

She returned her gaze to me and nodded. "No personal satisfaction."

"Exactly. And, even then, my satisfaction level is minimal." I got up and paced. Brenda waited for me to speak again.

I paused and looked at her. "I imagine I should feel terrified about getting caught, though I was profoundly careful. Perhaps I should even feel terrified of what I can and will do, but I'm not. I imagine regret or remorse should chase me in my dreams, but I sleep like ..." Our eyes met as the clichés, *sleep like a baby* and *sleep like the dead*, hung unsaid in the air. "I sleep better than I probably should."

"Your response is understandable. At least it's over and done with."

I walked to the window and fixed my focus on Caitlin's tree. "I'd do it again, if given the chance, and with an equal absence of guilt."

"You mean if forced into a similar circumstance, which I pray you never are."

"I meant exactly what I said." I returned to the sofa, picked up my mug and sipped as Brenda remained silent while wearing an expression I couldn't decipher.

Then I told her about taking the earring and what I'd done with it. "It hangs there like the sword of Damocles, a silent threat to all men who overpower women or think it's their right to."

"It's a two-way concept, Katherine."

"I don't follow."

"Every person who grasps power and clutches it lives under some form of fear."

"I've lived powerlessly under a form of fear, especially of men, and for just cause, nearly as long as I've been alive."

"That sword was held by a single horse hair, as you recall."

"There's a point you're trying to make."

"All I'm saying is that certain types of power are tenuous."

"You're advising me to proceed with caution."

"For what it's worth."

"Your opinion matters. So, noted."

"Please understand me—I side with you. My concern is for your safety and well-being. Always. I don't begrudge what you felt you had to do or that you did it. My concern is that there's a slippery-slope aspect to this path."

"Then I'll have to wear shoes with cleats." I hesitated a moment then asked, "Do you think my actions are indicative of someone becoming what your profession might call troubled?"

"No more, my dear Katherine, than the rest of us who've been traumatized. It comes with the territory, though perhaps not to the same extent."

I chatted with Brenda for five minutes more then left after receiving a comforting hug from her. She'd made a few comments, I assumed rote ones derived from her field of training, but I was certain of her support.

The lecture and scolding I'd anticipated were not delivered, only love and understanding and concern.

I couldn't speak as to members at lower levels of this extraordinary organization, but the ones at the top stood out in an exemplary fashion. These women didn't play around. No games. No subterfuge, especially among each other.

They also understood the need for revenge when and as appropriate.

They'd need to.

Because future plans had begun to form in my mind.

CHAPTER 50

Awhile back, Patricia had told me WAM women were involved in a revolution, one where women would be positioned to call the shots and rule the world. I hadn't asked for specifics then or as yet, nor had she expounded about this since that time, but I liked the sound of it even more now.

She'd also said her hope was that this could be accomplished in her lifetime, though her tone indicated she believed their efforts would continue into the next generation, maybe beyond, before fully achieved. I wasn't willing to be as patient. It might take a number of years, but the revolution would happen far sooner—it had to. I'd do whatever I could to make it so. A concrete plan was required. When I felt the timing was right, I'd ask her for more information, which was needed if I was to succeed in devising a strategy.

Patricia and I were alone one evening after everyone else had gone home for the day. I told her about my father, about Buster, about the others, and about my mother. I deliberately left out what Abigail had done to me.

She patted my hand and said, "I've heard numerous stories of every kind of abuse, but it still shocks me to hear the cruelty women are forced to suffer. When abuse involves children, my blood boils, and I want to hurt anyone who does such things."

"I'm glad to hear it."

Patricia tilted her head to the side and said, "Why do I feel there's something more to your comment?"

"I want revenge. I started with Eric. Buster's next."

"Ending with whom?"

I shrugged. "I'll have to see. For now, I have a list with several names on it—a starter list, you might say. I've recently added two names." My face wrinkled in disgust at the thought of Clyde and Jared. "One significant name is missing. Rather, I should say confirmation of a name is lacking. But I have my suspicions."

"The question mark you mentioned, reserved, I presume, for the man who killed your mother."

I lowered my head and nodded.

"Is it your intention to turn them all into eunuchs?"

"That's an unknown at this time, though a possibility. I suppose it depends on circumstances."

"If retribution truly is your intention, I suggest you avoid establishing a modus operandi."

"Point well taken. Any suggestions?"

"Considering your scientific and medical knowledge, and your developing skills, it seems, to me at least, that you have a cornucopia of options." She got to her feet. "I think it's time to expand your awareness of our more *particular* enterprises."

Directly behind Patricia's desk was a long credenza. Left of that was a built-in bookcase that stopped eighteen inches before that wall intersected with the side wall. She walked to the end of the bookcase and motioned for me to join her. I did, wondering which of the volumes held information reserved for those to whom she chose to reveal their contents.

She faced me, her expression stern. "I promised that one day I'd show you the laboratories. Remember?"

My pulse sped. "Is today that day?"

"Have you mentioned the fact of the labs or discussed their existence with anyone, even a member?"

I had the briefest thought of Abigail. Relief flooded through me that I'd refrained from saying more regarding this organization, especially about this aspect. I shook my head. "Not a word to anyone."

"One of the strongest bonds of our sisterhood is the secrets we know about each other and keep sacred. Your secrets are safe with me, but in order for me to involve you at the highest level, you have to swear to me, here and now, that what you learn beyond this point will go with you to your grave." She smiled and rested her hand on my forearm. "After you live a long and healthy life, of course."

My insides fluttered with excitement. I crossed my heart and held up my hand. "I swear on all I hold sacred."

She chuckled. "Accurate sentiment, if not a tiny bit dramatic."

"So it's different when you do it?"

"Touché."

Patricia pushed on the wall panel in the gap at the end of the bookcase, which was, in reality, a magnetic door. It swung toward us and opened to a tiny windowless room empty of everything but the paint on the walls and a keypad next to another door directly across from us.

She pulled the panel door closed and crossed to the keypad. The keypad had a shield around the top and both sides, so as to make it impossible for any bystander to see the numbers punched in. Fingers placed over the numbers, she keyed a code in to unlock the other door, which opened to a hallway several yards long and ended at an elevator.

At the elevator, she punched in numbers on another covered keypad that activated a screen positioned above it. Patricia stood completely still in front of the screen. A red light came on then shifted to green. The elevator doors opened and I followed her in.

"What *was* that?" I asked.

"Facial recognition is required for entry."

"I had no idea that technology was available yet, much less to the general public."

"It isn't."

She pushed a button marked 3L. The doors slid shut silently. I knew we were moving because the light shifted behind the numerals above the doors.

Patricia also watched the numerals confirm our descent. "I told you we have remarkable professional women as members, women committed to our goal. Geniuses, really, and easily persuaded to join us where they're not only compensated well but appreciated and respected.

"Their combined efforts created this system for our usage. And although I share at meetings that my husband is wealthy, that's an understatement. I put most of my fifty percent into solid investments, which allowed me to increase my settlement exponentially, and that amount continues to increase."

The elevator stopped. The doors opened, as did my mouth.

I stepped into the large gleaming space and said, "If I believed in heaven, this would be it."

CHAPTER 51

Patricia stretched her arms wide. "From the first door I opened, we began entry into our network of labs and areas restricted to high-ranking members and personnel I selected. Only the top echelon—a comparatively small number—know anything goes on below ground, or even that there is anything underground."

"Are you saying I'm now one of you?"

She rested an arm across my shoulders. "Yes, Katherine. After my many and sundry experiences, I'm an excellent judge of character and of what a member may potentially contribute to our organization and, specifically, to our cause."

My mind absorbed the fact of this equipment-filled room, including top-of-the-line computers at each workstation. Several scientists worked diligently at whatever would lead them to fulfill their purpose.

Patricia pointed. "See that door to the left at the far end?"

"Yes."

She smiled and winked at me. "If you look carefully, you'll see entry also requires facial recognition."

"I could ask what goes on in there, but would you tell me?"

"Better. I'll show you."

I followed her, eyes wide, as she nodded at or spoke to women who were able to glance up from what they attended to without spoiling a result. Each woman whose gaze shifted to me smiled. I beamed my delight back at them.

"You funded all of this by yourself?" I asked. "Contributions can't be that great, or are they?"

"A good portion comes from me, but not all. I'm not the only member with extensive funds."

She repeated the identification process in front of the screen at the left of the door, which slid open.

I followed her inside, mouth agape at the even more advanced equipment and computers the room contained, minus test tubes and beakers. "What goes on in here?"

"Ultra-secret projects." She gestured toward the computers and the women who sat focused on whatever they viewed on the monitors. "You're looking at some of the best programmers in the world."

"What are they working on?"

"They're also some of the best hackers." She smiled.

"Was your avoidance deliberate?"

"Sorry. Some of them are hacking government computers. Others are doing various research or addressing particular concerns."

My feet stopped moving. "Aren't you terrified their activities will be traced to you?"

"They explained why I shouldn't worry, but did it in their unique lingo. Once I got them to use words I could understand, they explained it as a buffer in a buffer to the two-hundredth power, whatever that means." She faced me. "Now that you've seen what's going on, what do you think?"

"Lao-tzu said, 'He who knows others is wise, but he who knows himself is enlightened.'"

"And that means what to you at this moment?"

"That I know myself. That I know I want to be an integral part of your revolution. And I want to do something great, something no one has as yet done."

"Such as?"

I shook my head. "I have an idea but it's only a seed. That seed was planted a long time ago. But right now, I feel as though a light switch just went on, more like a dimmer switch, really, that's been adjusted up a notch to a slightly brighter level of illumination."

"What kind of seed?"

"I'm not entirely certain as yet, other than it will put men in their proper place. But using your words, I've just been presented with a cornucopia of potential options."

Patricia laughed. "I knew you'd respond this way."

"Is the door in your office the only way in or out?"

"There is one other way, but only a very few people who work down here know about it. It's for emergencies only—the dire kind. Otherwise, the rooms are fire-proofed. I also had living quarters set up down here. Everything they need or want is delivered to them."

"It doesn't bother them to stay down here?"

"These women are basically hermits-on-purpose. Everyone's happy with the arrangements."

"I can understand that, considering the state of the world under male domination." I faced her. "When do I get my facial recognition set up?"

"I love your enthusiasm, and your level of commitment. Follow me."

CHAPTER 52

The single disappointment I had regarding moving up at WAM was that, although Patricia integrated my face into the recognition program and gave me the code, she insisted I wait until I was further along in my studies to use the science lab. I was, however, free to access both private labs anytime I wished, as an observer primarily, and was allowed to speak with the women there, as long as I didn't interrupt their projects or annoy them with too many questions.

She didn't need to worry. My desire to progress in my studies kept me busy and focused, so busy that I had to reduce my hours at WAM.

Classes and labs filled my days as instructors crammed fundamentals of the art and science of medicine and patient care into our brains. There was also massive, early preparation for the first licensing examination we were required to pass prior to proceeding to our third and fourth years of medical school.

Another time-occupier was my willingness to take advantage of the practice tests offered by the National Board of Medical Examiners. These tests were designed to increase our chances of passing Step 1 of the United States Medical Licensing Examination. It wasn't that I was concerned about my ability to pass, I merely wished to speed my completion time, like improving running speed in order to shave several significant seconds off a racing score.

Each time prior to Jenni taking the practice tests, she'd spend longer and longer hours attempting to stuff more information into her brain. I took this as a sign that she wasn't doing well. The point of the tests was to help us identify our strengths and what needed improvement. If appearances indicated fact, she needed a great deal of improvement.

"You really need to get more sleep," I told her one morning. "You have raccoon eyes and bags you could pack things in. Besides, an exhausted brain can't function as well as a rested one."

"Shut up! You think it's easy having you snooze away while I pour over books and notes all night?"

"I've told you a number of times that I'm willing to help you."

"Yeah. You'll help me. Right out of medical school."

"Ouch. Why would you even think that?"

"Just leave me the hell alone. Everything comes too damn easy for you."

"If you had any idea how wrong … Nevermind. I'm wasting my breath."

"And taking up too much of mine. Insufferable bitch."

Poor Jenni. It was painful to watch her grapple with herself as well as the material. It was even more painful when I, well rested, passed Step 1 of the USMLE with the highest, and perfect, score and Jenni failed. That is, if you consider her refusal to speak to me painful or a disadvantage. With the exception of her slamming every door for weeks, the silence was welcome.

Patricia threw a party to celebrate my passing that first exam and moving into my third year. She invited Brenda, Agatha, and Connie. A small, intimate gathering of those of us who knew at least some of my darkest secrets.

She treated us to fine dining in the best restaurant in the area, followed by brandy for them, tea for me, in her office.

"Although we miss having you around as much," she said, "we know it's temporary. And we're so proud of you."

They raised their snifters, I raised my cup and said, "It should be a more productive year. Aside from classes, I'll rotate through fundamental specialties required of students. I anticipate it being engaging, but I won't be able to choose rotations in areas that interest me until the fourth year."

Agatha asked, "Any early idea about a specialty?"

I shook my head. "So much captivates me. But I'll figure it out eventually. In the meantime, this is more fun than I've had in a while."

Connie chuckled. I looked at her and she winked.

I checked the time. "I need to get going. However, there is one thing I'd like to ask of you before I, or we, call it a night. Come with me to Caitlin's tree?"

Brenda said, "Of course," and drained her glass. The others did the same.

Minutes later, we stood in the moonlight before the young tree that was growing taller and stronger. A soft breeze wafted over us, shifting the laurel leaves. For a brief moment, the sword earring glinted in the cool light.

The four women encircled me with their arms. We stood there in silence. It wasn't that we had no words, it was that we each had too many.

Five women. Five friends. Untold measures of pain.

Abigail called me during the evening before the last day of the fall semester. The interruption annoyed Jenni, which caused me to answer the phone with a lighter tone than I might otherwise have.

"K, were you planning to come here for the holidays?"

"I'm staying here."

"That's a relief."

"Glad I could make your day."

She giggled. "I didn't mean it that way. Hubby-Buns has a cousin in Montana. He invited us to spend Christmas through New Year's Day there."

"That should be fun."

She yawned. "I guess. I'm not into all that wide-open-space stuff."

"Sounds serene, restful."

"That's so not my thing."

"I'm certain you'll make the best of it."

"I suppose."

"Life isn't always a party, Abigail."

"It should be."

Jenni slammed her book closed, turned around in her chair and faced me. "Can you *please* end that inane conversation so I can think straight?"

I bit the inside of my cheek to keep myself from making the remark that very much wanted to escape. "Abigail, I need to go. Enjoy Montana and the holidays."

I ended the call and said, "Better?"

Jenni faced forward and opened a different book. "A slug has a more interesting life than you do."

Some things are better left unsaid.

CHAPTER 53

I woke shortly after nine on the morning of the first day of Christmas break. Aside from attention on my studies during the prior months, I'd also given thought to what I wanted to do during this three-and-a-half-week interval. Many ideas were toyed with, but one particular idea continued to behave like a splinter in my thoughts.

I pulled the comforter to my chin and folded my arms behind my head, eyes affixed to an unseen point on the ceiling as I pondered how I might accomplish such a task.

My phone jangled, which caused Jenni, also in bed, to curse and bury her head under her stack of pillows. It was Patricia.

Before I had a chance to say more than hello, she said, "Let me treat you to brunch."

"Sounds good to me. There's something I want to discuss with you."

"I'll pick you up at eleven."

I stayed in bed until ten. As Jenni remained buried in a tangle of her bedspread, sheets, and pillows, my shower was a leisurely one, with it being my turn to use up the hot water.

Patricia was waiting out front as I exited the dorm, though it took honking at me to recognize her in the new silver Jaguar. I slid onto the heated leather seat.

Dressed in head-to-toe red, she said, "It's my Christmas present to myself. I deserved it."

"And so much more." I leaned over and kissed her cheek. "I'm embarrassed to say I have no idea what to get you, nor will it likely be up to your standards."

She put the car in gear and eased through the parking lot and onto the street. "There's only one thing I want as a gift from you. Spend Christmas day with me." She glanced at me. "Unless you have other plans."

"I don't. Gift granted."

We chatted about insignificant matters as we drove to a new bistro. Patricia had reserved a table near the small fireplace with logs that crackled and flames that cast an amber glow over us.

After the server delivered our food and left, Patricia leaned forward, resting her crossed forearms on the table. "What did you want to discuss?"

"Maybe it isn't a proper topic while we eat."

Her eyebrows went up and she grinned. "Then I insist you tell me."

"I so admire your courage."

"Back at you."

I lowered my voice. "I want to call in a few debts. They've gone unpaid for too long."

"Keep going."

"The first one is Buster, if he's even still alive. For all I know, some woman braver than my mother paid him back in full for his abuse. Only, I don't know how to go about locating him, though he may still be in Chicago. I can't imagine he motivated himself to move out of the city. I guess the thing to do is ask Connie."

"You said there are a few. Who else is on your radar?"

"That one is more complicated. I told you I had suspicions only about—"

"I remember."

We sat back and stayed silent as the waiter delivered our salads.

Once alone again, I said, "There are others, but because of the specific circumstances, they deserve lesser punishments. I'll have to track them down too, but later."

Patricia waved her hand holding the fork. "I can help with all of that."

"How?"

"Really, Katherine. Push pause on your emotions and think. I don't have a special staff for no reason."

"You'd let me employ their skills? Beyond just Connie?"

"That's part of why they're there. Trust me. They'd be delighted. I know their histories, which I won't share."

"I won't ask. Can we get started right away?"

Patricia laughed. "How about we finish eating first?"

I laughed with her. "I've waited this long. I can last a few minutes more." Another thought came to me. "Even if we find Buster, I'll have to travel to Chicago, if that's where he is, and find a place to stay. The cost may be more than I can manage. If you authorize it, I can work extra hours at headquarters during this break, though that means waiting to deal with him until spring break or maybe longer."

She rested her hand atop mine. "You weren't the only one unsure of what to give as a gift. All expenses will be mine, no matter how long it takes or what it takes."

I shook my head. "I can't accept. It's too much."

"You must. You owe it to all of us to let us share in justice being served. Not all of us have had or ever will have the satisfaction. Or the nerve."

My eyes filled and I choked up too much to speak.

Patricia retrieved a tissue from her purse and handed it to me. "Everything happens for a reason, Katherine, including my having the wherewithal to do what I can for other women. It's my choice how to use my money. You want to do great things with your skills and talents, and you want to do them for WAM and for women. I have full faith that you will. Let me do whatever will help get you there."

Unable to speak in response to her generosity, I nodded my agreement then melted into a puddle of tears.

I felt a fresh tissue being pressed into my hand, and I smiled between sobs.

CHAPTER 54

Minutes before noon the following day, I burst into Patricia's office. "They found Buster. He's still in Chicago. Now I have to figure out how to get there." I paced in front of her desk. "So many details to work out and in what now feels like a brief expanse of time."

"I'm not about to let you do this alone."

I halted my steps. "I refuse to involve you."

Patricia picked up her phone receiver, punched a few numbers in, and said, "Only thing I'm going to contribute is resources, including financial." She held up a finger to silence me and said into the phone, "My office. Pronto."

I suppose I should have guessed who was on the other end of that brisk conversation, but my excitement was too great. So was my relief when Connie bustled into the room.

Connie hugged me and said, "Season's greetings, all. What's up?"

Patricia unlocked her middle desk drawer and said, "Hold on. I'll tell you in a moment." She unlocked a small metal box tucked inside the drawer, counted out five thousand dollars in hundreds, fifties, and twenties, and handed the bills to Connie.

Connie tucked the money into an inside zippered jacket pocket. "Where am I going this time, when, and why?"

"Chicago, immediately, and you won't be alone. You and Katherine are to get in and get out as fast as possible. Use aliases. That amount should cover all expenses and your time. If it doesn't, let me know. Katherine will fill you in on the why."

Connie nodded and said to me, "Let's go. We've got arrangements to make."

I followed her through the panel door and down to the ultra-secret room three levels below ground. As we made our way, I asked why that was our destination.

"Our techs will arrange our flights, hotel rooms, and a rental car. They also need to set us up with authentic phony IDs and the all-important et cetera. When we're done with all of that, you can tell me why we're heading to the Big Onion."

"You'll likely figure it out when I give the techs the information they'll need."

"Probably. But with you, there's always more to the story."

The efficiency of WAM's operatives wowed me. Two sets of false IDs for each of us were set up, as were matching credit cards and bank accounts with histories going back a reasonable number of years, along with phony current balances. Then the creation of other data usually found in the system, in case someone in an official capacity decided to check up on us for any reason. Once these steps were completed, all reservations were made under the first set of our new names. As I said, efficient, and took two techs two hours each to complete the tasks, using programs they'd created.

We were assured our licenses and credit cards were identical to real ones in current use. Connie became a waitress who resided in Arkansas. I, a school teacher, now hailed from Mississippi.

Connie tapped me on the shoulder. "Let's go to my office."

I went with her to a locked door on the fifth floor. Once inside, she pointed to a chair, which I lowered into.

"Okay," she said, "start talking."

I filled her in on life with Buster, every last detail, as well as his current address and information about that part of town, the latter provided by the techs the day before. The light outside her window had started to fade by the time I sat back and waited for her to say something.

She picked up a pen and doodled on a tablet. Finally, she said, "You plan to have all the fun or will you let me share it?"

"Up to you. If you want to participate more than you already will be—"

"You bet your ass I do. It pisses me off when any sonofabitch abuses a woman. But a kid? That shit makes me feral."

"Feral is something Buster can relate to."

"I'll relate his ass. Right off the planet."

Buster wouldn't know what hit him, but he'd darn well know who.

CHAPTER 55

We got into the modest rental Ford at O'Hare International Airport and made our way into mid-afternoon traffic on the multi-lane highway, and onward to the chain motel holding guaranteed reservations for us—two rooms under our new names, and not reserved at the same time. We checked in ten minutes apart, put our overnight bags in Connie's room then went to mine.

"Remember," she said, "make it look occupied so housekeeping doesn't get suspicious when they do their thing in the morning. You do this part. I'll do the bathroom and vanity. There are particular touches that have to be done just right."

"Should I ask?"

"Maybe another time. Let's do this and get out."

Ten minutes later, Connie gave me a thumbs-up for my efforts. "Leave your room key on the dresser. And take the blanket."

Back in Connie's room, we sat on the double bed to review our strategy. She pulled out folded sheets of paper from her overnight bag.

"What's that?" I asked.

"Surveillance on Buster-boy procured by the tech fairies. You'd didn't think I'd let us show up with no intel, did you?"

"How'd they manage that?"

"WAM has far-reaching arms." She opened the papers. "Now I can fill you in on his comings and goings."

A few minutes after eight, and with overnight bags in hand and the blanket from her bed, we left the room key on top of the TV and exited. Connie drove to a favored burger place not far from the motel. We pulled into the drive-through lane, got our orders at the window, and parked in the lot to eat. Her appetite proved more stimulated than mine.

We ran inside to use the facilities then headed over to Armour Square, the squalid neighborhood where Buster now resided, so we could scope out his place and handy exit streets. Squalid was an understatement.

That task accomplished, we drove to a better neighborhood, found a strip mall, where we parked in the darkest corner available. I climbed into the back seat, handed Connie's bag to her, and we began our transformation into ladies of the night. Then it was back to Armour Square to wait until the appropriate moment presented itself.

We parked about fifty feet from Buster's building and on the other side of the one-way street. Scooted down in the front seat, I glanced at Connie. "I can't get used to you in a black wig and black eyebrows."

"Back at you, blondie."

A gust of wind blew sheets of soiled newspapers and other bits of trash down the broken sidewalk and rutted street. I followed one such item as it tumbled toward the corner, and then retrained my eyes on Buster's dilapidated three-story apartment building on the opposite corner.

"Not that I blame them," I said, "but no one's moving around outside. It's like being in a ghost town."

"No one's going to sit out on their stoop around here. Besides, most of these residents are probably passed out inside or getting high so they can enter oblivion." Connie checked the time. "Almost ten. He should be returning soon. If our intel is right, our boy will lounge inside awhile, snort some snow, and head out close to eleven to play with prostitutes."

"I don't want to know how the person who learned that did it. I am, however, certain that we're doing those women and the community a service."

"You bet your ass." Connie sat up an inch.

"What?"

"Stay down. He's just turned the corner *and* ... up the stoop he goes. Some people are such creatures of habit. Makes my job easier more often than I can count."

"They're positive he lives alone?"

"Yep. A woman would have to be pretty damn desperate to live with him in this place, or anywhere, for that matter."

I went quiet.

Connie looked my way. "Shit. I'm sorry. I wasn't thinking."

I shook my head. "It's okay. You're accurate in your assessment."

"Still …"

"That truth makes doing this even easier."

"All right then."

Connie handed me a pair of nitrile gloves. We slipped them on then covered them with black lace gloves. She slung the strap of a bulky purse over her shoulder and said, "Time to roll his rocks."

CHAPTER 56

We crossed the street and walked under a flickering street lamp, one of four that hadn't been shot out. Something on the broken sidewalk stuck to my shoe. I scraped it off against the curb. "What is that?"

Connie pulled a penlight from her purse, bent over and aimed the tiny beam at the unidentified thing. "Condom."

I bent over as well. "What's that pink stuff?"

She flicked off the light. "Lipstick."

"I'm going to be sick."

"You cut off a man's bits without a flinch, and this makes you sick?" She dropped the penlight into her purse. "Let's go. And no more distractions."

The smell inside the tiny foyer sent ripples of remembrance through me. "Shades of Cabrini-Green."

"What?"

"Nevermind."

Between the shoes Connie insisted I wear and the rickety wooden stairs leading us to the top floor, I stumbled more than once. "Why stilettos? And why a skirt that stops where it does?"

"Part of the uniform."

"To think that decades ago, when these buildings were constructed, the families that occupied them considered this a charming, safe place to live."

"You gabbing about architecture and days gone by 'cause you're nervous?"

"I suppose it's the memory of him coming into my room. He was so large. Everything about him was large. And brutal."

"Well, he's gone to flab now, and he's several years over a decade older. But he is big. Seeing him in my room would've terrified me too." Connie stopped and placed a hand on my shoulder. "If worms are wiggling in your innards, remind yourself of the women you're about to save and those you're about to avenge."

I nodded and stayed silent as we reached the third floor.

We moved toward his door as stealthily as possible across wooden boards that creaked no matter how softly we placed our feet down.

I stayed out of sight, about a foot and a half to Connie's left.

She took her position in front of the door, faced me and whispered, "Ready?"

"You bet your ass," I whispered back.

She grinned and knocked.

Heavy footfalls inside neared the door. Connie plastered a seductive expression on her face.

Buster yanked the door open. "What the hell? I ain't ordered no ho."

Connie looked toward me. I stepped into view, smiling as though this was the only place in the world I wanted to be. It was.

Buster ran his eyes over me then over Connie. "What the hell goin' on?"

Connie pretended to brush something invisible from her exposed cleavage. "We're your birthday present."

"It ain't my birthday."

Connie puckered her lips into a pout. "Freddie said you'd be happy to see us."

"Freddie who?"

She shrugged. "Didn't ask his last name. He paid us. That's all I care about. You don't want to party, we'll go. But no damn way I'm giving Freddie his money back. He can talk to you about that."

Buster scratched his crotch. "Guess we don't wanna piss ol' Freddie off." He opened the door wide and stepped back. Connie swished into the room. I swished in behind her.

The place reeked of body odor and too many other odors to identify or want to. Buster returned to his seat on the sofa, which had a leg that had somehow lost an inch. I knew that's where he'd been because he still had two lines of cocaine centered on the surface of the battered coffee table in front of it.

"I ain't sharing this with you," he said.

Connie gave a dismissive wave of a hand. "Freddie took care of us before we came."

He snorted the white powder into his nose then lit a fat joint, inhaling deeply. He leaned back and stretched his arms across the back of the dingy sofa. Eyes half-closed, he exhaled and said, "Strip."

Connie wagged a finger at him. "You first. I've heard so much about what we're going to play with—how *huge* it is—I want to see it. It'll get me in the mood, you know?"

He ignored my silence, and that I stood there like a pillar of stone. Connie's performance covered my inactivity.

She started toward him, bag still over her shoulder. "I'll help you peel those clothes off. Then this party can start. Baby, I'm gonna light your candle and let you make a wish."

Connie dropped her purse onto the end of the sofa. Buster stood. She helped him remove his pants and underwear over his growing erection, all the while making comments about how impressive he was down there. He began to raise his sweater over his head. As soon as his field of vision was obscured, Connie zapped his testicles with the stun gun. He crashed onto the cheap coffee table, which splintered beneath him.

I walked over and squatted next to him. I looked him in the eyes, ran my gaze down to his genitals and said, "It looked a lot bigger when I was a child."

Connie dragged her purse closer and dropped the stun gun into it. "Everything looks bigger to a child. However, this was one for the record books."

I grabbed his chin and forced him to look at me. "I doubt you recognize me. Katherine Barnes. You used to call me Little Katie when you forced yourself on me in my room, in the dark. Cabrini-Green. Remember?"

It took a moment but became obvious he did.

Connie said, "We don't want to spend a lot of time reminiscing here. Did you decide about giving him an Eric?"

"Patricia advised me not to establish a pattern."

"Then let's get this done and get out. Yes?"

"Ready when you are."

She pulled a small can of drain cleaner from her bulky purse. I pinched his oily nostrils closed and yanked his mouth open.

Connie removed the cap and said, "Let's see how well this stuff eliminates grease."

CHAPTER 57

The drain cleaner would work its magic without us staying to watch. We were certain of this because Connie had emptied the entire contents of the small canister into Buster's maw, even though a tablespoon's worth would have done the job. Its effects were kicking in at full force as we exited and closed the door behind us.

Twenty minutes later, our hooker attire and other disguises, as well as the empty can and nitrile gloves, were in a dumpster far removed from his neigborhood, but in an equally degraded part of the city. We drove off as the fire inside the dumpster whooshed to life.

It took a while, but we finally found a pay phone somewhere we likely wouldn't get mugged or worse. Connie reached the tech waiting to hear from us. Fifteen minutes later, the phone rang. I listened to the one-sided conversation.

"We're all set," Connie said as she ended the call. "Now to find another hotel or motel closer to our destination."

"You were amazing back there. I would have taken care of it by myself, but I'm glad I didn't have to. I doubt I could have made the pretense as convincing."

Connie took a bow. "What can I say? I got skills. C'mon. We need to boogie."

We found a motel in the desired vicinity, drove to the back, parked front-end facing out, and locked the doors. I took the back seat, Connie stayed in front. Wrapped in one of the blankets, it took longer than I thought it would to fall asleep. Too many memories cropped up. Nor was I spared in my dreams. I didn't dream about what we'd done to Buster. I dreamed about what Buster had done to Mama and me.

At first light, Connie said, "Rise and shine, partner. It's next-step time."

I crawled over the seat and yawned. "I'm starving."

"You'll have to wait an hour or so." She reached into her purse and handed me a candy bar, taking one for herself. "This will have to hold you." She started the car and headed for our next destination.

We parked in the long-term lot at Midway International Airport. Before we got out, we exchanged our fake IDs and credit cards for the second batch of false ones, and wiped our fingerprints off the interior and exterior of the car. We checked in and retrieved our boarding passes under our new names.

It would be another three hours before our flight left to return us home. We located the food stalls. My appetite had definitely returned, much to Connie's amusement. On the way to the departure gate, we passed a gift shop.

"Hold up," I said. Connie followed me to a display case.

"What are you looking for?"

"I'll know it when I see it."

She shrugged and wandered around while I looked for what I wanted. Purchase made, Connie trailed me out of the store.

"What'd you get?"

I stopped at a trash receptacle and removed two small cards from the plastic shop bag. Each card held a pair of earrings.

Connie crinkled her eyebrows. "Wieners-in-buns? That doesn't seem like your style."

"They're not for me. Not exactly." I removed one earring from the card, stuffed it into my front jeans pocket, and threw the other away.

Connie put her arm around my shoulder. "Caitlin's tree."

I nodded and sniffed back tears.

"And the small hearts?"

"One for Mama, one for me."

CHAPTER 58

Connie and I went directly to the techs the moment we arrived at headquarters. Because ours hadn't been a direct flight, deliberately, it was after nine at night, so the building was mostly empty. Patricia was likely at home, planning how to take over the world.

We handed over our sets of fake IDs and credit cards, which the tech with spiked purple hair and a tiny diamond stud in her left nostril tossed into an incinerator. "Since we're doing business, the name's Lavender," she said.

I avoided saying the obvious and held out my hand. "I'm—"

She ignored my hand. "Already know, don't I?"

"Of course. Apologies."

She returned to her desk and said, "I'll clear the fake stuff from the system in a bit." Looking directly at me, she added, "I made some headway with your other project."

Excitement rushed through me. "What did you find?"

"Let me show you." She swiveled her chair so as to face her computer. "Coeur d'Alene police had a strong suspect but no evidence conclusive enough to avoid the reasonable-doubt trap in court. Plus, he had an alibi. Flimsy as shit, but it stuck."

"Was it Anthony?"

She shook her head. "Still in prison, but maybe getting out in about another year or so, if he's a good boy. The guy they arrested and released is Ralph Johnson."

"I don't know who that is."

"Maybe his mugshot will help."

She made rapid-fire keystrokes I couldn't follow. Seconds later, a police report appeared on the monitor screen, which included the front and profile photos.

I grabbed onto the desk.

Connie said, "Whoops. Girlfriend needs a chair."

I plunked onto the one she provided.

"Who is it?" Connie asked.

"Someone I never would have expected." I told them about the *nice* man on the beach and his Irish setter. "I never knew he and Mama had further interaction. She never mentioned him."

Lavender summarized as she read from the police report. "Says here that he told them he and your mother spoke on the beach a few times. He visited your mother at her apartment a couple of times, and they did things socially on a couple of occasions. Said although he felt sorry for her, their acquaintance didn't last, because they were too different. That they came from different worlds in every sense." She leaned back in her chair. "He was clever about covering his ass regarding his prints being found in your mother's apartment. They couldn't pin her death on him, but feel pretty sure it was him. What about you?" She looked at me and waited.

"The police were proficient regarding Anthony, but I never heard more from them about Mama's killer. They should have told me about Ralph."

Connie leaned over and studied his face. "Probably preferred to have a sure case. They had to let him go. No choice."

"If it is him," I said, "he planned it carefully. All this time I thought ... It doesn't matter, only proving it was him does."

Connie said, "Bet it's him. And like so many of the guilty damn bunch of them, he's walking around free."

"Not for long," I said.

Connie punched my arm. "Friggin' A."

Lavender nodded. "Times two."

CHAPTER 59

I put my fork and knife down, slouched back in the upholstered dining room chair, and undid the button on my jeans. "I'm stuffed."

Patricia laughed. "I'm not surprised. You ate almost an entire half of the turkey by yourself."

Connie picked a piece of dark meat off the bird and tossed it into her mouth. "Yeah, what's with that?"

My cheeks grew warm. "Sorry if I made a pig of myself. I've never had turkey that wasn't in an aluminum tray before, and even that's been in the last couple of years only." At their stunned expressions, I added, "We always had spaghetti and meatballs for holidays."

The fact that such a holiday meal of spaghetti came later in my life was one I chose to keep to myself. We were each too full of turkey and well-being to bring up bologna or peanut butter sandwiches or the fact I'd been unable to enjoy my favorite dish since that day I'd found Mama. The last thing I wanted to do was turn this into a pity party, a term I'd learned from Connie.

Connie halted her reach midway for another bit of dark meat and said, "No one ever invited you for a holiday meal?"

How many times had Abigail invited me? Each holiday since Mama had died was the answer to that question. I found myself relieved that she was in Montana. "I was invited many times but declined."

"Why?"

"I had my reasons."

Patricia stood and said, "No one get up. I'll start the coffee. We'll let the food settle before we even think about cleaning up."

She left Connie and me at the table. We sat in companionable silence until Patricia returned a few minutes later bearing a tray with cups, et cetera, and a French press coffee carafe. With a deft hand, she poured and handed each of us our steaming cups.

Once seated, she said, "It's off-topic, and you can tell me if this isn't the time to discuss it, but something has been weighing on my mind." Facing me she said, "I wish there was a way to confirm that Ralph is complicit in your mother's death. I hate the thought of you not being positive it was he who took her from you."

Connie blew across the top of her cup, took a sip, and said, "I've given that some thought. There's a way."

We listened attentively and discussed options for how to bring justice to Ralph Johnson, if justice needed to be meted to him. To use Patricia's phrase, we had a cornucopia of options worth consideration.

CHAPTER 60

I swiveled left and right a number of times in front of the full-length mirror in Connie's bedroom. "You can't be serious?"

Connie shrugged. "If you want to catch a big fish, you gotta use the right bait."

"It's winter. I'll freeze my backside off." I turned and stared at my exposed rear in the mirror. "Literally."

"You want this to work, don't you?"

"I'll get arrested for indecent exposure before I can do anything worthy of incarceration. Or I'll die of hypothermia." I stared at my reflection and the tiny fabric triangles that did nothing to cover my breasts. "And what's with this pitiful excuse for a top?"

"The more of your *girls* you show, the better you'll get his attention. We want Ralphie-boy focused on your fore and aft so he doesn't notice me."

"This ought to accomplish it, I suppose."

"Just do what I told you to do. If you confirm it was him, we follow through with the plan. If you confirm it wasn't or can't confirm anything, we'll call it a day and keep looking."

"I'm getting dressed. I can't look at myself like this another second."

"Relax. It'll work. That's all that matters. Unless you'd rather wait until summer, when it's warmer *and* crowded, with some lifeguard watching everyone."

"No. If he's guilty, his reprieve has lasted long enough."

"Atta girl."

Two days after Christmas, we headed north to Coeur d'Alene in a rental car secured with yet another false name assigned to Connie, though we both traveled with false IDs again. Since we were heading

188

into my home territory, she said it was best if I made the drive disguised so no one who knew me could ever say I'd been there. With Abigail and Hubby-Buns remaining in Montana through New Year's Day, there was no chance of bumping into her or him.

We made the several-hour drive with me wearing a wig and makeup that altered me enough so that I barely recognized myself in the mirror. The plan was to spend the night at a motel in the area and avoid Mama's apartment and Mr. Hopkins. Better if we got in and got out without anyone knowing I'd been there.

That night, we dined in the room—with me still in disguise—and reviewed the strategy Connie had devised. The next morning we slept in and ordered breakfast from room service. When the server knocked, I hid in the bathroom since I'd yet to alter my appearance. Connie placed the do-not-disturb sign on the door after the server left. After we ate, she did a thorough check of the paraphernalia needed to accomplish our task. At two that afternoon, I got ready to fish or cut bait, as Connie phrased it.

A quick call was made to Lavender, who reconfirmed Ralph had indeed remained in Coeur d'Alene for the holidays—no last-minute change in plans, was spending it alone, as well as that he and his dog walked to the beach around three thirty every afternoon, rain, shine, or snow, and always stopped at the same spot.

A local weather report predicted a cold but sunny day. As the sunlight would start to wane by the appointed time, it would be frigid.

It was easy to recall where that spot on the beach was located. Mama and I had always parked and sat in the same place, which was about twenty yards from where Ralph and Irish played fetch. At three twenty, I got out of the car, pulled the collar of my too-snug fleece sweatsuit tight around my neck then scrunched through the sand in slip-on tennis shoes and waited.

The long curly black wig was secured to my own hair with so many bobby pins that even a strong gale wouldn't have budged it from my head. Black wrap-around sunglasses stayed perched on my nose so I could look in any direction without indicating where my eyes were aimed. Connie had done my makeup, or I should say overdid it. The only cosmetic I typically used was tinted lip gloss. She was adamant that I had to look like someone else, as well as enticing, hence the Cleopatra eyes, too much blush, and pronounced red lipstick.

Initially, I kept my gaze focused to my right. Minutes later, Connie, decked out in a diving suit and gear, duck-walked into the lake. I watched her swim out a distance then bob low in the water, her focus on me.

A few minutes after that, a dog barked to my left. I felt sorry for the four-legged creature. Then I remembered proof was still required. He might yet return home with his master.

Ralph threw the ball into the water. Irish barked gleefully, frantically wagged his tail, and then dashed into the waves to retrieve the yellow tennis ball.

I got to my feet and started in their direction.

CHAPTER 61

In the diminishing light, I made sure to sashay the way Connie had instructed, which was no easy task on sand. When I reached Ralph, I paused to watch Irish bound back into the water after the ball, as well as to see Connie give a subtle signal from her position, now opposite me and yards out in the lake.

"That's a beautiful dog," I said. "What's his name?"

"His name's Irish. Mine's Ralph." Ralph gave me the once-over, grinned, and extended his hand.

I gave him an award-winning smile and shook his hand, wishing I could wash it as soon as he let go, which took seconds longer than I preferred.

Irish maneuvered through the water and rushed forward. He skidded to a stop right in front of us and shook the water from his fur.

"Sorry about that," Ralph said.

"No problem." I laughed, patted Irish on the head, and said, "Good boy." I meant it, too, because it gave me a nice segue into what was to come next. "I think I'll join him."

"You're crazy. The water's freezing."

I removed the sunglasses and waited. No recognition response came from him. I let the glasses slip from my fingers. "It's like that club—Polar Bear, I think is the name—only I won't be going in naked."

"My loss."

I smiled, kicked off my shoes and felt the first shiver run through me. My galvanic skin response to the cold was immediate and I worried that I'd resemble a plucked chicken more than a vixen. I unzipped my top and dropped it to the sand. Ralph's eyes became transfixed on the tiny bikini-top triangles, which were now more like pyramids.

I faced the water, shimmied my pants down my thighs—bending over just enough—and stepped out of them. At his intake of breath in response to my thong, I turned, licked my lips and said, "Come in with me."

"Much as I'd like to, I can't. No swimsuit. But I'm happy to watch."

I sidled up to him and stroked his chest with a finger. "If it were nighttime, we could go in naked."

He wrapped an arm around me and rubbed my exposed buttocks. "I'd like that. A lot. Although, I think my hot tub is a better idea."

I looked around. "It's dark enough. Close enough to nighttime, don't you think? What are you wearing, tighty-whites or boxers?"

"Boxers. But—"

"C'mon, Ralph. Look around. There's no one anywhere near enough to care what we do. Besides, they're all leaving. We'll go out just far enough so we keep our footing. We can keep each other warm, if you get my drift. Or do you get these kinds of invitations so often that I'm boring you?" I gave him a red-lipped pout and ran my finger down his chest and thigh.

"What the hell. Why not?" He began to strip.

Irish dropped the ball at our feet. Ralph paused long enough to toss the ball a good distance down the beach rather than into the water.

I ran into the lake first so I could keep his attention on me, not that Connie would be obvious to anyone who didn't know to look for her. A few yards in I turned and held out my hand. He sloshed into the water with a yelp, took my hand, and we continued further out, laughing at our naughty endeavor.

Irish barked at us from the shore. Ralph yelled at him to stay. Irish wasn't happy but resolved himself to the command and stayed amused by chewing on the ball.

When we reached a depth where the water came just below my breasts, I made sure Ralph's back was to the opposite shore and held onto his shoulders. A quick glance behind him allowed me to see Connie waiting for my signal.

CHAPTER 62

"You know, Ralph," I said as I stroked a finger across his shoulder, "I haven't been entirely honest with you."

"What about?"

"We actually know each other. Well, not really know, but we've met."

"I'm sure I'd remember meeting you."

He shifted the triangles until they no longer covered me. I let him grope me wherever he directed his hands and made sounds that seemed appropriate so it kept him entertained while I reminded him who I was.

His eyes widened in recognition and his hands dropped away.

I hung onto him and left the triangles askew. It seemed a more non-threatening thing to do. "Did you and Mama ever see each other here at the beach after I left for college? She was impressed with you, you know."

"Uh, yeah, I saw her here. Couple of times." His gaze shifted around, like someone looking for a way to escape. "Who've you been talking to?"

"I don't know what you mean."

"Did someone here—anyone—say something to you about your mother? About me?"

"I haven't spoken with anyone here. After her funeral, I cleared out and never looked back. I'm only here now because I felt sentimental with the holiday and all."

"What about the police? They say anything?"

I shrugged. "They had no leads by the time I left, and I never heard from them again. I figured they didn't care." I stroked his chest. "Mama would have loved to have gone to dinner with you. She told me that after that first time we met you. Did you ever think to ask her out?"

Ralph fixed his attention beyond my left shoulder. "No. No offense or anything, but we weren't a match."

And there was the lie. "But you were friendly with her when your paths crossed here?"

"Sure. No point in being rude."

I rested my hands on his shoulders. "Ralph, since you were so nice to Mama, would you mind if I kissed you to express my gratitude?" I bounced up and down just enough in the water to draw his attention back to my breasts, watched the wheels turn behind his eyes, and thought about how easy men are.

He licked his lips. "You can thank me any way you want."

I wrapped my arms around his shoulders and my legs around his torso, pressed my mouth to his, and held up one finger. I let him paw me and stick his tongue down my throat until the moment I'd been waiting for.

Wide-eyed, he broke the kiss, looked down and around, as though he might be able to see anything in the shadowy water. "What the hell? Something just brushed my leg."

I released him and flung myself backward, careful not to let the water alter my wig and makeup. Down Ralph went, surfacing only once before Connie did whatever she'd planned to do to him—she'd refused to divulge that part of the plan—while I kept watch. The only soul paying attention to us, or on the beach, was Irish, who barked, picked up the ball in his mouth and wagged his tail. I shouted for him to stay.

Connie remained underwater for what seemed to me a long time. Occasionally, I'd glance at where Ralph had submerged.

Long minutes later, her head popped up about fifteen yards from where I waited. She submerged again, and I grew concerned, fearful he'd dragged her down. Moments later, she emerged two feet from me, pointed and said, "You might want to fix those."

I tracked where her finger pointed and adjusted my triangles.

"Atta girl. I'll meet you at the car."

"What about Irish?"

"I always wanted a dog, and this one's already housebroken."

Irish barked and wagged his backside when I returned to shore. He stared out at the water then back at me a number of times. While I got dressed, I talked to him in soothing tones, or at least as soothing as chattering teeth allowed, and scanned the beach—we were completely alone.

I retrieved his leash and attempted to attach it to his collar. No dice. He wanted to play. I started toward the car and called him to follow me but he wouldn't budge. I picked up his ball and tossed it in the direction of the car. His attachment to the game too strong, he galloped after the dingy yellow orb. We repeated this activity until Connie and I got him into the backseat.

Connie opened the trunk, stripped the wet suit off, dressed, and then got in and started the engine. She put the heater on high, the car in reverse, and started forward. "He's got white flecks on his snout. How old is he?"

"Irish was a puppy when I met him, so, probably elevenish."

"He's in great condition. Usual lifespan for his breed is around twelve to fourteen years, though I read about one who lived to seventeen. His former owner obviously took care of him. I thought about getting one like him once."

I scratched Irish behind his ears. "And now you have."

"We need to get him some food and stuff."

I gave her directions to one of the large chain stores, where she parked so far from the entrance that we were the only ones there. Irish and I stayed in the car with the doors locked and the heater still on high to dry us. Connie returned with two large plastic doggie bowls, a giant bag of top of-the-line kibble, treats, chew bones, a canister of tennis balls, a cushy comforter, two towels, and a case of water.

We decided to drive fifty or so miles south and find a roadside motel rather than let someone see us with Irish. Connie asked for a room at the back so we could sneak Irish inside, but told the desk clerk it was to avoid traffic sounds from the highway. Better not to say anything about having a dog, she'd said as we parked. Once in the room, she used pliers retrieved from her trunk to remove the extra tag on his collar that identified his former owner and phone number.

That night, Irish took turns sleeping with us, as we each had a double bed. We left before the sun came up and after he tended to his business outside.

The ride home was definitely different from the ride up, with occasional stops so that one of our trio could use the grass and sniff everything in sight. And like Irish, I spent a good deal of the time staring out the window but without leaving smears on the glass. Whereas Irish's thoughts revolved around food, intriguing smells, adoring pats and hugs, and a giant chew bone, I contemplated the path my life had led me down.

Marcus Aurelius once commented, "For everything that exists is the seed of that which shall come from it." Too bad men, who considered themselves superior in all ways to women, never heeded that fact. A great number of them had planted seeds of disquiet in a great number of women over the ages. They would suffer as a result of the fruit produced by those seeds, if I had anything to do with it.

It took effort but I found earrings shaped like flip-flops, which I secured to Caitlin's tree with a thin strand of wire—one for Mama, one for me.

CHAPTER 63

I put my avenger cape away for a period of time so I could focus on my studies and maintain the required pace through my third year, which included doing rotations to get exposed to various fields for consideration.

We were guided to consider a number of aspects as we progressed, such as, if we found we enjoyed solving puzzles, we should consider internal medicine as our chosen field. If frozen section fascinated us, we should consider becoming a "physician's physician" and choose pathology. Whatever we inevitably chose, our comprehensive essay, used for the purpose of residency matching, had to demonstrate a passion for the field, and that our personality and goals as a physician were a good fit. Applications for residency were to be made during September, before interviews were held in the early part of the following year, our fourth.

Additional advice given was to take copious notes about meaningful interactions with patients, as well as what it was about a particular specialty that appealed to us. This level of detailed information would be looked for in the essay.

My days were full ones, and the months seemed to zip by. Abigail sounded genuinely disappointed that I wasn't going to Coeur d'Alene during any of my breaks—she called to check before each one, and didn't press the issue when I stated my schedule was far too tight for her to come here. She had to be satisfied with our twice-monthly calls. No way would I trust her to come here. If she wanted to engage sexually with someone other than Hubby-Buns for one or more nights, she could do it someplace where it didn't involve me.

My third year now completed successfully, I sat across from Patricia during one of the brunches she treated me to whenever my schedule allowed, and remained animated as I discussed the highlights of what I'd learned, particularly how clinical immunology intrigued me.

"Something I've always considered compelling, even as a child," I said, "is phagocytosis, where the body defends itself against a foreign body."

Patricia gave me a small smile. "How apropos."

"What do you mean?"

"Consider how often you, as well as WAM members, and most women, I suppose, needed to defend herself against a foreign body or, I should say, an unwelcome and abusive body part."

"That never occurred to me, but I see what you mean. That lines up with immunodeficiency, which is when the immune system fails to provide an adequate response or defense against an attacker. I've certainly experienced that *and* behavioral immunity a number of times."

"And that is?"

"Disgust aroused by an encountered stimuli. Our inclination to get far away, and fast, from a bad smell is one example. It's nature's way of conditioning us to avoid what isn't good for us or might destroy us."

Patricia sighed and said, "And yet we women consistently pick the wrong men, like moths to a bright light, and stay with them longer than we should."

"That assumes right ones even exist. However, there is an exception to what you said. There are those of us who are selected by them, and without our consent."

"Point taken."

"It does make an odd sort of sense, now that I think about it. I'm immune to what are supposed to be the charms or appeal of men. I suppose I'm stuck in disgust mode and have been before the age of five. Simultaneously, I behave like an immune system ready and willing to go after my attackers. Life shouldn't be that way, but it is. Women should be able to live their lives without constantly being on guard. It's time to reverse the long-standing power and overpowering pattern of the opposite sex."

Patricia raised her glass of champagne. I tapped my water glass to hers and said, "I intend to fulfill WAM's goals, as well as my own."

"I'm counting on it."

After brunch, I returned to my dorm room. Jenni was in the shower. I made the *tsk* sound at her piles and piles of notebooks, each line crammed with her scrawled writings. For every ten notebooks of hers, I had one. And those were kept primarily to appease instructors who got snippy when I, at first, didn't take notes. Only once did I attempt to explain that my ability to retain information was pronounced. This skill wasn't received well by that particular instructor or fellow students.

I called Connie and connected with her in her Jeep. "It's been a year. Still no word from the techs about Ralph being discovered yet?"

"Nope, and if I was effective, which it seems I was, don't wait any longer for him to surface—pun intended. The police think he did a runner. Since the evidence matter was a problem for a conviction, they didn't waste manpower or funds to look for him. Word is, neighbors who were initially concerned gave up, because he took his dog with him." She laughed and cooed, "*Good Irish. Good boy.* Gimme some dog." Returning her attention to me, she said, "He gives the best kisses."

I chuckled at how mushy Irish had made my otherwise life-hardened friend. "As you wished, I left what went on underwater to you, but how did you manage to keep him submerged all this time?"

"Even if you think you want to know, you don't want to know."

"I'll take your word for it. Looks like you and Irish are definitely family now. He never misses his former master or tries to run away?"

"Not a chance, not with all the pampering I give him. *Good boy. What a good boy.* Sorry. He's just so damn adorable. He heard you say his name and smiled at me before sticking his head back out the window. I love how he's happy at both ends."

I laughed and said, "Later. I just heard the shower turn off."

"Give your roommate a big kiss from me."

"That just triggered my behavioral immunology."

"Your what?"

I laughed again and ended the call.

CHAPTER 64

At the end of January, I had two significant meetings. The first was the interview regarding my residency, to be assigned during this fourth year, with my request being infectious diseases. The confirmation would come in March.

The other meeting was less formal but equal in importance to me.

In response to my request for more details about the bigger plans of WAM, Patricia got up from the chair behind her desk and walked to the window. She kept her back to me as she looked past the glass. Knowing her as well as I did, I could tell she looked past the landscaped grounds as well, and that what she surveyed was inside her mind.

After several moments she said, "It isn't just that some men—too many of them—treat women poorly or abuse them. It's all the other things they've done throughout history. Some rulers *they've* been. Chaos and deception and violence run through their veins.

"Granted, some women have gone rogue, as well, but nothing like the numbers of men who have. And most women did so as acts of preservation. Men are at the forefront of every massacre perpetuated on humans. Millions and millions of people slaughtered or enslaved. They're most often the ones wielding weapons used in mass shootings and terrorist attacks. All for the sake of power."

"I recall reading years ago about cultures where women lead."

"Too few, and too far removed from society at large." She turned and faced me, arms crossed at her chest. "A few years ago, a single-question, anonymous survey was taken at several universities, the results of which shocked the survey-takers to no end. But not me. I wasn't surprised in the least."

I studied her expression of disgust mixed with anguish. "What was the focus?"

Her eyes stayed fixed on mine. "The question was put to males only."

I sat up straighter. "This should be interesting."

"More like revolting. The question was, If rape were no longer a crime, if there were no punishment involved, would they engage in that activity?"

"We know the answer."

She nodded. "The majority—*the majority*—said they would, and as often as they chose to. Even in this modern age, we still have cultures of men who believe rape is their right, and in some instances, their obligation. It's up to us to do something about this."

"I agree. However, it can't be anything standard."

"I'm listening."

"It can't be anything they could imagine, much less expect."

"Subterfuge. I like it. Keep going." She joined me on the sofa.

"We have to hit them where it hurts, in a manner of speaking. Get them focused on one direction. While they're looking where we cause them to look, we weaken them and infiltrate their power structure."

"I have my own ideas, but tell me yours."

"We know what our desired end result is. All we have to do is create a problem that gets them anxious and screaming for a solution. We present them with ours, but the camouflaged version, not the real one. We let them believe our focus is the same as theirs. We make it convincing. And in the meantime, in gradual increments—"

"We take over. Is this the seed you've mentioned?"

"Yes, in part. It's the what and how that I'm still waiting for an inspired idea about. What about WAM's strategy? You've never clarified that for me."

"Like you, we have a goal but not the precise how, at least not one we've as yet agreed on, despite having some of the brightest minds on board. At present, our primary focus has been on empowering women and helping those in need. That's an all-encompassing task at the best of times. But we share a commitment that women must become the stronger sex."

"We are the stronger sex."

"Not in men's minds, nor in many of our sisters' minds."

"In the words of Matsuo Basho, 'Do not seek to follow the footsteps of the men of old; seek what they sought.'" I reached out and took Patricia's hand in mine. "I'm committed to making your goal a reality. Along with that, I'll include punitive measures on behalf of myself and all women."

"All I ask is that you keep one thing in mind."

"Which is?"

"It isn't our goal to destroy men or eradicate them. That would be foolish for a number of obvious reasons. However, it is our goal to retrain them."

I thought of Irish. "Like teaching a dog to do his business outside."

Patricia grinned and said, "Imagine what the world would be like if men were as loyal, loving, and so eager to please us."

"I might even be able to tolerate them. Or not."

CHAPTER 65

It was my habit to visit Caitlin's tree once a day, even if it was dark out, and no matter the weather. The sky was a canopy of clear blue and the sun made everything sparkle. Especially the silver trinkets attached to the growing laurel tree now several feet taller than I stood.

Had things gone differently, my daughter would be growing as well, charming me and every woman at WAM, and being spoiled by Patricia and others.

I sat on the grass beneath the tree and watched the ornaments glint in the light as a soft breeze caused them to dance. For some inexplicable reason, Abigail came to mind. Perhaps she was thinking of me at the same time. Alhough we'd stayed in contact by phone, though once a month now rather than twice, it had been a long time since we'd seen each other.

Somehow, I couldn't imagine her announcing to me that she had entered the world of mothers-to-be. I doubted if she ever would. It might ruin her fun. She'd have to put a child's needs above her own, and I wasn't certain she could do that.

A distinctive sensation coursed through me. If Abigail ever did get word to me that she was carrying life inside her, I'd be inclined to hate her, perhaps not immediately, but eventually, or the other way around. Rationally, I knew she had nothing to do with my losing Caitlin, but had all to do with my daughter's conception. I found it difficult to separate the two events, though I did try.

I'd given thought to why I maintained any form of relationship with her and always returned to the fact that she was my only link to the past. As long as I avoided allowing her to trick me into a bad situation, I could keep my ties with her.

I'd spent no time at Mama's apartment, though I still made the payments each month. Mr. Hopkins never questioned me about this. He did report that he cleaned inside weekly to make sure everything stayed in good shape and no repairs were needed. Each month I sent extra funds to cover this expense. I should let the apartment go, let someone who needs a place to live have it, but I can't. It's like Caitlin's tree—a memorial for someone I've loved and lost.

Besides, my need for close friendship—in intimacy and proximity—was fulfilled where I was, and with women who offered more mental stimulation and loyalty than Abigail ever could.

Other than these snippets of time by the tree, my hours stayed filled for the most part. However, I made sure there was time, even if only a segment of an hour, to learn more about the scientists and what they were working on in the underground laboratories.

One thing missing from their work and their equipment was what might facilitate genome research. I made a mental note to discuss this with Patricia at some future time. A DNA sequencer, along with additional equipment, as needed, would facilitate my immunology research. My desire about this wasn't solely for that purpose. The topic had fascinated me since I was a child. DNA was the mystical spiral of vast information revealed and mysteries to be solved.

My seed idea developed a fissure, and a tiny shoot began to emerge through the casing. I didn't understand what it represented but believed I would. When the time was right.

I'd learned that life is, more often than not, all about the timing.

CHAPTER 66

My fourth year included the usual. I sat for Step 2 of the USMLE, receiving the highest—make that perfect—score.

I applied to and was accepted at UCSF Medical Center for a residency in infectious diseases. It meant commuting from Palo Alto to San Francisco, but I didn't mind. Time alone as I traveled proved soothing. Patricia made it an even more comfortable ride by surprising me with a new car—a silver Audi—stating I'd earned it, and argued that I had to let her behave like a proud substitute mother when I protested the expense. I wept when she said that and hugged her when she agreed to let me keep Mama's car tucked out of sight in the empty spot in her three-car garage.

It became apparent to me almost from the start of my residency that patient care was not and never would be my forte. I didn't mind dealing with women but found a prejudice existed when it came to men. Unless a male was ten or younger, I had great difficulty looking at or touching any part of their bodies. I hid this abhorrence as best I could, but it cast a definite shadow over my days. Despite this, I never allowed my feelings to affect patient care. I couldn't afford to. I needed to know as much about male physiology, and something about their psychology, as possible.

I also recognized that I wanted to accomplish something greater, such as find or create cures for deadly diseases. This would mean dedicating myself to research, and I knew the precise laboratory that would fulfill this as well as my other desired goal.

This was the topic of conversation over brunch with Patricia on a day off.

She sat back in her chair and studied my expression. "One thing I know about you, Katherine, is that whatever you put your mind to, you achieve, and with fewer complications than most people experience."

"I appreciate your faith in me."

"You still intend to get licensed, right?"

"Definitely."

She gave me a wide grin. "Dr. Katherine Barnes."

"Technically, I've been Doctor, or rather, Professor Barnes for a few years."

"You never told me. I would have introduced you with your proper title. Why didn't you ever say anything?"

I shrugged. "It's never been about the titles for me. It's about being allowed into the scientific realm where discoveries and advances are made. Of being able to select a high-level laboratory to work in." I grinned and said, "I happen to know the perfect one that will suit my objectives."

"As soon as you're licensed, every resource at headquarters is yours to use."

"I'm just asking, but why have you had me wait?"

"It's a code of ethics of sorts, devised by the scientists who work there. They're adamant that only the best and the brightest, and the licensed, be permitted to share their space."

I thought about Abigail, Jenni, and the others, and their less than stimulating dialogue and thought processes. "I completely understand. It means that I, too, will not be forced to suffer fools."

"We suffer enough of them in this world."

"I'll find a way to end one half of the population's suffering while inflicting it on the other half."

Patricia nodded and sighed. "They drove us to this."

"And I—we—intend to take over the wheel."

CHAPTER 67

In my attempt to cram as much into my residency as possible, I worked twelve-hour shifts and several double shifts for four weeks straight. The hospital finally forced me to take three consecutive days off. They didn't mind using residents as much as possible, but burnout was frowned upon.

On one of my days off, I found myself assisting Patricia with volunteer work, which consisted of distributing toiletries, clothing, and food at a homeless shelter for women and children.

It proved to be a long day in more ways than one. On the ride home in Patricia's car, I said, "That was painful on many levels."

"I know. It always appalls me to see the degradation and conditions some women are forced into."

"Do you go there often?"

"Twice a month. I would have invited you sooner, but I thought it better to let you stay focused on school, et cetera. Each first week of the month, I bring supplies to them, donate funds of course, but I also hold a meeting there at the middle of the month. The sad thing is that only a percentage of the women choose to let us help them climb out of the hole they're in."

I turned my face to her. "I'd think each of them would want that."

"Some of them are so used to seeing themselves in one way only, they can't imagine anything can change, much less work up the energy to make the effort it takes. Their experience of life has exhausted them."

I nodded and looked away. "My mother was like them. She had it better in a way. She never reached the point of being homeless, but she easily could have gone over that edge. In an odd way, we were fortunate." For the next several minutes, I gave her a summary of my younger years, keeping it brief, and including things I hadn't shared before. "It took losing me to foster care to find the motivation to change her life and mine."

"That took more courage than, perhaps, you comprehend."

"You're right. I didn't fully understand it at the time. That came later. I wish there were some way to help those children to skip over degradation and go straight to self-reliance."

Patricia turned into the parking lot of WAM headquarters, pulled into her designated spot, and turned the engine off. "Come with me. I have something to show you."

I grinned at her. "You have a plan, don't you?"

"When do I not?"

Patricia uncoiled several large rectangular papers across the surface of her desk and placed weights on each corner. An architectural rendering of a three-story facade was the top sheet. "As we speak, this building is in the preliminary stages for construction to begin a mile from here. On fifty acres I purchased several years ago."

I traced the dimensions with my fingers. "It's massive."

"Every worthy undertaking should be, in some measure." What you're looking at will be a privately funded school for homeless and under-served girls. It'll function like a private school, meaning they'll be housed there, with family visitation rights of course, supervised, if that's required. We'll even provide transportation on weekends and holidays for family to visit them at the school. Depending on the history, visits may be for an hour or an entire day."

She removed the top sheet and tapped the blueprint. "This west wing will house girls from kindergarten to eighth grade." She moved that sheet to reveal the next one. "This is the north wing, and where ninth- through twelfth-grade girls will be housed." That sheet was moved. "This is the eastern side, which will be an accredited college, complete with dorms, and so forth. Everything needed will be provided to each student."

"I love it. But how will—?"

"Funding? I read your mind. Let me remind you that a good number of our top members are wealthy. Seriously so. Plus, there are the worldwide contributions. Naturally, each group has to keep some of what they collect for their own purposes, but they send ten percent to headquarters. Some of the wealthier members have agreed to sponsor several girls, some as many as twenty a year or even throughout their entire time here."

"It almost sounds as though they know your ultimate goal."

Patricia winked. "Some of them do. Some of them live in places where women are oppressed. They put up with it because they have to. However, they're committed to changing this, no matter if it takes a generation or two."

"And, I assume, some of them do this under the noses of their male overlords."

"They're women of vision and hope for women's futures. I leave what they tell their husbands about this expenditure to them."

"I'm more than impressed."

She rolled the papers up and put them away. "The only way to make a long-term difference is to start them young or, if older, as soon as possible. Even if we have a young woman for one year, she'll leave here believing in herself and her rights as a woman, and with skills that will never fail her."

I walked to the window and fixed my gaze on Caitlin's tree. "Borrowing from John Milton, we'll untwist 'all the chains that tie the hidden soul of harmony.'"

"The only way for peace and harmony to ever exist on this planet is for women to take over."

"Men aren't going to know what hit them."

CHAPTER 68

The next three years went by in a relative flash as I continued to complete requirements to become licensed. Patricia's school was still under construction, but closer to being completed than not. The slight delay was a result of safety modifications she decided to add, plus expansion—she wanted to go big—and issues over décor.

For my twenty-eighth birthday, Patricia gave me a relatively new invention—an iPhone—and prepaid my bill for two years. It was yet another extravagant gift from her.

I no longer had to wait for Jenni to be out of the room so I could talk on my landline phone. This wasn't a result of now being able to talk anywhere. It was a result of my having moved into a furnished efficiency apartment, inexpensive, but adequate for the little time I spent there. As did others at the hospital, I kept the phone on vibrate. Each time a call or text came in, it never failed to bring Mama to mind.

It was while scrolling through the directory that I saw Abigail's name. It had been awhile since we'd spoken. I thought of the topics we usually discussed when we did speak, and the ones I never brought up or ever intended to. Things were going well in my life, and I wondered if she'd still be as happy for my successes as she'd once been.

Nostalgia has a way of cropping up uninvited. Depending on circumstances, I found such times either soothing or annoying. At the moment, I found myself wishing to hear her voice, no matter what she chose to discuss.

I pressed the call button, only to decide after the first ring to disengage. Abigail's sexual proclivities and extracurricular activities, which did and didn't involve Hubby-Buns, were not topics I relished. It was, however, Abigail's favorite topic, and she would go on and on about this, as though I wasn't even there, unless I stopped her. When it came to men, Abigail was magnetic, or easy—I couldn't decide which—and with a strong tendency to attract trouble.

She knew how I felt regarding this and expressed dismay that I no longer was curious as when we were teens. I tried to explain my why to her but she couldn't or wouldn't hear me. I'd been curious about her adventures back then solely because of the scientific aspect. Her tales served as edification regarding something I had no personal desire to experience. I'd experienced enough of the up-close-and-personal aspects prior to that time, and since, and continued to regard it as distasteful.

I slipped the phone back into my pocket and felt it vibrate. Abigail, calling back. I thought about answering. That's as far as it went. This decision was partially my reticence to hear about her latest foray and also because I'd never entirely forgiven her for what she'd subjected me to, and the consequences. I didn't want to feel that way toward her but I did.

I'd speak with her again one day.

Today wasn't that day.

CHAPTER 69

Patricia handed me a cup of tea then took a seat in her chair. "You once told me you had a list of men's names. As far as I know, you've scratched a line through two of them."

"That number hasn't changed. One was a definite name, the other was the question mark. I didn't write his name in. He didn't deserve it."

"What about the others? Any special plans for them?"

"I'll deal with them when the time is right."

Patricia nodded and rested her cup and saucer on the small table next to her. "Any chance you're available this Saturday?"

"I can arrange it. What's going on?"

"Membership has expanded quite a lot since you joined us."

"I noticed."

"In order to facilitate and protect our short-term and ultimate goals, we—me, Agatha, Brenda, and Connie—realized we needed to create two membership groups. There will now be the regular members and a select group. Regular members will know only what the public and government know about our organization. The others will know more, based on their performance over time."

"You're saying they'll have to prove themselves, like I did."

Patricia smiled. "I had no doubts about you or your value to us, but I did need to be certain you were dedicated."

"How do you decide who's who?"

"We've assigned ten women, who don't know more than we've told them, to keep their eyes and ears open as they engage with non-member meeting attendees as well as existing and new members. They look at or for women who've been through a traumatic event perpetuated by a man and are ready to take a stand, and or those who can contribute to our goals in a significant way."

"And you trust these women to discern this?"

"They were carefully selected. These are women who've dealt with the public and individuals in particular ways. They can read people quite well. They include a social worker, lawyer, cop, a counselor—all women who know what to look for." She laughed. "One is a bartender. But they're all expert at body language and watching a person's eyes."

"What's my role in this?"

"Sit in with me as I conduct interviews."

"I'm happy to, but why?"

"I value your opinion."

"Reading people is not an expertise I possess."

"You're better at it than you know."

I'd managed to switch shifts with someone so I could have the weekend off. Good thing, too. There were three hundred interviews scheduled for that weekend. It took four women—Patricia, Connie, Agatha, and Brenda—two days to interview seventy-five women each.

In a room other than Patricia's office, I listened to the Q&A, made comments to her during the intervals we were alone in the room, and, with Connie's help, took the files to the tech fairies at the end of each day. The files stayed in four batches so that each interviewer received her specific files once whatever the techs did was completed. Apparently, it was an all-hands-on-deck situation, as twenty-five techs occupied a computer each down in the lab.

That Sunday, when we returned upstairs, Connie took our orders and left to get take-out food. We ate and waited for the techs to finish their tasks.

While we waited, I asked what the techs were doing.

Connie said, "These particular members have to be vetted down to their toenails."

I glanced at each of the four women. "What exactly do you look for?"

The others turned to Patricia, who said, "A variety of things. Finances, marriages, divorces, other relationships, criminal records, and ..."

"And?"

"Religious affiliations or beliefs."

"Does that matter?"

"Absolutely. The one type of woman we don't want in our exclusive group is one with strong religious beliefs that align with submissiveness of women to men."

"That could be tricky," I said. "Most members, at one time or another, and in some measure, have been submissive."

Brenda leaned forward in her chair. "The difference is that the women we're interested in are the ones who were forced into submission by cultural or religious beliefs and rejected it. Neither do we want the ones who volunteer to submit, whether that's a result of dogma or a desire for a man to take care of them."

"I'm not religious," Patricia said, "though do believe in a higher power. However, I question—make that adamantly disagree—with submission of women cited in the Bible. I suspect when Constantine did his machinations at Nicea, he had his minions omit passages about women being equal and changed texts in order to subjugate women.

"Women who attain specific roles and responsibilities in top levels here cannot succumb to dogma that proclaims men as natural rulers, heads of households, or the boss of women."

I nodded once. "That explains some of the questions."

"Indeed. But people are prone to lie if they think it'll get them where they want to be. We not only have to be careful about our selections, but make certain we avoid infiltrators."

"No Bible believers, then?"

Patricia snorted a laugh. "*Good book*, my fanny. Not one of those tomes proclaims women as equals. One thing I'm certain of is that a new book will be written and followed one day, one we or those who come after us write."

We discussed this and other things for another two hours, interrupted only when the hidden door opened and four techs brought the files to us with the reports tucked inside each file. The techs left as silently as they'd arrived.

Patricia and I took the sofa. The others went to a conference table at the other end of the room. A few hours and a lengthy discussion later, fifty women were selected.

Among those chosen were doctors, research scientists, engineers, educators from various grade levels and areas of expertise, psychologists and therapists, a few policewomen, a few bank executives, one CPA, and one sanitation worker.

I sat back and yawned. "A diverse group for certain."

"Yes," Patricia said. "We need to be covered when specific knowledge is needed or particular tasks need to be done."

"I get that about all but the sanitation worker."

"Everyone has a role. Use your imagination. Can you think of even one instance when someone in that field might prove useful?" She tilted her head and waited.

It didn't take long. "Definitely."

Connie stood and stretched. "No grass grows on her head."

CHAPTER 70

This interview process was held once a month after that first one I attended. I wasn't always available but made a point to try to be. How many women were interviewed varied, sometimes almost as many as the first batch and sometimes only a small percentage of that number. The women accepted were put on probation, without their knowledge, of course. I'd asked Patricia if each woman interviewed knew what it was about.

"Better if they don't. At least, not until their probationary period is over, and if they warrant being elevated to the level just below the top one."

"How long is probation?"

"A minimum of two years. It all depends on how involved they become, how well they perform, and how trustworthy they prove themselves to be."

"What do you tell them? After all, if they talk to some of the regular members who've never been interviewed, won't they, and the regular members, get suspicious?"

"We say that we occasionally look for women with particular skill sets. If necessary, we say it's for placement purposes, either within the organization or in the general public. Most of our members are content to receive the basic care and advancement we offer."

I chuckled and said, "You and the other three are adept liars."

"Dearest Katherine, women have been forced to lie *with* men and to them since the beginning of time."

My smile departed. "Forced is the right word."

She made eye contact with me and said, "Only until we turn the tables on them." She smoothed her hair and said, "They should have been smart enough to realize they could piss us off only for so long."

"They should have never, to use your words, pissed us off in the first place."

Four months later, I sat for and aced Step 3, received my license as a qualified medical doctor, and gave notice to a disappointed hospital. I spent time in the lab at headquarters, exploring the equipment and conversing with the scientists. But the need for medical care at the headquarters facility became greater sooner than anticipated.

A select number of members who were doctors and nurses, which included me, joined Agatha in her efforts to tend to the homeless women and children and some of the more destitute or abused new members. Those who could pay nothing received free care. Those who could afford to contribute toward costs, even if only a dollar, did so.

I split my time between the medical facility and adhering to Patricia's request that I learn more about the administrative side of the organization. She started by explaining the financial aspects then gave me limited responsibilities, all the while monitoring how I did. Always good with numbers and logic, I did well. Soon, I oversaw the handling of contributions, regulating expenses, and managing payment of full- and part-time staffers who were compensated by salary or hourly. Fortunately, I wasn't involved with any aspect regarding volunteers, of which there was a substantive number.

Patricia did something else for me—she threw a massive party to celebrate my certification, complete with giant banners proclaiming my success and party favors for guests. Thankfully, the day was sunny and comfortable, because women and girls of all ages and backgrounds crowded the appointed rooms inside as well as spilled onto the grounds. Caterers and wait staff—all women—bustled about at warp speed, keeping food trays and platters filled and fluted glasses topped.

"Did you invite every woman in Palo Alto and its environs?" I asked.

Patricia laughed and grabbed a fresh glass of champagne for her and one filled with punch for me. "It certainly looks like it. I couldn't have gotten this kind of response and promotion by running an advertising campaign, which would have cost a bundle."

"What's this party going to cost WAM?"

"Nothing. I'm paying."

I faced her, eyebrows arched. "Do you realize how much of this could be deducted as a legitimate expense?"

"Katherine, there are expenditures and there are investments. You need to distinguish between the two." She wrapped an arm around my shoulders. "You're one of the best investments of my life."

Tears spilled onto my cheeks.

She grabbed a clean cocktail napkin from the tray of a passing waitperson and handed it to me. "Surely, after all this time, you know how I feel about you. You're the daughter I always wanted."

I nodded and used the napkin to dry my eyes. "You mean as much to me. But I can't help but think about Mama and what she'd say if she were standing here with us."

"She'd be so proud of you, as we all are."

"I'm going to tidy myself up. I'll be back shortly."

"Find me outside. I'm going to make the rounds."

The cold water I splashed on my face in the ladies room revived me somewhat, but the heaviness in my heart about Mama's absence refused to diminish. Only one thing could lighten that burden in some measure. I found a room off-limits to guests and called Abigail. No answer. I sent her a text and asked that she call me right away. Five minutes went by with no response. I needed to return to the party.

I fixed a smile on my face and joined the women who'd given my life purpose.

The future would be ours.

Or I'd die trying.

We stayed to help staff with clean-up, which took several hours. Thirty minutes after I got home, I got a call from a sobbing Connie.

"Irish is gone," she said.

"How could he get out?"

"Not that kind of gone."

"Connie, I'm so sorry."

"I got worried when he didn't meet me at the door. Found him on the bed surrounded by a dozen tennis balls. He'd slowed down—age, you know—but hadn't acted sick at all. He scarfed his food this morning and acted normal. I hate that I wasn't with him. That he was alone."

"I understand."

"That's why I called you."

"We three had a history." I got to my feet. "I'll be there in fifteen minutes."

"Thanks, but no. I want to spend some time with him before I take care of ..." Weeping, she hung up.

The next morning, when I visited Caitlin's tree before starting my workday, I saw a new sapling had been planted several yards to the left—a red maple.

CHAPTER 71

During a mid-morning break, I sat sipping tea with Agatha in the medical facility lounge. We were recounting highlights of the party when one of the nurses sprinted into the room.

"Homeless shelter just dropped off a pregnant woman in labor."

Agatha stood and stretched. "C'mon, Katherine. Let's see how long this little one takes to enter the world."

"Not so simple," the nurse said. "The mother's a heroin addict."

Agatha scowled. "Damn it. What else do we know about her?"

"She told them she's been on methadone for almost a year. Somehow, she got herself to the shelter. Told the administrator her boyfriend held her down and injected her with the real stuff against her will. Heart rate and oxygen levels are unstable."

The three of us sped from the room. The woman screamed and thrashed on the table, making it difficult for staff to tend to her. During her flailing, she tore the I.V. from the back of her hand.

"We need to restrain her," Agatha said.

The nurse opened a cabinet and retrieved the restraints. The woman's breathing became shallow.

"Intubate her," Agatha ordered. "And someone get a fetal monitor attached. Stat!"

The woman's lips and nails were turning blue. Her blood pressure dropped, as did her pulse. Muscle spasms were followed by seizures. Ventricular tachycardia progressed to ventricular fibrillation. We had her set for defibrillation within seconds.

Agatha yelled, "Clear," and sent the electrical current to the woman's heart.

No pulse, and the same heart rhythm.

After two more attempts, time of death was called. Everyone in the room went quiet.

Agatha checked the fetal monitor. "We don't have long. Prep for a C-section. Just the basics. No time, or need, for this to be pretty. We're going down-and-dirty, team."

Despite the frantic pace she worked at, Agatha's surgical skills left me even more impressed than before. "You're an artist," I told her as we cleaned up.

"An artist angry as hell, you mean. What the hell did her boyfriend mean to do, kill them both? I guess that would have cleared him of any responsibility for them."

I glanced toward the table where the nurse was nearly through tending the newborn. "What are her chances?"

"With the right care, and time, she can make it."

"Poor little thing is shaking so hard."

"She'll do better once we can get her swaddled and out of bright lights and away from noise. At least she was full-term. She would have arrived any day now. We'll have to keep her here as long as it takes. It's best if we set up a rotation of women with soothing voices and personalities to hold her, probably around the clock."

"They'll need to be told what to watch for. Any seizures or respiratory issues start, they have to get help fast."

"Not to worry. We have a neonatologist on call. I've already had someone text her. She should be here soon. This little one will get the proper care."

The nurse picked up the baby and walked to where we stood. My gaze fixed on the dark-haired wailing infant. "Okay if I hold her?"

"Of course." The nurse handed her to me.

I cradled the child to my chest and stroked her hair. "If I hadn't been present at her birth, I'd think she was wearing a wig."

Agatha stroked the infant's tiny fist. "We'll have to make sure she's in perfect condition before we turn her over to an agency. It'll be up to them to find the right parents to adopt her."

I glanced at the covered body of what used to be a living, breathing woman who'd never hold her child. "What about the mother?"

"We'll treat her with respect."

"Of course. What I meant was what about her death certificate? Someone needs to call the shelter to learn her name."

The nurse said, "Already done. They don't know, nor did she come here with any ID. Unless police can find someone who knew her, she'll have to be listed as Jane Doe."

I cuddled the infant closer to me. "I can't tell you how furious all of this makes me."

Agatha frowned and nodded. "You're preaching to the choir, my dear."

Two hours later, the coroner's office picked up the mother. Police interviewed Agatha, though she said it was more like an interrogation. We learned the shelter administrator received the same treatment, despite explaining the woman had never been to the shelter before.

During a break, I went to the room where the newborn was being looked after and held the fretting child in my arms.

The unidentified boyfriend—I presumed the father of the child—would get away with his crime.

I kissed the infant's forehead and whispered, "At least it was one murder, not two."

Men. They were going to pay, every last one of them.

CHAPTER 72

For the next week, every spare moment I had during the day was spent with the infant. I slept each night in the assigned room at the facility, with the baby cuddled to me. Despite her symptoms, which were waning due to our staff's excellent care, I became more entranced with her the more time we spent together. I wasn't alone in this. Patricia was equally affected.

We were together in the dimly lit room one night a week later. I sat in the rocking chair with the baby in my arms, moving the chair slowly, gently, while we spoke in low tones.

Patricia smiled and said, "That little one has gained a few ounces."

"She's eating better now. I was more than a little concerned."

"She's calmer than before."

My phone vibrated. I checked the caller—Abigail—and returned the phone to my pocket. I shifted my focus from the tiny face to Patricia's. "I don't think I can let her go."

Patricia studied me for a moment. "Then we won't. We'll adopt her."

"Can we do that? Aren't there laws about that? People know she's here."

She waved a dismissive hand. "Documents can be created. Lies can become truths—they often do. Our techs are skilled at that kind of thing."

"You truly think we can get away with it?"

"I don't think, I know. We'll need to name her. Why don't you choose one?"

"I've already been calling her by one I looked up."

"Somehow that doesn't surprise me. And?"

"Lauren."

"I like it."

I stroked Lauren's soft cheek. "It's French. For laurel."

"How very fitting, Katherine."

"What about her last name?"

"Barnes, of course."

"I think Lauren Hill sounds better. Besides, you could get away with the adoption aspect better than I could, legally speaking."

"I assure you that won't be a problem. As for the name, what about Lauren Hill Barnes? That way she has both our names."

Lauren stirred in my arms then settled again. "I can live with that." I looked at the baby and said, "What do you think, Lauren? Do you like that for a full name?"

She stretched one of her tiny arms out. I knew her hand was curled into a fist because babies don't uncurl completely for a few years, but it made Patricia and me chuckle.

"However," Patricia said, "don't think you'll get the joy of raising her alone. With your schedule, you'll need help."

"Your schedule is far from light."

She grinned and stroked the back of Lauren's hand. "I've already spoken with the others. Among the five of us, we'll manage. When Lauren is able to leave the facility, we'll take turns having her with us. She's also inspired me to add a nursery and daycare room to the school. One of the biggest issues for some of our mothers is a safe place for their children, including infants, while they work or go to school."

I kissed Lauren's head. "Look at that, little one. You're already stirring things up in a good way."

"Like I said, it's best to start them young. That way the differences they make will be significant."

"She's making a difference, all right."

I wiped the tear from her cheek that had fallen from mine.

CHAPTER 73

During the wee hours of the morning, Lauren woke. Her wailing still lingered in weakness, but was improving. I didn't mind. It meant she was getting stronger. And fighting to live. I'd make certain she also thrived in every way.

I moved from the bed to the rocker and spoke in calming tones to her. Some might have thought the topic was inappropriate, but I found myself thinking aloud. She didn't mind. I believe she felt comforted by my voice, even when I became more animated when the proverbial lightbulb went off in my head about how to make men pay.

Ten minutes before seven, sirens wailed nearby then faded. Lauren whimpered in response to the high-pitched tones then went still again. At seven, my replacement tapped gently on the door and entered. I made my report, gave instructions, kissed Lauren's forehead and handed her over.

There were many things I could have done upon being relieved of my watch, but my eagerness to share my idea with Patricia was too great. I'd get the pot of coffee going in her office and be there to greet her when she arrived at eight or before, as was her habit.

I sprinted across the grounds, rounded the corner to the entrance of headquarters, and skidded to a stop. Three police cars and an ambulance covered the parking spaces at the entrance to the building. Yellow crime tape cordoned off the area.

The expression worn by the officer nearest me indicated he wouldn't allow me through. Then he noted my white lab coat and ID clipped to my pocket.

As he raised the yellow tape for me to walk under, I asked, "What happened?"

"Some of the place got torn up. I'm not sure how many men were involved, but they got away."

"How do you know it was men?"

"Couple security people saw them. Also said they got 'em on video."

"That means you can identify them from the tapes."

He shook his head. "Ski masks."

Tires screeched to a stop not far behind us. The officer and I turned our attention to the car, and to Agatha, who dressed in her lab coat and ID badge, got out and hurried toward us. "What's going on?"

The officer repeated what he'd told me.

She lifted the tape and crossed under. "Anyone hurt?"

He nodded and pulled a small notebook from his pocket. "Patricia Hill. She said she was working late, heard noises and went to check. They caught her. Really did a number on her."

Agatha and I looked at each other. She said, "At least she's talking."

I grabbed her hand and we bolted inside.

We dodged displaced furniture, shattered glass, and plants ripped from their pots. Ran past offices with file drawers open, folders and papers strewn everywhere, computers smashed. Dashed past framed photos once proclaiming accomplishments from their places on the walls that now littered the hallway floor.

"We should have asked him where she is," I said.

We turned a corner and Agatha said, "We've found her."

Coming toward us was a gurney propelled by two emergency medical technicians. We jogged to meet them.

Agatha said, "You're not taking her anywhere but to the facility on our grounds. We'll take care of her there."

The EMT at the foot of the gurney shrugged. "As long as we get her someplace quick."

At the sound of our voices, Patricia turned her head toward us. Her eyes were swollen shut. She moved her equally swollen lips but no sound came out. The attempt to raise a hand proved too much and she passed out.

"She keeps doing that," the EMT at the head of the gurney said. "Seems it was hours before security found her in her office during rounds."

As we headed for the facility, the EMT gave his report, starting with her vital signs.

"Looks like they tortured her," he said. "Some of it, you can see for yourself. Lacerations, contusions, cigarette burns, broken bones, probability of internal organ bruising, and signs of rape."

As he expounded, Agatha glanced at me. We knew if visuals counted for anything, Patricia's condition was dire. We also knew we'd do everything in our power to save her.

Once inside the facility, Agatha assigned an administrator to deal with the EMTs. We rushed Patricia into one of our private emergency rooms. I quickly set up the I.V. and made sure the saline was dripping at the appropriate rate. "As much as I hate what it'll do to her, we have to examine her," I said.

Agatha sighed hard and nodded. "She's in agony every time she comes to. I'll give her enough morphine so that what we have to do to her is bearable."

Connie burst into the room. "Sonofabitch! Was off duty when I got the call. I didn't want to believe it. When I learn the names of the bastards that did this, they're going to pay through their asses."

"They wore masks," I said. "Didn't security tell you? And that they got away?"

Connie sneered. "That last part is what our security team told the police."

"What are you saying?"

"They caught one of them. I seriously doubt the others are going to report to police that he's missing and where."

"That means they may come back for him."

"I hope they do. Right now, security is adding to their numbers. And not just their numbers. Tasers are good for some things, but these bastards come back, they're going to be looking down barrels aimed at them by some seriously pissed off women."

Agatha prepped a syringe with morphine. "Why the hell didn't they discover Patricia sooner, or that we had *visitors*?"

"Whoever did this screwed with the alarm system *and* the video feed. Nobody knew any shit was going down. Our system is so sophisticated, security made rounds inside and outside the building every five hours. That's changed, effective now."

I removed the cap from the I.V. portal. "I thought the intruders were captured on video."

"They were. We have a backup system that records in case something happens to the main one. Means we only watch the main one, unless it goes down. Then we use the other one until repairs are done. Way they dicked with it, everything looked normal, quiet. They didn't know about that second one, because only top-tier security know about it. And Patricia, of course." She turned her stern expression on us. "Not a damn word about it to anyone."

Agatha and I nodded a silent oath.

My phone vibrated—Abigail.

Patricia moaned. We clustered around her. Agatha inserted the needle into the I.V. port and began the gradual administration of the drug.

I stroked Patricia's hair. "We've got you now. You rest and let us take care of you. We've got you."

CHAPTER 74

Lauren continued to improve. Patricia struggled to do so. Over the next week, I split my time between the two of them, each needing me in their own way, I needing them in mine.

Patricia had intermittent periods of alertness, if you could call it that, and always between doses of morphine.

It was during one of these more alert intervals that she spoke to me for the first time. Being frail, a whisper was the most she could manage. I put my face close to hers and stroked her hair.

"How's Lauren?" she asked.

"Growing. Improving. She's going to be a beauty with her curly black hair, tawny complexion, and blue eyes."

"Her eye color may change."

"It might, but her mother's eyes were blue."

"I got the paperwork started before ... before this happened. It's all taken care of. Get the documents from Lavender. Lauren is yours."

"I'll take care of it soon. That's not the most important matter at the moment. Getting you well is."

Patricia did her best to give me a smile through her battered lips. Tears leaked from her still-swollen and bruised eyes. "I'm not doing well."

"Nonsense. We're doing everything possible to ensure you get better. We're a crack team."

She looked away for a moment then looked back. "This wasn't the first intrusion, though it was the worst."

"No one mentioned anything about a prior one."

"Katherine, I have to make sure you know that ..." Her eyes closed.

I tapped her shoulder. "Patricia." When she opened her eyes, I said, "Know what?"

"We have a traitor in the organization."

"You can't believe that."

"The men knew about the secret passages and the underground facility. They got as far as the first room inside the panel and tried to force me to give entry, but I wouldn't. Thank goodness Lavender thought to make each person's key code individual." She made a feeble attempt to reach for my hand. I took hers gently into mine. "That's actually top-secret. No one but Lavender and I know this. Everyone thinks their codes are identical. Now you know, and you aren't to tell anyone."

"I won't. So, when you refused to help them, they hurt you."

"They would have done it anyway. There's a type, you know."

"Too well."

"At least I prevented them from getting to the women below, as well as our secrets."

"You saved them, just like you always save everyone, including me."

"You have to find out who … you have to be careful …"

Patricia's breathing altered, as did the data on the monitor. Her body lurched as she went into cardiac arrest then crashed. I called a code blue and began CPR. Staff, including Agatha, rushed in with the crash cart. For the next five minutes, we did everything humanly possible.

But she was gone.

Agatha called time of death.

I climbed onto the bed and pulled Patricia into my arms, sobbing without hesitation or restraint, unable to believe this had happened to me again.

Agatha told everyone to leave. She sat on the end of the opposite side of the bed and stared unseeing at the wall.

I don't know how much time passed before I could speak again, but when I could, I said, "I've lost two mothers. I don't think I can bear it."

Agatha swiveled to face me. "You must. She's counting on you." She came around to my side of the bed and placed her hand on my shoulder. "You need to let us tend to her now."

I kissed Patricia's forehead, stroked her hair, and gently released her. "I'll help."

"You'll go. You have an infant who needs you. I insist you take the remainder of the day off and spend it with Lauren. If you can, get some sleep."

I got to my feet then fell into Agatha's arms, where we wept until she insisted I leave.

The attendant was finishing Lauren's bath when I returned to the room. One person I loved was about to be bathed for the last time. The other would have many baths for years to come. I had a daughter now, and she needed me.

"I'll take over," I said.

"You're not scheduled until eight tonight."

"Tell them to change the schedule. Have someone relieve me at seven tomorrow morning."

"Maybe you ought to reconsider. You look like you need as much care as this little one."

"I'll be fine."

"I heard a lot of activity out there. What's going on?"

"You'll find out soon enough."

She handed a swaddled Lauren to me and left. I curled up on the single bed, placing my daughter between me and the wall. We cried ourselves to sleep.

The next morning, I found Abigail had left three messages on my phone and an equal number of text messages. She'd have to wait.

CHAPTER 75

A blown-up photo of a laughing Patricia rested on an easel next to her closed coffin. Thankfully, the weather cooperated. So many women attended, the memorial had to be held outside on the grounds. The procession to the graveyard was the largest the city had ever had to coordinate.

Afterwards, everyone returned to headquarters, where testimonial after testimonial was offered long into the night.

At one point, Connie sidled up next to me. "We're going to have to do something about our prisoner. We're getting tired of feeding him."

I pulled her away from anyone who might overhear. "I'd forgotten about him. With what was going on with Patricia and Lauren, and the arrangements for this."

"We know. And don't worry about it. Keeping him on ice isn't a problem. But we can't do it indefinitely, nor do we want to."

"What have you done with him so far?"

Connie shrugged. "We've asked him politely to tell us who he is and what's going on."

"And?"

"He's a clam. Now it's time to ask him a little less politely."

"I want to be there. I have questions and won't leave without answers."

"I figured as much. That's why I waited."

My phone vibrated in my pocket. Abigail. "Excuse me while I take this."

I answered and told Abigail to hold on while I looked for a place where I could be alone. "Sorry. I had to get where I could hear and speak."

"I'm surprised you answered at all."

"A lot has been going on here."

"Don't try to tell me you couldn't find even one second to text me back."

"It wasn't the right time."

"Speaking of what's right, you have no right to ignore me. I've always been there for you."

I allowed the silence and distance between us to hang in the air for several moments then said, "I have more important things to be concerned with than your exploits."

"That's only because you don't have any of your own."

"I'm hanging up."

"Sure. Run away from your problems, just like you always do."

"You couldn't be more wrong."

I ended the call and located Connie. "I say we conduct our Q&A tomorrow."

"Friggin' A. Mind if I warm him up ahead of time?"

"Whatever works for you works for me. But just warm him."

"Like a toaster set on light."

CHAPTER 76

I'd arranged to take the day off, at least until eight that night, when I'd take over with Lauren. I met Connie in her office at nine that morning, and together we made our way to yet another private space below ground level, one Patricia had never revealed to me, and located in another part of the building. It was a basic utility room, minus the security entrance features required for the other rooms.

I followed Connie into the small brightly lit room constructed out of concrete everywhere but the ceiling, which was comprised of solid wood beams. Three women from the security team were seated at a folding metal table. They looked up and nodded when we entered.

At the opposite end of the room, their captive sat duct-taped to a metal chair positioned over a drain installed in the floor. His head hung toward his chest. Dried blood smeared his face. His pinkie fingers lay on the floor on either side of his chair.

"You warmed him up all right," I said. "Any results?"

"Nope."

The man raised his head, sneered and spit blood in our direction.

I whispered something to Connie. She nodded and left the room.

"You will talk," I said to him.

He laughed and grimaced in pain. "If these Amazon bitches couldn't get me to say anything, what makes you think a runt like you will?"

"I know something they don't."

The briefest flicker of fear mixed with doubt reflected in his eyes.

Minutes later, Connie returned carrying a glass bottle sealed with a glass stopper obtained from the science lab. "They didn't even blink when I asked for it."

I took the bottle from her and walked closer to the man. "In this bottle is H-Two-S-Oh-Four." I turned to Connie. "How's the ventilation in this room?"

"Top-notch. And there's that."

She pointed to a large ceiling fan, like an attic fan found in older homes before central air and heat became a staple. It was recessed in the corner of the ceiling to my left, which was why I'd failed to notice it. "Does it run quiet?"

"Yep."

"Better switch it on."

I turned back to the man. "Since your expression went blank at the mention of the chemical formula, I'll explain. In this bottle is sulfuric acid, otherwise known as oil of vitriol." I sneered. "Now it's registering. Then you know about its strong acidic properties, especially if it's concentrated, which the content of this bottle is.

"When applied to the skin, it causes burns upon contact, as well as secondary burns through dehydration. Did you know that?" He didn't answer so I continued. "This acid is hygroscopic. That means it absorbs moisture from the air. Imagine what that means for skin. You can stop me from using it if you answer our questions."

"Go screw yourself."

I removed the glass stopper and allowed one drop to fall onto the jean-covered thigh of his right leg. He screamed obscenities at us in response to the agony caused.

"Will you talk now?"

"Screw you and every bitch in this place."

"Unzip his pants."

His eyes opened wide as Connie moved toward him.

"You're all crazy," he shouted.

Connie undid the button of his jeans.

He struggled against his restraints. "You're not fooling me. You're not going to do it."

Connie dragged the zipper down. She pulled nitrile gloves from one of her pockets and slipped them on. "No way am I touching that thing bare-handed."

When she opened the fly on his boxers, he said, "Wait. Okay. I'll talk. First, give me some water."

Connie picked up a plastic water bottle from the table, popped up the drinking nozzle and held it to his mouth." He gulped half the bottle.

"Who are you?" I asked.

He licked water droplets from his lips. "My name doesn't matter."

"That answer doesn't satisfy me." I glanced at Connie. "Does it satisfy you?"

"Nope."

He looked from Connie back to me. "Damn it. My name's not in any system. I'm a ghost."

I moved forward, my hand on the stopper. "Do ghosts dissolve in acid?"

"*All right.* I'm part of an elite team."

"Keep going."

"We were hired by the government to take WAM down."

"Why?"

"They know what's going on here. The stuff the public doesn't know about."

"How do they know?"

He pressed his lips into a tight line. I twisted the stopper.

"All right, damn it. There's a mole in the organization."

"Give me a name."

"No way the government's going to let you bitches carry out your mission."

"Who's the mole?"

"I don't know."

I pulled the stopper out. "Tell us, and I won't use this. Tell us, and I'll let you live."

"I swear I don't know. We weren't given a name, just that it's someone at the top."

Connie and I looked at each other. Her stunned expression shifted to one of fury in a flash.

"Any suspicions?" I asked her.

"Zip. You?"

"I can't even begin to imagine."

The man coughed and spat off to the side. "That's all I can tell you because that's all I know. We were told how to get into the first room and given a code that was supposed to give access to a hallway. We were told entry after that required facial recognition, which is why we had explosives along to blow the other doors so we'd gain access to the underground sections. The code we were given didn't work."

"What was the code?" I asked.

He shook his head. "It was given to the team leader only. When we found out the code didn't work, we started prepping to blow that door as well. Then that Hill woman came into her office and found us in the anteroom. We thought we hit the jackpot, but she wouldn't cooperate."

"How many of you raped her?"

"Shit, lady."

I removed the stopper.

"All of us had a turn."

I said to Connie, "How many were there?"

"We counted nine."

I faced him. "Nine."

"It usually takes just the first one, maybe three guys, to get a woman to talk."

"In those circumstances, what do you do, toss a coin?"

He shrugged.

His indifference turned my anger to ice. "She wouldn't cooperate, so you all—"

"It's the adrenaline rush, you know? It makes you do crazy shit."

"Did you beat her before or after the rapes?"

"She wouldn't cooperate."

"Same question."

"After." He grinned. "Too messy if you beat 'em first. Ruins the moment, if you get my drift."

I pulled the stopper from the bottle and walked up to him.

He squirmed against his restraints. "I told you everything. I swear. I told you everything. Look, just take me to the woods somewhere and drop me off. I can't go back to the team. If you're caught, you're out. Out of all of it. I'm on my own now. Persona non grata."

Carefully, I poured a third of the acid onto his genitals. As the acid did its work, I poured a third over his heart. The top of his skull received the final third, and the acid worked its way through his skull to his brain. His screams lasted longer than I'd anticipated.

I faced Connie and the other women. "I suggest you hose him down and wear protective gloves and clothing when you remove him."

Connie said, "We'll handle disposal. We have someone who's an expert."

"The sanitation worker. You can trust her?"

"Tested and proven."

One of the women rushed to a corner and vomited.

One of the other women, whose eyes were fixed on the man, said to me, "I didn't know you had it in you, Katherine."

"It was the adrenaline rush, you know? Makes you do crazy shit." I placed the stopper into the empty bottle. "He was a fool, or thought we were, if he believed we'd let him go." I shook my head. "Men. They still don't comprehend what we might do if they push us to the edge. Or over it."

Connie blew loose hair from her face. "Friggin' A."

CHAPTER 77

Agatha called a meeting of the top women, which included me. I counted thirteen of us around the table in one of the larger conference rooms. Fourteen in total, with Agatha standing at one end. I'd had limited or no interaction with most of them.

Agatha tapped her pen against the table. All present ceased talking. "Patricia left instructions, should anything happen to her, which are in this sealed envelope." She took a moment to compose herself then held up a letter-size envelope from the WAM stationary supply. "It was to be opened and read in front of all of you, in the event of her ... which I'll do now." She used a letter opener, withdrew the folded single sheet of paper, and began to read.

"It's a line said in movies and novels, and though I don't mean to sound trite, it fits the moment, because if this letter is being read to you, it means I'm no longer with you.

"What a remarkable life I've had with all of you at my side. You've given so much of yourselves—your time, energy, and, yes, funds—to fulfill our purpose in, and for, our world.

"Some of you have been with me nearly from the start. No matter how long you've been a dedicated member, I can never thank you— each of you—enough. And I hope you'll understand when I say—call it intuition, perhaps, or simply commonsense—but after great consideration, I began to groom one of our members to take over for me in such an event."

A number of women at the table glanced at Agatha, Brenda, and Lavender.

"Katherine Barnes is that person. She is to take over my position as head of WAM. Access to everything is hers. I know she's capable. More than capable. I trust each of you to give her any assistance she needs, to heed her advice and directions, and to give her the same loyalty you've given to me and our organization. Our sisters depend on each of you, and we depend on each other.

"I ask you to do everything possible to succeed beyond our most dearly-held desire to achieve our goal.

"With all my love and heartfelt appreciation. Patricia."

Agatha folded the letter, placed it back in the envelope and said, "Katherine, as our new leader, the meeting is now yours."

She walked around the table to where I sat speechless. I scraped back my chair and stood, too baffled to say anything.

Agatha handed the envelope to me then embraced me. "Go on, Katherine. Your chair at the head of the table is waiting. We're all waiting."

I took my position and looked at each woman in turn, noting their expressions of anticipation, puzzlement, and so forth. Connie winked at me.

I cleared my throat. "First, I must tell you that I had no idea this was Patricia's plan. I thought her involving me with new responsibilities was solely to assist her, to familiarize me with the inner workings so my assistance was accurate and productive. But this …

"Because I'm as surprised as you are by this transition, I ask you to give me a few days to comb through Patricia's records to further familiarize myself with all she took care of. There may be several rough patches as we move forward, but with your help, we can get through and beyond them. For now, I suggest four of you alternate leading the monthly meetings. You can decide among yourselves who's best suited to that task." I lowered my head. "I'd give anything to have her standing here instead of me."

I brushed tears from my face, remembered how often Patricia had handed me a tissue, and looked up. "She's entrusted me to fulfill the various purposes of our organization. I'll do my best to pay tribute to her. And to you. We'll meet again in the next several days, once I have a more thorough understanding of what's involved. Meeting adjourned."

The women scooted their chairs back and made their way to me. Hugs and congratulations were exchanged. It seemed to me their generous comments were genuine.

I reminded myself that one of them was a traitor.

CHAPTER 78

Agatha, Brenda, and Connie followed me into Patricia's office, now my office. I closed the door and started a pot of coffee.

Brenda settled onto one end of the sofa. "Katherine, you really had no idea what Patricia had planned for you?"

I turned and rested against the credenza. "None whatsoever. I was as gobsmacked as I'm certain all of you and the others were." My gaze drifted to Patricia's favored and empty chair. "I can't get used to the idea of her being gone. It doesn't seem to matter how many people you lose, does it? Regarding the pain and vacuum it creates, I mean."

Brenda nodded. "Each one is a unique loss."

We sat in silence until the coffee was made and distributed in Patricia's china cups. I took a sip and turned to Connie. "What about security? They may come back."

"Beefed up, like we're expecting an invasion. Any man tries to get in or even puts a toe on the property without authorization, he'll regret it faster than he can blink. We'll be cautious about women not known to us as well."

I nodded and looked at Agatha. "Obviously, my schedule will have to change."

"I'll be sorry to lose you."

"Any medical service I can provide in a pinch, please ask. However, keep me scheduled for nights with Lauren. How long before you think she'll be well and strong enough to leave?"

"Another month, to be safe. Maybe a bit more. However, you'll need sitter care during work hours once she's released. We'll help you arrange that here so you have constant access to her anytime."

Connie said, "I'll set up a designated security team to take care of her. Don't want to take any chances, not even with members we trust. Anything happens, they wouldn't be equipped to handle it."

I gave her a small smile. "Thank you."

Agatha nodded her approval. "Is there anything we can do for you now?"

I shook my head. "I need to start going through everything."

Agatha stood. "Then we need to let you get on with it. Come, ladies. We all have work to do. Katherine, let us know if you need anything."

"I will. Connie, please stay for a moment."

Brenda and Agatha kissed me on the cheek and left.

Connie leaned forward and rested her elbows on her knees. "You didn't mention the mole to them. Any reason?"

I made eye contact with her. "It's a delicate predicament."

"No kidding. Any plans for how to find out who it is?"

"I was going to ask you."

"I'll give it some thought, but I'm mostly blank about that. Probably because it's so damn hard to believe. Seems to me, whoever it is needs to somehow slip up in a way we notice." Connie helped me pick up the cups and place them on the credenza. "Changing the subject, I got a puppy."

"I'm glad. What kind?"

She smiled. "Irish setter. Called him Irish Too. T-O-O."

"You must hate being away from him."

She leaned against the credenza. "Yeah. With all that's going on— your promotion and all, okay if I bring him here?"

I grinned. "Absolutely. He'll be our mascot."

"Call if you need something."

Alone, I stared at Patricia's desk and chair for several moments before taking a seat. Hours later, I'd, at a minimum, perused every file label of every manila folder in her office, as well as every computer document label, knowing it would take days to read through everything. It would take months to know most of what Patricia had known about the organization, anything on paper or electronic, that is. I had no doubt there were other things she knew that had not been committed to paper or computer document.

I did come across rough notes regarding Patricia's ultimate plan to move women into leadership roles around the world, but nothing concrete. No clarifying bulleted list or strategic outline to guide me. I called Agatha.

"Was a strategy ever firmed up regarding Patricia's master plan to attain WAM's goal?" I clarified which goal.

"We tossed around ideas but never landed on a fixed strategy. Why?"

"I found notes. They're incomplete, more like brainstorming. I'd hoped you could tell me more."

"We were still in the early stages about that. I'm sorry, Katherine, we just had an emergency arrive. I'll catch up with you later."

I leaned back in the chair, regretting that I hadn't pushed Patricia for more details or her thoughts. Regretting that my chance to tell her my own brainstorm would never happen.

That's when I recalled the drawer with the metal box filled with cash. It wasn't money I was after, it was more about making sure it was still there and to see if anything else important was inside.

I followed her process and opened it. Inside was a small envelope with my name on it. She'd secured the flap and edges with tape. It took a while to carefully open the envelope so as not to tear the paper it contained.

Inside were instructions as to how to find her hidden safe. In the note, Patricia stated that no one at WAM knew the safe existed. I locked the office door and returned to her desk. Following the instructions, I stood to the left of the center drawer and felt around on the left inside panel of the recessed part of the desk, an uncomfortable position that caused me to question what she was up to. My fingers reached a raised square with a button at its center. I pressed the button. A small hidden drawer sprung forward from beneath the center drawer, hence the need to be out of the way.

Only one item was in the drawer—a tiny cassette tape.

I needed a recorder, and was certain I should listen to the tape alone. Knowing Patricia, it could contain information about anything.

CHAPTER 79

It was six fifteen. A little under two hours before my time with Lauren would start. I shoved the tape down far in my front pants pocket, put everything back, hidden as I'd found it, turned off the computer, and moved at pace to my car parked out front. I drove to the nearest store I thought might have recorders for that size tape—it did. I purchased one, and batteries. The next stop was a drive-through for a hamburger. Then to a nearby park, where I put the batteries into the recorder and listened while I ate.

Patricia provided a list of names of women, members of course, who were located around the world, and enough of their biographies to familiarize myself with their specific contributions to the organization. Their membership wasn't a secret, only the true level of their involvement, and this secret was to remain sacrosanct.

The tape held fifty or so minutes of content. I'd thought that, after looking through her filing cabinets and computer, I had a grasp of her responsibilities and interactions, but what I'd reviewed was the proverbial tip of the iceberg.

Toward the end of the recording, Patricia said, "Katherine, I made this tape for you right after I began to train you. You're listening to it, and that means you've now taken over for me because it was time, or something unanticipated has happened."

I used one of the paper napkins from the burger place, since, once again, I had no tissues with me.

"In the bottom drawer of my middle filing cabinet, all the way to the back and behind the folders, you'll find a USB flash drive Lavender jazzed up for me, as well as for the women listed in this recording. The USB is taped to the back of the space-adjustment thingy inside the drawer. Whatever program she loaded onto it allows you to send and receive encrypted messages to and from these women via computer.

"You start the communication by using a key you type in. Ours is a symmetric key, meaning we all have the same key, known only to this elect group. But for extra protection, Lavender set us up with a password authenticated key exchange, PAKE for short. That way, we can each be assured that the person we communicate with is the person we are meant to communicate with.

"We use a 4,022-bit key to get the encryption request started. You'll find that key and the PAKE one on a card taped to the underside of the drawer above the one with the USB. Whenever you use that information, be certain to return that card to the same spot. Same for the USB. Unless you come up with a better hiding place. Never let anyone find either, but definitely not the card.

"When a message goes to one, it goes to all. That was our agreement. Always use this computer encryption as your sole method to communicate with them. Don't worry, so far, we've seldom had cause to use it.

"Sorry if you find this message redundant. I know what a steel-trap memory you have, but I thought it best to make sure you had this as back-up. I've already explained to you the circumstances that must exist for you to reach out to them and when to do this. And that you're not to discuss this with anyone. I know you'll follow my instructions. Love and hugs, my dear."

I stared open-mouthed at the recorder then slammed my hands against the steering wheel. She'd planned to explain all of this to me long before I took over. I'd have to figure it out for myself, just as soon as I figured out what to figure out.

I returned to Patricia's office and put the tape back in the safe drawer. A quick trip to the filing cabinet drawers allowed me to confirm the USB and card were where she'd claimed. Afterwards, I went to the facility to cuddle and care for Lauren, whispering many things to her as she stared into my eyes as though fascinated by every word.

The next day, I made certain a letter went out via e-mail to every WAM member, announcing Patricia's passing away and my taking her place upon her written request. I read every response. To a woman listed on the tape, they sent their condolences about Patricia and welcomed me as their new leader.

***

Connie found me in my office the next morning. She'd brought Irish Too to meet me. I fawned over the adorable puppy, who was around the same several-months old as Irish had been the first time I'd seen him.

Connie tossed a tennis ball across the room. Irish Too scampered after it. "You're WAM head now," she said.

"Yes."

"You've adopted a daughter."

I looked from the puppy to her. "This is going somewhere."

"I want to set up secured living quarters for you inside here, and select security teams for you and Lauren."

"I see your point. Can you have a space ready by the time she can leave the facility?"

Connie grinned. "Sooner than that. I've already started. A furnished suite of safe rooms will be ready by tomorrow. I suggest you sleep in one of the underground beds tonight."

"Always thorough. But I'm spending it with Lauren."

"I'll assign a detail at the facility. I want no mistakes. Not if I can help it. Favor?"

"Name it."

"Let that little guy stay in your quarters with you, once you move in. He's housebroken, and I'll get security to walk him. You won't have to do more than feed and water him. And play with him and give him loads of affection. Just when you're there. The team and I will do the rest."

"Of course. Lauren won't appreciate him until she's older, but they'll enjoy each other eventually."

"That's one less thing to worry about."

"How long is your list?"

"Probably as long as yours."

CHAPTER 80

The next several months passed more like a whirlwind than moments linked together by a ticking clock. I still had no idea who the mole was, but neither had we had another attack at headquarters or, thankfully, at any of our other structures. My encouragement about this remained limited. The original elite team, or a new one, might prefer to let us grow lax, comfortable that the threat was long over, and then return.

Connie and several women, hand-picked by her, were in charge of my security, though I didn't reveal any of Patricia's secrets I was to keep. At times, I felt alone, being able to trust people only so far, but my caution was necessary. It even became necessary to take care with what I said to Lauren, who would one day start to utter words then sentences.

At the end of August the following year, I cut the ribbon at the opening of the Patricia Hill School of Early and Higher Learning. Lauren received star treatment in the nursery part of the daycare center. No one commented about my toddler's security team inside and outside the room. At least, not that I heard about.

The first time I brought her there, I gazed around the room, at the children, and wished Patricia could see this aspect of her dream fulfilled.

I'd turned twenty-nine mid-April. Lauren had turned one in May. I was head of WAM, had opened a school, and was the additional mother to a puppy whose antics caused laughter to bubble or erupt out of Lauren—a sound that made my cells shimmer every time.

This reality was so far removed from my Cabrini-Green days, it almost made those earlier years seem as though I'd dreamed them.

Almost.

School and daycare staff I approved had been scrutinized and carefully selected by Connie and her security team, with the assistance of the tech fairies digging deep into applicants' pasts as recently as the day prior to their first interview.

Lavender sat on the office sofa with me, her eyes fixed on Patricia's favorite chair, which no one ever thought to occupy. "I think we should continue to monitor the new staff's activities."

"The vetting was more than thorough."

She shrugged. "Still. At least until we're convinced of their loyalty."

"How long might that take?"

"I don't know." She flashed a smile. "Twenty, thirty years maybe. I think that's probably what we should do for every new person and member. Wished we'd started that a couple years back."

I kept my expression as unremarkable as I could. "Did someone say something to you?"

She pulled at a loose thread on her jeans seam. "I've been able to add two plus two and get four since I could crawl."

"Meaning?"

"Only one way those bastards knew what they did, and it wasn't because Patricia told them." She made eye contact with me. "You know it too, don't you?"

I got up from the other end of the sofa and walked to the window. Caitlin's tree had grown a couple of feet, its young, outstretched branches laced with leaves. "Do we have the resources to do that on a consistent basis?"

"Won't take me any time to write a program that makes it easy to track anything they do online and by phone. It's not full surveillance, but it's something, especially if they have no idea it's going on. Better safe and all that."

I turned and faced her. Patricia had trusted Lavender enough to set up the encryption method. "How did you and Patricia connect? I never asked and she never volunteered the information. If you don't want to answer—"

"She found me in an alley. I'd run away from a sexually abusive family member. I was a kid and alone. Filthy. Smelly." Lavender looked away. "Didn't stop her from taking off her cashmere jacket and putting it on me."

"So, you're the one."

Her eyes met mine. "Yeah. She put me up in her guest bedroom. Fed me. Clothed me. Listened to me, once I felt safe enough to talk— make that trust. No one else had even wanted to look at me. Couldn't get away fast enough when I begged for spare change."

"And your computer skills?"

"Once she learned I had a keen interest, she got me the best training anywhere. I did the rest on my own. We spent a lot of evenings talking about her plans for WAM."

"Do whatever you think needs to be done. I'm sure if you detect anything as off, you'll let me know."

"Count on it."

I leaned back and fixed my eyes on the ceiling.

"Something's on your mind. What?"

"I need a laboratory." I glanced at Lavender. "It has to be as secure as what we have here. Sizable. I was just wishing I'd realized this before the school construction began, or even was completed, though I'd prefer it to be in this building. I'll have to consider an addition, but wish it could be underground as well. That's not feasible."

"Would 2,500 square feet be enough space?"

I sat up and faced her. "Definitely."

Her lips stretched into a smile. "Follow me."

CHAPTER 81

Lavender led me through the laboratory then into her workspace. We continued to the less-well-lit back of the room, where shelves littered with supplies and spare and antiquated equipment lined large portions of two walls. In that corner was a gap between the ninety-degree angle formed by the end shelves. She pushed on a panel like the one in the office and a door sprang open.

"It's not so much that it's a secret," she said, "but that we mostly ignore it's there or forget about it. Patricia said to use it only if it became absolutely necessary."

She reached in and flipped on a switch. I followed her inside.

"It's perfect," I said. "Large enough for my purposes. More than enough space, actually. Secure. Private enough, as long as I can make it clear no one is to enter without my consent."

"Easy to do. Those of us who work down here can make sure of it." She raised the back of her sweatshirt and pulled out an automatic pistol. "Connie armed and trained us. You know, in case someone manages to breach the other security measures. I'll add, in case anyone tries to stick their nose where it doesn't belong."

With the help of Lavender and Connie, I equipped the room with all I needed within two months. Four months later, I stepped into my laboratory and cursed at the sight before me.

The latest experimental female chimpanzees had died, like the others before them, as had the female mice before them.

I'd intended to accomplish this task on my own, but the truth was I needed help so conferred with the scientists at headquarters. None of them had a desire to switch focus, but each provided five or more names of women to consider who were members and had the required credentials.

I put my project temporarily on hold while I gave my attention to accruing physicians with a scientific bent, or vice versa, to assist me. Using Connie and Lavender and all our resources, after six weeks, I'd hired eight women from the U.S. and various parts of the world, all single, all childless with no intent to change this. All dedicated scientists on board with WAM's ultimate goal, my specific goal, and their terms of employment.

With a few modifications done by a thoroughly vetted team of members who had construction skills, a dorm-like room was created in my lab, with enough beds for each of us, an equipped kitchen, three bathrooms, and a big-screen TV connected to a secured satellite dish positioned on the roof.

The women worked in shifts around the clock. I worked as few nights as possible, but on the ones I did, Lauren's security team acted as sitters. At three every afternoon, they'd take her from daycare to our secure quarters. Connie was in the process of creating a number of safe rooms on each floor there and at the school.

Involving more brains in the lab than just mine proved invaluable. We modified the existing non-lethal, non-steroidal, anti-inflammatory COX-2 inhibitor enough so as to reduce progesterone levels by an even greater percentage than the original formula. This prevented implantation of a fertilized egg as well as inhibited ovulation in our experimental mice, though produced no adverse effects on the eggs. As expected, our new formula proved more efficient. Empirical tests of the original formula we modified had determined the effects were reversible. We calculated it would be the same for the new one.

After several successes with mice, we advanced to chimpanzees. As with the mice, their ovaries ceased to release eggs, or if an egg did get released, it had no nourishing uterine tissue to take root in. The males caught on to our process and would screech and yank on the cage bars when it was time to mate with the females. My fellow scientists observed this part of the process with impassive expressions. I did my best to hide my disgust, or else *suddenly* had to use the restroom or do something for the duration. If they noticed my consistent absence during such times, they kept it to themselves.

At that point I split the team into two groups—one to focus on this part of the equation, the other to begin to find a way to fulfill the more complex one.

We were ready to advance to testing our formula on human females. The other part of my goal would have to stay with chimps for a while. I fully believed it would be successful, so had two of my scientists work on a formula to reverse the inability for women to conceive, while the others assisted me. As in nature, the remedy plant is usually within a few feet of the poisonous one, so I believed the solution was close at hand. The scientists I assigned to work with me to find a way for male chimps to conceive stayed on task.

We were on our way.

CHAPTER 82

Through our resources of Connie's security team and the techs, along with heavy vetting based on a specially designed questionnaire, we found eight members willing to volunteer to advance our cause. They were in their twenties or early thirties—no one over the age of thirty-five was approached. All were single, childless, still menstruating but had no desire to ever conceive, and were "ready and willing to stick it to men," as one of the volunteers stated.

We'd also included one specific qualifier—the women's menstrual cycles had to be stable at every twenty-eight days, and their next cycle had to begin within the same one week we'd targeted. This prevented us from having to stagger initiating the test by too great a difference in timing. We told them it was a new, safer form of birth control.

Each of them took the formula for ten days, starting on the tenth day of their cycle, when their ovaries were preparing to release an egg. Ultrasounds of their ovaries, as well as blood tests to measure hormone levels, were required. It took four months for some, five for others, for egg release to decrease significantly then cease.

Sperm was required for the human tests, so I engaged Connie's services yet again. We happened to be together when mention was made on the local news that someone had broken into a Los Angeles sperm bank and made a rather large *withdrawal.*

Despite the success, a problem did crop up. I sat with the eight scientists as we discussed this.

Gretchen drew her brow into a frown. "The formula to make irreversible is proving most difficult."

"Did you adjust the level of diclofenac?" I asked.

"Ja."

"Reduce it another ten percent. Test it on mice then on one of the chimpanzees first."

"This I already did."

"I'll work with it. I want all of you to continue with the other side of our project. Eventually, one male chimp will conceive. It must happen."

Everything depended on it.

CHAPTER 83

Lauren, who'd turned two, used her small legs to run everywhere rather than walk, which kept her security sitters more active than anticipated. They didn't mind. They especially enjoyed having the word *auntie* before their first names.

Our human test subjects were healthy in every respect, other than their bodies either failed to release an egg each month or, if an egg escaped and conception did happen, their uteruses refused to house and nurture the zygote. We still struggled to find a way to create conception in the male chimpanzees, our one failure.

Then success, once we realized what had to be done. A healthy chimp uterus was transplanted into the chimp we'd named George. His team did everything to prepare his body, including widening the pelvic inlet to make space for the uterus to accommodate a chimp fetus, and gave him a steady infusion of anti-rejection drugs. Connecting the uterus to appropriate veins and arteries for adequate blood supply took delicate work and a number of hours. I was extraordinarily proud, as were they, of their accomplishment.

One of our other successes caused us to celebrate with champagne for the others, apple juice for me. We refined the particulate aspect of the anti-conception formula and tested it as a spray, the same as one might use an air freshener, and were rewarded with the desired results.

"I think it's time we test our product outside the lab," I told my scientific team. "I calculated that three years of consistent application is required for the full effect to be the one desired, especially to ensure its reach is global."

Gretchen scooted to the end of her chair. "How will you do this? We cannot use water supplies. Too many complications."

Faye said in her Texas drawl, "She's right. There's a whole lotta people that still have their own wells. And there's underground springs that get bottled."

"There's only one way," I said. "Aerosol distribution. That's why we created it the way we did."

"But how?" Gretchen asked.

"I've already addressed this. Months ago. One of our members has a high-level position at the Environmental Protection Agency and is willing to assist."

"She knows what is what? She has no problem doing this?"

"She confided her why to me. Her animosity toward men matches ours."

Gretchen nodded. "But how will she convince these people at EPA?"

"She's already done so." They stared at me and waited for an explanation. "The general public, as well as many of those in office, have been conditioned to respond a certain way to a particular buzzword: *Sustainability.* She said that word means one thing to some, and quite another to those in the know. It required little effort on her part to introduce legislation to use of our formula."

Gretchen tilted her head and said, "Again, how? Surely, she did not tell them the truth?"

"She told the EPA that this new organic compound could be included in the cocktail usually dispersed in the atmosphere via chemtrails. That it's a non-toxic fertilizer that promotes and increases crop growth, and that the test results are irrefutable." I laughed at the play on words. The others joined me.

"Ja. Jets flying all around the world will routinely spray our formula over an unsuspecting public. I see now why you say it take three years."

"As soon as I knew the formula worked, I gave it to our other lab personnel, though I tweaked it to speed effectiveness. They'll have significant quantities ready to go by the end of the month and will continue to fill orders."

"Is good idea," Gretchen said. "Jets here fly everywhere. No need to get it to other countries."

"I agree. I don't believe that'll be necessary. However, time will tell. If need be, we'll distribute it to members elsewhere who are in a position to get it into public consumption."

"You do understand, ja, what this might mean? We still have no way to reverse the effects."

"We will."

Not long after that conversation, George's uterus nourished a fetus and did so for an exciting month. But the fetus died, as did George, during the surgery to remove its lifeless form. His two minders applied themselves to figuring out what had gone wrong and how to prevent it from happening again. They determined a fine-tuned hormone adjustment was required.

We'd have to start over.

CHAPTER 84

By the time Lauren turned three the following May, a distinct decrease in conception had occurred worldwide, though initially more so in the more heavily populated areas here and abroad. Fertility clinics soon found themselves visited by a stream of affluent clients eager to create the next generation for themselves or their adult children, all to no effect.

Pundits spent an increasing number of minutes during nightly news segments exclaiming how this decrease in birthrate, if not reversed, would lead to the eventual end of humankind.

Certain conspiracy theorists speculated the decrease in conception was some type of alien intervention. They were correct, of course, but not in the way they imagined.

Young men believed this to be a tremendous opportunity to have all the carefree sex they desired. However, women's desire went the same way as their ability to conceive. To alleviate men's *enthusiasm*, we started work on a formula that would calm them down, emotionally and sexually, also for aerosol distribution.

By the next year, human conception around the world was zero. The public not only was in a state of panic, they were despondent. It appeared to them that the effects of whatever had caused this catastrophe were permanent.

We were concerned as well. I'd thought that by this time, we would have successfully created a way to reverse this.

The bright spot in all of this was Michael. Our chimp had a healthy embryo growing in his transplanted uterus and all looked well. This had its own complications. Waste removal from the fetus had to be set up surgically, cautiously, and taken care of by machine. Michael was not happy with us, which required administration every four hours of a measured dose of tranquilizer, one we deemed safe for the embryo we prayed would become a fully formed fetus.

Along with the boost in hormones, I'd created a drug designed to keep the uterus healthy full-term. I named it PH-244. PH—Patricia Hill.

We watched our host chimp like a child watches an egg expected to hatch. At the end of 240 days from implantation of the zygote, we did a C-section and removed a perfectly formed, healthy male chimpanzee. Michael, only slightly worse for wear, was fed his favorite foods once his appetite returned.

"I thought of a name for our first conceived chimp," I said. "Mada. It's a feminine Irish name, but because of what it represents, I say we go with it."

Faye popped the cork from a bottle of champagne. "What's it represent?"

"It's Adam in reverse." I laughed and they joined in.

Seven glasses filled with champagne, and one filled with apple juice raised in celebration.

Faye said, "To Katherine, a true genius."

"I didn't do it alone."

"Maybe not, but somehow I think you could have."

"I'd still be at step three without each of you." We clinked our glasses and sipped. "There's a way to go before we announce our success. I want several certain successes before we go public. In the interim, we work on the next part of our plan."

We had to continue to succeed, and so well that this process of conception could be transferred to men.

They were paying for their misdeeds in some ways, but not in the way I intended.

We tested the initial calming formula on the male chimps. The results fell short. It was back to the drawing board.

But at least we had Mada.

CHAPTER 85

My team and I spent a private New Year's Eve in the regular labs with the others. Connie and Agatha joined us. Brenda had a prior engagement.

Connie, like me, stuck with sparkling apple cider. She raised her glass. "Here's hoping 2013 is everything we want it to be. May it be a fruitful year in the ways we desire." She winked at me.

I grinned, held up my glass and said, "Everyone say it with me."

All present raised their glasses, and as one chorus shouted, "Friggin' A."

Of course, fruitful was a relative term. Humans hadn't conceived during the last two years. Correction—a few had managed to conceive but were unable to go past the first trimester.

I recalled that Thomas Huxley said, "The chessboard is the world, the pieces are the phenomena of the universe, and the rules of the game are what we call the laws of Nature."

That reminder should have dissuaded me from my ultimate goal, but it didn't. Far too many men demonstrated no hesitation about breaking the law, especially regarding women.

I had to succeed in punishing them. Especially now. Now that women's interest in sex had waned dramatically or disappeared altogether, certain segments of the disgruntled male population decided that, willing or not, women would fulfill their physical needs. Sexually transmitted diseases erupted, mostly because condom manufacturers were unable to keep up with demand from the multitude of impatient males. Pharma companies were months behind in production of antibiotics, most of which proved ineffectual as viruses mutated beyond scientists' capabilities.

Never in my imagination had an escalation in disease and crime, particularly against women, been considered a possible outcome.

We scrambled in the lab to produce a formula to diminish the male chimpanzees' sexual desire, what you might call a prophylactic measure. Yes, there was a drug on the market that accomplished this, but the challenge was to get men across the globe to get it into their systems voluntarily, which we knew would never happen. Another aerosol was needed.

That's when I began to panic.

That's when I began to wonder if my hatred of men *would* lead to the ultimate destruction of humanity. Men were paying for their crimes, but not to the degree women were.

***

I returned to my living quarters. Irish Too bounded toward the door to get his share of affection before Lauren could reach me.

Lauren's security team, aka sitters, had fed and bathed her. After they left, we had our cuddle time then a snack. As I tidied the kitchen area, I watched and listened to my daughter.

She propped her baby doll in the toy highchair. "My baby is hungry."

She fed invisible food to the doll with a plastic spoon. "My baby is full." She looked at me and frowned. "And *she* doesn't like peas *either*."

I bit back my smile. "Noted."

She undressed her doll and placed her into a plastic tub. "My baby needs a bath." After the pretend washing, with her singing and talking to her doll, she dressed the doll in pajamas.

I watched her every move, mesmerized by her attention to the doll in her care, as she cooed, petted, and showered her *baby* with affection. Like a loving mother.

Lauren's mouth stretched open with a yawn. Doll clutched to her, she took my hand and pulled me to the rocking chair, climbed into my lap and said, "My baby's sleepy, Mommy. We'll rock my baby and tuck her in."

Irish Too went to his cushioned bed, turned in circles until something about it was just right, and lowered himself. He rested his head on the raised rim and watched us with half-closed lids. He snuffled once then drifted to sleep.

I wrapped my arms around Lauren, rested my cheek atop her soft curls, and began the gentle back and forth of the chair as my daughter sang to her doll.

She yawned mid-lyric and said, "My baby is so sweet. I love my baby, and my baby loves you, Mommy." Another yawn followed.

Moments later, she said, "Mommy, you wet my hair."

After a few hard swallows, I said, "Sorry, Lauren." I tilted my head back so my tears ran down my neck instead.

CHAPTER 86

I sat at my workstation, eyes focused on the latest failed chemical formula displayed on the computer monitor. My thoughts strayed to Lauren and how she lavished attention on her doll. The signs presented as though she'd make a good mother, and that she'd want to be one, just as I had.

The previous night, I'd stared at shadows on the ceiling created by a rotating night light with cutouts in the cylinder that surrounded the bulb, and mulled over my conflicted feelings.

Such thoughts were resolved by a particular one: Motherhood was not restricted to giving birth. Lauren was a perfect example of this truth. Nor did giving birth necessarily result in the best of maternal instincts rising to the surface. Mothering came from a deep desire to nurture. It's why a hen will warm kittens tucked beneath her feathers, or a female dog will nurse kittens.

I told myself not to worry. That by the time Lauren was old enough to choose motherhood, everything would be resolved.

It had to be.

I was stuck in this musing when Faye approached me.

At near-whisper volume she said, "Katherine, we have a problem, possibly a big one."

"I know. I'm working on it."

"I'm not referring to our work. Leastways, not exactly."

I faced her. "What then?"

"I suggest we speak elsewhere. Can you go now?"

"From the expression on your face, I think I'd better. Let's go to my office."

I wasn't in the habit of explaining my actions, so left without a word, and with Faye trailing me. As far as I could tell, no one paid attention. On the trek up, Faye watched the numbers, her breaths rapid, her hands shoved into her lab coat pockets, though I could see her hands clenching and releasing beneath the fabric.

Once in my office, I had her sit on the sofa while I made cups of chamomile tea. I settled at the opposite end of the sofa. "What's the problem?"

"Chloe. I think she's losing it."

I set my cup into the saucer. "Explain."

"She thinks you don't know what you're doing. We disagreed vehemently with her. Our dialogue quickly became arguments. She ended by saying she believes your plans are evil."

"Did she say why she feels this way?"

Faye avoided looking at me and took a sip followed by another.

"You're delaying," I said.

She nodded. "Chloe believes it has to be a form of madness possessing you to reverse what God designed. That men are not meant to conceive and hold that place in the maternal world. That God gave women more effective mammary glands for a specific reason. Her words, almost verbatim."

"Did she say anything else?"

Faye trained her eyes on me. "She believes it's your intention to end the world."

How had someone with such strong spiritual beliefs made it past the vetting process? Only one way—she had to have lied. Unless some epiphany had struck her while working on our projects.

"Katherine?"

"Sorry. Has she paid any attention at all to the news?" I got to my feet and began to pace. "Is she aware of how these developments led men to even more vile behavior?"

"She blames you."

"How remarkable. And how like a man it is for her to blame women for the actions of men."

"She doesn't blame *all* women, just one. I'm sorry to say this, but I'm afraid she may be willing to betray us, specifically you. She's showing the earmarks of someone contemplating going to the authorities."

I stared at my tea, as though an answer or suggestion about how to proceed might float to the surface.

Faye leaned forward. "What're you gonna do?"

I went to the window and fixed my gaze on Caitlin's tree. "Only one thing to do."

CHAPTER 87

I sent Faye back to the lab then called Connie and asked her to come to my office ASAP. More pacing went on as I waited the few minutes it took for her to arrive.

We sat on the sofa as I explained what I'd just learned.

Connie whistled and said, "After all we've been through to get where we are, there's only one solution."

I made eye contact with her, saw the steely resolve in her eyes and in the set of her lips, and shook my head. "Killing women is not in my playbook."

"Even one who means to destroy you and everything you—and we—have worked for? That Patricia *died* for?"

"I'll talk to her. I'll convince her this is for the greater good. She believed that at the start. She just needs reminding."

"A lot of good that'll do. She thinks you're evil."

I shook my head. "She thinks my plan is evil."

"Believe me. If the two haven't merged in her mind yet, it's only a matter of time."

Chloe and I were to meet on a bench by the lake at the nearest off-site park. The risk of allowing her off the grounds was addressed—Connie had two of her security team follow the woman. Connie and four of her team followed me.

There was a strong possibility that hours confined in the lab had affected Chloe, akin to seasonal affective disorder. I'd advised all of them to spend some time in the sunlight on the grounds every day, and they usually did this. Their dedication to our common goal had kept them focused. Our successes, and how well the scientists were catered to, had kept them content. If it turned out Chloe wasn't suited for such long-term focus and confinement, we had a problem indeed.

I stopped at the popular, always crowded Palo Alto Coffee Haven to get coffees for each of us. I paid limited attention to what went on inside because one of my security team had followed me in, while the others kept watch from one of their personal cars parked next to mine. Connie suggested this vehicle rather than being obvious by using one of their tricked-out SUVs.

Order in hand, I pushed the door open to leave and heard some-one say the name Abigail. My head snapped around and I raked my eyes over the crowd, but didn't readily recognize anyone. Nor did I have time to look more thoroughly. Abigail was a somewhat common name, or at least, that's what I told myself as I continued to the car and headed for the park.

I'd never called Abigail back after that last call. My activities in the lab and with Lauren had pushed my friend from my mind. By now, perhaps Abigail was relegated to the designation of former friend. Perhaps it was the same regarding me in her mind.

Again, the usual tug was there. I was the one who was supposed to call her back. For the sake of history, I should call her and apologize, though what explanation I could give would have to be thought out ahead of time.

These thoughts diminished as soon as I spotted Chloe seated on the bench. I parked my car and kept my attention on her for a few moments. One reason was to allow my security team time to park in a convenient place but not draw attention. The other was to focus on the set of Chloe's shoulders—tension radiated from her.

I picked up the small tray holding our coffee cups and got out. One deep breath in then out, and I started forward.

In my mind I told her, *For all our sakes, you must hear what I say and agree.*

CHAPTER 88

We sat in silence and watched ducks paddle on the placid lake while others of their kind landed or took flight. Sunlight warmed us in a soothing way, and the effect I'd desired by picking this spot became evident—Chloe's posture relaxed in some measure. I glanced at her then back at the lake. "Are you happy working with us?"

She went still. The stiffness returned. "Someone's been talking."

"Please answer my question."

"What you're doing is wrong."

"Which part?"

"All of it."

"Tell me why."

"No one can play God. No one should try."

"Perhaps you should have thought of that before becoming a physician and a research scientist. After all, isn't that what people in those—our—fields do?"

"There's a difference between playing God and assisting God with His work."

At the earliest opportunity, I'd be certain to ask Connie how Chloe had passed the vetting process. Her initial response when I'd told her about Chloe had driven the question from my mind. Until now. "That's a matter of perspective," I said.

She looked at me then away again. "I don't see how."

"You knew our goal before you signed on."

"I thought I did."

"You said you were on board with our master plan."

"I was. At the beginning. Then I saw the results."

"Speaking of beginnings, you have to realize this is the beginning of the end, but not of the world, Chloe. It's the beginning of the end of men believing they're superior to us. An end to them believing they're our owners. Our minders. They've never appreciated what our full purpose is, what we contribute to the bigger-picture of life, or what we could if no one stopped us. Never appreciated what it's like to carry a developing human inside, to feel it move, to go through agony mingled with ecstasy in order to deliver a child into the world."

"They were never meant to. And to my knowledge, neither have you."

She was only partly right about the latter, but I was in no mood to expound. "The majority of men are clueless. They think nothing of harming us, of brutalizing us physically and mentally." I glanced at her. "Even spiritually."

"Not all men are like this."

I faced the lake. "First, we'll show them how inferior they are, which I believe we've accomplished, in part, by robbing them of the ability to experience a female's conception solely as a result of their precious prowess or degrading, brutal force. They've long deserved to be humbled. It's a kindness, really."

"It isn't working the way you'd imagined. In fact, you've escalated such behaviors."

I watched a duck land then glide across the water. "The next step is to weaken them physically. Not entirely, you understand. Just enough to let them feel what it's like to be as weak as they believe us to be."

"Everything we're doing is an abomination."

"Once they're weakened enough physically and egotistically, we'll take over. Our domination will be kinder, gentler. They'll discover what equality should look and feel like because we'll demonstrate it fairly. We won't demean or abuse them."

"We're doing it now."

I looked at her. "In this matter, the end justifies the means."

"You would reduce this to a hackneyed phrase?"

"I'm not reducing anything."

Chloe harrumphed. "Just the population and the continuation of the human species, not to mention women's safety."

"All temporary issues. We'll resolve them."

"One failure after another."

"I'd like to think you'd be with us as we restore balance and sanity to the planet."

"To use another hackneyed phrase, it appears 'The lunatics are running the asylum.'"

CHAPTER 89

Chloe raised her face to the sunlight and closed her eyes. "You're treating all men as though they're evil. That's a gross misjudgment of character as well as a misappropriation of power. You have this image of men fixed in your mind, and it's wrong. My father was a perfect example. He was firm, as a mindful parent should be. But he was also kind and caring. He was always there for me, my family, and his friends."

"Someone hurt you, though. Otherwise, you would never have agreed to work with us."

She lowered her head. "Only one out of many who didn't."

"Then you're one of the fortunate ones." I told her my story—all of it—starting from Buster and ending with Eric, though I left out how the story ended for each of them. I omitted any mention of Ralph. I reminded her of what men had done to Patricia, and repeated Patricia's words about how brutally men had acted throughout history and still to this day.

She sighed heavily. "I'm very sorry about Patricia as well as your own experiences. Now that I know, it explains a great deal about your motivation. But this doesn't mean you have a right to do what you've done and what you intend. Besides, men have been battered by women."

"Their percentages are far lower in number than ours."

"They're battered because they won't strike back."

"As I said, too few in number to count as equal in significance." I turned on the bench and faced her. "Can't you see how important it is that we take over control?"

"No."

"That's only because you believe I'm trying to end the world. I'm going to save it."

CHAPTER 90

Chloe shook her head. "You've judged the entire male population based on the actions of a few."

"A few million, you mean. Perhaps even billion. And that's solely contemporary times. Some incidents are never reported, especially when it involves children. Some victims never live to report their abusers."

"Your thinking is flawed in the worst way. You're so intent on punishing them, you can't see this."

"It's more than their actions. It's their attitude."

"It's discrimination. No different from someone of a particular race doing something wrong and others blaming the entire race. The reality, Katherine, is that evil emerges from those willing to engage in it, with no regard for genetics or upbringing. Surely you know this."

"You're right, but in a limited way. There's no race, culture, or—since you mentioned God—religion able to claim their men are free of violence against others, including or especially toward females. Not one. Do your research. Some men still hold the belief that we're just above cattle to be fed so we live to fulfill their usage of us as providers of children. It's time they get a dose of their own medicine, *Doctor*."

"Except in this situation, they can't take their medicine, as you put it, without our being subject to the pernicious side-effects as well."

"If someone set up a site online where women around the world could hold up a virtual hand to be counted among those who've been harassed, abused, and or raped by one or more men, the site would crash in the first ten seconds."

Chloe rose to her feet. "It's impossible to speak with you. Impossible for you to see reason."

"I can say the same about you."

"Judgment belongs to God, as does vengeance. He said so and it is so. But that's yet another way you attempt to take over His role. Someone else, someone higher than you in creation, attempted this and was cast out of heaven, damned for all eternity, with any chance of redemption lost."

"In my opinion, your God hasn't dealt fairly with us. Quite the opposite. Someone down here needs to do it. And it'll never be a man."

"You need to read the Bible."

"I've read it."

"Then you missed reading about women who were prophets and in positions of power."

"Far too few."

"Everything you're doing and saying is blasphemy. You'll pay for it, just as you're making the world pay."

She walked away. I turned to watch her move toward her car, shifted my gaze to Connie and shook my head.

CHAPTER 91

Chloe's words echoed in my mind as I drove back to headquarters. Aspects of her comments contained truth, and it was those particular truths that nagged at me.

Was it time to abandon my goal, and Patricia's? If I did this, WAM and all the good it was doing for women might disintegrate. The women might disperse, leaving torn about all they'd given of themselves, only to have this situation and their dreams end in utter failure. It would mean a return to status quo. Or worse.

Could I live with that?

Although I felt certain we would succeed on all fronts eventually, there was no denying that the possibility of ultimate failure haunted me.

I pictured Lauren in her later years, living in isolation because she was the daughter of the woman who'd been responsible for ending human life on our planet, if there were even anyone left alive to condemn her for this.

What would she think of me? How would she feel about my denying her the chance—even the right—to bear a child or children? Or my being the cause of her having to live virtually sequestered and surrounded by a security detail until they died off as well? Unless they and others abandoned her before that time, if they even allowed her to live.

I'd have to push my scientists to work harder to create a formula to reverse the anti-conception result. It, too, would have to be dispersed as its predecessor had been.

Once obtained, we'd hold the proven formula in storage, at least until we succeeded with causing the first man to carry a child to full-term. Then the next and the next, until a good portion of the male population had experienced this. We'd start with rapists and murderers of women and children. They deserved it most.

***

Connie joined me in my office. I made my nearly verbatim report of Chloe's and my conversation. "She has something like a field of self-righteousness around her, which I was unable to penetrate with logic and facts."

"Field or no field, she's wrong. Patricia was on target about the need for a revolution. We can't stop now. We've put too much blood, sweat, and tears into it." She paused then added, "You're not thinking of dumping your projects, are you?"

I slumped back on the sofa. "I have concerns, but no, I'm not giving up."

"Friggin' A."

We sat in silence for several moments before I said, "How *did* she manage to get selected for an interview? We said no one with spiritual beliefs."

"I had the same thought, so checked her file. On the question about spiritual beliefs or religion they were raised with, she said her parents were atheists. Plain and simple, she lied."

I sighed and shook my head. "No, she didn't."

Connie fixed her gaze on me. "Explain that to me."

"We need to modify the question because it never asked about *her* specific beliefs."

"Crap. A loophole."

I sat forward. "I need to get back to work. Have your team keep careful watch of Chloe—phone calls, e-mails. Lavender can help with that. Trail Chloe if she leaves the grounds. We want to know where she goes and whom she speaks with."

"That's a big risk. Kind of 'Too little too late,' if you ask me."

"It can't be helped."

"That's *not* a WAM motto."

"No. It isn't."

Connie slapped her thighs and got to her feet. "Let me get this surveillance thing set up. Gotta move fast in this situation."

After Connie left, I stood at the window, arms crossed. Initially, Chloe had insisted she believed in our cause, but she didn't. Had she deliberately lied about that? Had Connie deliberately *missed* this? She'd gotten the others right.

An even worse thought occurred to me: Was there a specific reason the identity of the mole had never been discovered? If someone was in the position to keep us guessing or to cover the truth …

The intruder had said it was one of our top members. It made my head spin to imagine someone I trusted implicitly might be the person who stood willing to betray us at any moment. I'd have to be even more cautious from now on. I no longer knew who to give my full measure of trust to. In its own way, it was Abigail all over again, multiplied.

Now I understood why Patricia had kept so many things to herself, limiting knowledge, in part, to no more than one person, depending on what the matter was.

How odd to be surrounded by so many, yet feel so completely alone.

I returned to my lab. Chloe occupied her workstation, but avoided looking at me or the others, and spoke only when spoken to.

Little work got done by me, as I was too focused on watching Chloe.

CHAPTER 92

My mirrored reflection made plain how poorly I'd slept. By a few minutes after five, I'd abandoned all chance of getting any sleep in the time left before my alarm clock would sound.

Chloe was a problem that needed a solution, but I didn't care for the obvious one. Certain this was some temporary reaction to the heavy schedule and predominantly isolated lifestyle, I resolved to speak with her again. But what to say? We needed to ramp up our endeavors, not decrease them.

A sleepy Lauren toddled into the bathroom and took hold of a leg of my pajamas. She wobbled in place, eyes closed. I'd woken her. I scooped her into my arms, carried her back to bed and tucked her in next to Irish Too, who opened one eye and gave a half-hearted wag of his tail. I scratched the fur behind his ears. He stretched and draped a foreleg across Lauren.

I brushed dark curls from her forehead and studied her serene face. "I'm doing it for you as well as for all of us. I never want you to have the experiences I had. It's my job to protect you, and I will, no matter what it takes. I only hope you'll understand when you're old enough."

I kissed her forehead and went to the kitchenette to start a pot of coffee.

Chloe had been attacked as an adult in her twenties. She was childless. She didn't understand.

How could she?

My mother had felt so powerless that the only way to forestall Buster's abuse of me was to allow him to abuse her. Giving in to his demands had also been her attempt to keep his temper and treatment of her from crossing the line from abuse into brutality. She'd succeeded only modestly in her attempts. I refused to allow this to be the predominant recourse for women like my mother, to self-protect or protect their daughters while trapped in a living hell.

I grabbed hold of the counter to steady myself as a reality washed over me: I would do anything, including sacrifice myself, to protect Lauren. Just as Patricia had done to protect the women beyond the paneled door. Just as my mother had done for me.

Tears streamed down my face as memories of what my mother had put herself through for my sake bombarded me, and without me realizing it or ever thanking her.

This was why I had to succeed. So that such a need for protection from men ceased, finally and forever.

I managed to eat a slice of toast with my coffee and waited for Lauren's security aunties to arrive at seven thirty.

Prompt as usual, they called first to confirm they were at the door then entered.

Lauren sat up, rubbed her eyes and yawned. She kissed Irish Too on the snout then slid from the bed. "I want oatmeal with cinnamon for breakfast."

"Lauren," I said, "you know the proper way to greet people is to say hello first."

She stopped in her tracks, mouth agape, and fixed her blue eyes on me. The twinkle she gets in her eyes flashed. She straightened her spine and said, "Hello first."

As anticipated, she got a laugh from all of us. I kissed her goodbye and made my way to the office to check e-mails and so forth. Twenty minutes later, I headed to down to my lab.

The women were already busy at their workstations. I scanned the room.

"Where's Chloe?"

CHAPTER 93

Faye frowned and said, "Chloe's still in bed, sleeping like there's nothing to do."

Gretchen nodded. "Ja. Her work, it be less than it should be lately. You talk to her, ja?"

"I'll talk to her all right."

I started toward the sleeping quarters, relieved that Chloe was still here. That relief lasted another two seconds, when another thought crossed my mind. What if her sleep was the eternal kind? We certainly had a variety of tranquilizers on hand for the chimpanzees. She wanted out, and likely realized what an impossibility it was that we could allow her to leave.

I sped my steps, flung open the door and stopped at the threshold. Her form was indeed under the covers, head to foot, in the last bed near the far wall. Her usual toiletries and miscellanea cluttered the nightstand to the left of her single bed.

"Chloe. Time to get up. We need to talk."

No response.

A second, more pronounced tremor of fear radiated from my chest to my stomach. I forced my feet to propel me forward. Once at the side of her bed, I poked her back, surprised at the level of give.

I yanked the covers away, impressed with how carefully she'd constructed a representation of her form with clothing and towels.

No report had come from Connie about Chloe's movements or disappearance during the night. Suspicion crept up my spine.

I returned to the lab and said, "Chloe's gone. I'm going to find out what I can, if anything. Please continue with your work. I'll join you later."

I left as the volume of their comments increased, partially from excitement, partially because most of them hurried toward the quarters to gape at the bed.

Once in my office, I called Connie. Before she could say a word, I said, "I need to see you immediately."

"On my way."

Tense minutes later, she entered my office and I shouted, "Chloe's gone."

"Yep. Problem solved. Permanently."

I collapsed into my desk chair. "What have you done?"

"Saved your ass and saved WAM in the process. She was doing a runner. You know as well as I do we couldn't allow that."

Perspiration beaded on my scalp. "What am I going to tell the others?"

"Tell them I found her wandering the grounds last night, blathering nonsense. Tell them she's had a complete mental breakdown, or whatever the proper lingo is. Tell them I got her placed in a safe, secure hospital—make that rest home—and staff are taking good care of her. No expense too great. Yada yada yada. And that there's little chance she'll ever be the same."

"They'll ask why I didn't know about this when I showed up for work this morning."

"Blame me. Tell them it happened on my watch and I didn't want to disturb you and Lauren, since I was handling it. That I meant to tell you first thing, but because I was up until dark-thirty getting her settled, I didn't wake in time to tell anyone."

"If they'll even buy that story."

"My security team did. But then, they aren't prone to asking questions."

"My scientists are all about the questions."

"Then you'd better make this explanation sound good." Connie sighed. "Look, is my story plausible or not?"

I exhaled hard. "It is. It has to be."

"Since it's the one I put out there, we have to stick with it. You'll tell them only what I told you, right? No alterations?"

"Yes."

"Then you're in the clear." Connie waited a moment then added, "I understand how you must feel. I'd feel the same way if one of my team went off the rails and became a threat to us."

"Would you take the same action in that situation?"

"I'd have to. I wouldn't like it, but I'd do what I was supposed to—protect you and WAM at all costs."

I scrubbed my forehead with my fingers. "I had a similar thought just this morning, but about something else." I turned my gaze to her. "Thank you, Connie. For looking out for Lauren and me. For all of us."

"We're a team."

"We're more than that." Understanding registered in her eyes, and I added, "If you truly are in need of rest, get some. I'm sure someone can cover for you for a few hours."

"You don't need to worry about me. Fix that attention of yours on the bull's-eye."

She left, and I took a few moments to splash cold water on my face then returned to my lab, where I repeated Connie's fable as fact.

Gretchen patted me on the arm. "Too sensitive, was Chloe. That is never good for lab, ja?"

I nodded.

Faye put an arm around my shoulder. "Probably had mental illness in the family that skipped a generation, which would explain her recent behavior. She probably didn't even know about it. You know how family is about keeping skeletons in the closet."

Gretchen shrugged. "Anything, it is possible."

"So I've discovered," I said.

I scanned their faces as they watched me and waited for whatever I might say. "We wish Chloe well where she is now, but it's time to aim for what's possible and necessary."

They took turns hugging me then returned to their workstations. As they walked away, I repeated silently what Fra Luca Pacioli had said, "A thing may endure in nature if it is duly proportioned to its necessity."

Chloe had negated her necessity.

Connie had deleted Chloe.

I inhaled a deep breath, held it several moments then released it.

It was time to get back to work.

CHAPTER 94

Our latest formula designed to calm men and weaken them physically, but only slightly, succeeded once we adjusted the dystrophin protein, the lack of which results in muscular dystrophy. Naturally, it wasn't our intention to go *that* far, nor did we. It took several attempts to devise a way to make this formula attracted solely to Y chromosomes then reduce the protein by fifteen or so percent. I blended this formula with the anti-conception one, added in the one to calm men, using the same Y chromosome attractor factor for the latter one. Once results with the chimps proved satisfactory, I gave our other scientists the revised formula.

The head scientist studied the formula on the printout. "The men at EPA approved this?"

"I don't see any reason to burden them with making a decision about it. Let them think it's the same product. My contact there knows. That's all that matters."

"Yet another reason Patricia singled you out."

I patted her on the arm then returned to my workspace.

By 2014, it had been three full years since any human had conceived, with the exception of one fluke—Amber Lake. Progress about her pregnancy, which was announced later in the year, was updated each Friday evening on all news programs around the world.

I'd commented to my scientists how much I wished I could run tests on Amber to determine how she'd bypassed effects of our formula, but that was out of the question.

We celebrated my thirty-third birthday in April, Lauren's fifth in May, and Mada's second during the first week in December. Mada's party included banana cake for everyone, including the chimps, though we regretted the clean-up that followed.

While enjoying the festive occasion, we reminisced, especially because getting Mada to this age was a hard-won success.

Nature's design is for the mother to nurture and care for her offspring until old enough to fully separate. Chimps reach puberty around age eight or nine, can deliver a first infant at age eleven or twelve, and by age fifteen, males demonstrate social maturity. Initially, they learn from their mothers, and then from other chimps in their grouping as they mature.

Mada's *mother*, for all intents and purposes, was her father, Michael, who had no clue about how to tend to a newborn, nor demonstrated interest. And there was the breastfeeding matter to contend with—there was none, for obvious reasons.

The females remained curious about Mada, including the female whose egg contributed half of his DNA. But as the inherent processes had not been present to establish an immediate bond at a natural birth, she'd demonstrated no interest in taking care of him either.

This care had become our task.

Research assisted us, and we'd kept careful charts as to what Mada was supposed to do development-wise and when. It also meant each of us had taken turns wearing him in a harness strapped to our chest. Mada also wore diapers, as all our chimps did, our least favorite chore. Giving him a bottle proved the most pleasant.

At two months, he'd begun to suck his thumb, reach for objects, struggle to get out of his harness, and when large enough, began to stand upright by holding onto the legs of the person whose charge he was in that day.

The next month, he began to wobble on his feet and push and pull on us, developed his first tooth, and enough coordination to grab objects and hold on. This, of course, quickly became problematic.

He took his first steps at five months. That's when we put him into a cage adjoined to his biological mother's. It delighted us to see she took more interest in him then, especially when he began to imitate her facial expressions and grooming habits, which amused her. She'd make faces, watch him repeat them, and do her version of a chimp laugh in response. He also began to climb the sides of the metal cage.

Gretchen put her plate and fork down. Frowning, she walked to the cage of our latest impregnated male. Her shoulders sagged. Shaking her head she said, "Three this makes to die."

I joined her and rested a hand on her shoulder. "Out of eight, five are thriving. That's something. The odds are in our favor."

"Better odds would I like."

"So would I. We keep going until we have a one-hundred-percent success rate of gestation and birth."

Faye joined us with the sole infant sleeping in the harness she wore. "We've got four impregnated chimps now." She patted the bottom of the one she carried. "And one recuperating. If all goes well, we could find ourselves needing to recruit infant-tenders if the others are delivered and survive. Otherwise, we'll be spending more time on infant care than anything else."

I smiled at her. "That's what they call a good problem to have."

"In the wild they aren't weaned until age five. Will we keep them that long? Even keep them as test subjects?"

"I'm not certain about that yet."

"Like I said, we could get overwhelmed."

"Let me worry about that." I glanced back at the chimp that had died. "Take care of him in the usual way. Then it's back to work."

CHAPTER 95

At 5:21 p.m., January 7, 2015, I was still in the lab, but getting ready to leave for the day. My cell phone vibrated. I read Connie's text message and said, "Something's happening."

Faye, nearest to me, looked up. "What is it?"

"Connie said to turn the TV on now, on the Global Media channel. Some big news is coming on after the commercial break."

We clustered around the big-screen TV. Remote in hand, I pressed the on button and watched the screen come to life.

After the commercial ended, Sasha Aspen, wearing spiked magenta hair this week, looking paler than usual, aimed tear-filled turquoise eyes at the camera.

"Gotta be contacts," Faye said.

I shushed her as Sasha drew in a deep breath and announced that Amber Lake had miscarried.

We listened to the remainder of the brief report. I turned off the TV as the others returned to their workstations. None of us said a word.

I closed the files on my computer. "I'll see you in the morning."

Heads nodded but stayed lowered.

I understood their response. I was heading to my quarters.

To be with my daughter, one of the last children born.

Relief, sadness, and something I didn't want to feel—guilt—engulfed me like dense fog.

CHAPTER 96

Two months later, perspiration dampened my underarms from the heat of the overhead lights inside the Global Media Studio located in San Francisco. I shifted in the chair positioned at a slight angle and to the right of Sasha Aspen's usual chair. A few feet to my right were four cages. One held Mada, the other three each contained a pregnant male chimp. We'd hooked up opaque bags to the waste-collection tubes protruding from the chimps' abdomens, so as not to upset viewers.

Gretchen and Faye stood nearby but off-camera, in case they were needed. Connie and seven of her security team stood guard offstage right and left, but close enough to reach me in a hurry. More of her team had taken positions inside and outside the studio.

Sasha leaned back and tapped her pen against her chin. "And you're certain there's nothing you can do that allows women to conceive again?"

"As I said, we're working on it. It's easier to fix something when you know the cause."

She pointed the pen at me. "You honestly expect us to believe you created a way for male chimps to conceive and carry to full-term?"

"Yes."

"I'm certain our listening audience, which is most of the planet awake at this time, is as eager as I am to hear how you managed this."

I gave her a slight smile. "I'm afraid the methods are proprietary."

"Then how can you prove this *miracle*, for lack of a better word? Although," she smiled at the camera, "scam is a word that comes to mind. For all we know, those three might be fat. Or maybe you inflated their abdomens with air or whatever, and it has something to do with those bags attached to them."

I withdrew a stethoscope from my lab coat pocket. "Follow me."

I led her to the nearest cage, where a pregnant male, who like the other two, lay prone on a long cushion.

"What's wrong with him?" She glanced at the others. "In fact, what's wrong with all of them?"

"Nothing is wrong. They're in perfect health. I gave them sedatives so this experience would be easier for them to tolerate, especially the pregnant ones."

I opened the cage door and used the stethoscope to locate the fetus's heartbeat. I kept the bell in place and handed the ear tips to Sasha. "Listen." When her eyes grew wide, I said, "Even if you aren't familiar with chimp physiology, you know the position of that heartbeat is too low to be *his* heart."

She handed the ear tips to me and turned to the camera. "It's true." She aimed her gaze at the control booth. "I don't care who gets upset, I don't want one commercial break until this hour is up. This is monumental news."

I introduced her to Mada, who lazily grabbed the finger I thrust through the wire mesh. He puckered his lips at me then nodded off. That netted a slew of questions from Sasha about care of the infants and other matters, some of which I answered, some of which I didn't.

"And you intend to transfer this ability to human males?"

"Once the process is perfected, we'll arrange for human trials."

"So men will have chimpanzee uteruses plugged into them."

"I suppose that's one way to put it."

"Why not transplant them in healthy women of ideal child-bearing age?"

"We can't risk having whatever systemic cause that affects double-X chromosome carriers affect, infect, or waste even one chimp uterus. That leaves us with males." I gestured toward the cages. "As the evidence demonstrates."

"How much do you intend to pay these bold men?"

"It will be on a voluntary basis only."

She looked at the chimps then into the camera. "It'll be interesting to see who'll step up."

During the last minute we had left, she said to viewers, "You heard it here first, folks. Dr. Katherine Barnes is working her way to a miracle for the rest of us. This is Sasha Aspen, who, though I've seen a lot in this job, can honestly say my mind is blown."

Thank goodness Connie had brought the security team numbers she had for our excursion. Otherwise, we would never have made it out of the studio and through the throngs waiting outside the building.

Back inside our private lab, I made sure the chimps were okay and sleeping off the tranquilizer. I left Gretchen and Faye to share their interpretations of the event with the others.

I found Connie waiting for me, seated in her usual corner of the sofa, arms and legs crossed.

In response to her odd expression, I said, "What?"

"You really think men will volunteer to do this?"

"If they want the species to continue, they'll have to."

One of Connie's team burst into the room. "Turn on your TV."

"Why?" I asked.

"Just do it."

CHAPTER 97

I found the remote and aimed it at the big-screen TV mounted to the wall opposite the sofa. "Which channel?" I asked.

She chewed on a cuticle. "Doesn't matter."

A tall, thin man with a comb-over revealing more pink scalp than hair stood in front of a bank of microphones. The banner at the bottom of the screen listed him as The Right Reverend Stephen Jones. With a flourish, he removed a white handkerchief from his pocket and wiped the sweat from his scowling, florid face.

"How long has he been on?" I asked.

"Couple minutes. I ran here as soon as I heard about it."

We sat or stood as still as statues, transfixed.

The reverend slammed a fist against the Bible in his other hand. "What this so-called scientist has done is an abomination."

I thought of Chloe then let the memory go.

A reporter said, "Others see it as a glimmer of hope, a miracle, if you will."

"I will not. This is Satan's work, pure and simple. Thus sayeth the Lord, 'My people are destroyed for lack of knowledge: because thou hast rejected knowledge, I will also reject thee.'" He waved the Bible and said, "I'm speaking to you, Katherine Barnes. Repent. Abandon being the servant of the father of lies. As it's written, 'Thou hast forgotten the law of thy God.' And he'll forget you after he casts you into the lake of fire. Repent and desist, you vile whore of Satan. Find a Christian man to obey and give him children."

I muttered, "Bastard."

Others in the crowd began to shout him down. One woman close to the microphones shouted, "Idiot. Other than Amber Lake, there's been no conception for several years."

"With God, all things are possible. All throughout the Old Testament, he gave barren women children. What's happening now is His punishment for the multitude of sins rampant in our world. Repent, all ye heathens."

The crowd erupted.

Connie rested her elbows on her knees. "I'd pay good money to be there now. I'd sneak up on him and zap him with my stun gun. Right in his self-righteous nuggets."

The security woman with us said, "I'd hold him still."

The outspoken woman shoved her way to the microphones. "Don't listen to him. He's a man. What does he know about the pain we women feel about this catastrophe. He *can't* know."

The reverend moved to stand in front of the woman. "Jesus himself said the end times would be like in the days of Noah. As it's written in Genesis, 'And God said unto Noah, The end of all flesh is come before me; for the earth is filled with violence through them; and, behold, I will destroy them with the earth.'"

The same reporter from earlier said, "Are you saying this possible miracle to save the species is part of the end-times myth?"

"It's no myth, son. It's a promise from the Almighty. We are on the path to perdition. Repent, all of you. Before it's too late."

The woman bumped him out of the way with her hip. "What a load of superstitious crap. We stand on the brink of a chance to repair whatever it was that got broken in us. We need children. Not just so humans continue. We need them for more reasons than *this* guy can comprehend." She raised her fist and shouted, "Success to Katherine Barnes and WAM." She continued to repeat this phrase as others in the crowd joined in.

The reverend stormed away amid the uproar.

I hit the off button. The three of us were silent for a moment then I said, "Is she a member?"

Connie answered. "I'll try to locate her and check. If not, I'll see if she wants to be." She got to her feet and gestured to the other woman. "Let's go. Time to review our security measures."

I placed the remote on the coffee table. "You think we'll have problems?"

"It would be a miracle if we didn't."

Throughout the remainder of the day, my mind whirled with many thoughts, so it wasn't until I got into bed that night when I realized I'd heard nothing from Abigail about my appearance on TV and what I'd achieved. Surely she'd either seen it or heard about it from someone. I'd checked the news before going to my TV-less secure quarters. Regularly scheduled programs on nearly every channel had been bumped to allow coverage and discussion. It was all anyone was talking about. All they wanted to talk about.

I fell asleep before another thought about this or anything else could clutter my mind.

CHAPTER 98

Donations and membership applications flooded in, as did phone calls and e-mails and personal appearances by women eager to join our organization. We had to recruit volunteers solely to handle the volume.

Lauren's and my security teams doubled from five to ten, all armed in multiple ways and trained in martial arts.

The first attack happened two weeks later. Bullets shattered every large window in the lobby and a number of windows on other floors facing the front, though no one attempted entry. Nor would they have succeeded or liked what and who would have been waiting for them had they tried.

I joined Connie in the lobby the next day as a crew installed new panes. "They'll just do it again," I said.

She tucked her thumbs inside her weapon-laden belt. "That's why I'm replacing all exterior glass with aluminum oxynitride. Much more effective than traditional bulletproof glass. This stuff can stop .50 caliber armor-piercing rounds."

"That should do it."

"To a point. Nothing is completely impenetrable, say, like if someone used a rocket launcher."

I glanced at her. "You don't anticipate someone doing that, do you?"

"I stay busy trying to anticipate what someone might do. I suggest we replace every window at the school with this stuff."

"Whatever you need to ramp up security, do it. Funds coming in from around the world seem nearly unlimited." I faced her. "I'm not saying your budget is also unlimited. Just keep me apprised of expenditures."

"Good. Because I have other ideas about what's needed."

Connie's planning and efforts were exactly what were needed. Two more attacks happened within a six-month period, thankfully restricted to the headquarters building, always from a distance, and always minimal compared to what it could have been. Connie had seen to the barrier aspect as well, and applied the same protective measures at the school and the medical facility.

The other day, Lauren told me she sometimes feels like a chrysalis. Were conditions different, I would have taken that as a positive statement by a child anticipating the moment she broke free of her protective cocoon and her wings fluttered open and wide. A child, as most children are at that age, eager to enter the larger world waiting to be interpreted and improved by them.

But I knew she meant something else entirely.

CHAPTER 99

At the beginning of December, after a number of discussions—some of them heated—with Agatha, Brenda, and Connie, we began arrangements for the first human trials.

From the safety found inside headquarters, I initiated necessary outside contacts. This included the warden of the nearest maximum security prison with inmates on death row and California's governor. We scheduled a Skype meeting for the second week. At the appointed time, I initiated the meeting. Present on my side were Agatha, Brenda, and Connie.

"You can see," I said ten minutes in, "why men condemned to die are ideal for our initial purposes."

The governor puffed air into his cheeks then expelled it. "I'm not comfortable with the idea of swapping their sentences for this."

"Understandable. But some of them may die during the trial. We lost a number of chimpanzees before we had our first success."

"But then you did have a success. More than one."

"True, but that was chimps."

"Let's say some of these guys survive. I can't release them back into the public arena, no matter how famous this may make them. Some of these guys are the worst of the worst."

"I'm not suggesting you release them. Once they've fulfilled our purpose, put them back in prison, but off death row. It's the only way those who fit our criteria might agree."

"I suppose I could live with that. Warden?"

The warden leaned forward. "What about security?"

I gestured to Connie who nodded. "Not a problem."

He scowled. "Could you be a bit more forthcoming?"

"Sure thing. They'll each be in a secure room with 24/7 security details."

"Confined to bed," I added.

"Why?" the warden asked.

"One reason is they won't feel like doing much of anything once the transplant is done. Another reason is they must remain still so the uterus has a chance to integrate with the body and become viable. It's the same for the in vitro part of the process. Once the embryo begins to develop as anticipated, it's imperative they remain mostly immobile." I continued with an explanation about the waste removal aspect for volunteer hosts and fetuses. "So you see, they not only won't want to move about, they won't be able to. Any movement required for the process, and their well-being, will be severely restricted and monitored."

The governor cleared his throat. His face bloomed red. "Where will the, um, female contributions come from?"

"Volunteers. Keep in mind that human female eggs are still good. The fault is in their uteruses and ovarian release of an egg, which we can retrieve through a simple procedure."

"They aren't hesitant about a criminal being the father of their child?"

"Understand this," I said. "Your volunteers are in no way the parent, merely the host. Their roles end as soon as we release them back to you. That's included in the agreement they'll each sign—no claim on any child born. No responsibility at all, for that matter, and absolutely no contact ever with the child or parents, not that we'll release names and whereabouts to anyone. Our volunteer members donating eggs are married women, all in the appropriate age range, all in stable marriages with husbands who'll donate the sperm. We felt obligated to start with established couples we've vetted intensely beforehand. Think of it this way: It's no different than other surrogate arrangements, relatively speaking."

"What about those other two women sitting with you? What's their involvement?"

I introduced Agatha, who said, "I'll supervise all medical treatment and care." She listed her degrees and so forth, and then gestured toward Brenda.

Brenda smiled in her grandmotherly way. "I'll address their psychological needs." She provided the same type of information as to her qualifications as Agatha had.

The warden tapped his pen on his tablet. "And you're positive about the security matter?"

Connie grinned. "Our only competition would be Fort Knox. Maybe."

Discussion continued for another half hour, but primarily to finalize details. We agreed to swap appropriate documents via e-mail and ended the call.

I smiled at the three women. "Looks like we'll be in business starting the first week of January."

After several moments of congratulating ourselves, Brenda and Connie left. Agatha remained.

"There's something I'd like your approval on," she said.

"I'm listening."

"I'd like to use the scientists—the others, not your personal ones—to expand an idea I have in the oncology field."

"Which is?"

"I want to work on a cure for cancer."

"You have time to focus on that and our project?"

"I will if you let me use the services of at least two volunteer scientists who will agree to follow my instructions."

"Sounds like a worthy pursuit. As long as it doesn't detract your attention from—"

"It won't. I promise."

"Then go for it."

Agatha gave me a quick hug. "Patricia would be so proud of you."

"I hope so."

"She took to you and believed in you from the start, even when …" She reddened from her neck to her hairline.

"Even when what?" When she didn't answer, I said, "Did others have questions about me?"

She aimed her eyes at the floor. "Just a few." Eyes focused firmly on me, she said, "It didn't take long for them to realize Patricia was right about you."

"Should I be worried about them?"

She shook her head and smiled. "Not at all. It was mostly about jealousy. They wanted Patricia to hold them in the esteem she held you. They wanted to *be* you."

"I'd like their names."

"Don't make me tell you, Katherine. It wouldn't be fair. Not after all this time. They've proven themselves over and over. You have nothing to worry about, and more important things to focus on. I'm sorry I mentioned it."

She kissed me on the cheek and left.

Nothing to worry about.

I had everything to worry about.

CHAPTER 100

The second day of January was the turning point for us. Four shackled prisoners arrived, delighted to no longer be on death row and no longer behind bars. Connie's team took over the transfer outside the medical facility, refusing entry to our facility by prison guards. They were unhappy about that. We didn't care.

Connie had addressed security in more ways than I could have fathomed. Only one of the prisoners attempted to get away. Personally, it pleased me to see him try it in front of the other three. They learned quickly that any further attempts were futile, painful, and humiliating. Connie and her security team could be referred to as any number of things—which the men initially spewed—but *lightweights* was not one included in their more colorful adjectives.

We decided to stagger the transplants a week apart, more for our convenience than any other reason. We repeated the procedure used for the chimps, but modified for human biochemistry and physiology. After the tenth month, the first uterus proved healthy and ready for insertion of the fertilized egg.

Six months in, and after some discussion, another Skype call, and arrangements we needed resolved and met, we had four new prisoners with transplants. Agatha referred to it as a backup plan—a necessary evil. We hired additional female doctors and nurses specifically trained in organ transplants and neonatal care.

It's remarkable how an invasive procedure or two, plus the addition of sedatives and restraints, make an otherwise violent man compliant and uncomplaining ninety-eight percent of the time. This also served to make Brenda's involvement with the men seldom required.

Tending to the needs of a full-grown man, especially once the machines were hooked up to remove embryonic waste, proved far less appealing than for chimpanzees. But it was a necessary, time-intensive occupation. They and the fetuses had to be kept healthy at all costs.

Monitoring our hosts and fetuses became a 24/7, exhausting, yet rewarding occupation.

The first prisoner host presented a problem I hadn't anticipated. He, like the others, usually slept through the sonograms. However, the first time he felt the fetus move, he wept. Afterwards, he forced himself to remain awake and asked endless questions.

Two months into the second trimester, while I was conducting a sonogram, he wrapped his hand around my wrist.

His eyes fixed on mine. "I know I signed off on no contact, but will you let me see him when he's born?" He rubbed his expanding abdomen and smiled as the developing baby responded on the screen.

I hadn't been allowed to experience that kind of moment with Caitlin while she grew inside me. Rage welled and coursed through every cell in my body. I halted the sonogram and started for the door.

"Please," he said quietly.

I kept my back to him as my eyes filled. "I'll decide at the time."

At the beginning of the eighth month, which was during February of the following year, Agatha and I stood at the bedside of this host.

She sighed and shook her head. "The vitals of both are starting to fluctuate."

"What do you want to do?"

"I suggest we deliver this one."

"I agree. I'd rather face the usual challenges with a month-early infant than risk it."

"I'll get everything set up. I want to do this as soon as possible."

Atypical of usual C-section procedure, we put the host all the way under. Within ten minutes after the incision, the first human baby was born after years of what could be termed an infant drought.

"I would have preferred a girl," I said.

"So you mentioned a number of times. You may change your mind when you hold him." Agatha frowned. "We have a bleeder here."

I assisted her in her efforts to save the prisoner. He didn't make it. I almost felt sorry that he hadn't had the chance to see his son or hear the first sound he made.

Almost.

Agatha called time of death, a task I'd witnessed too often.

I did a quick check on the infant being tended to by a nurse then joined her at the wash basin. "We need to find a way to make sure the men survive."

"They will. This one was a fluke, an ulceration waiting to burst that didn't present, possibly because he was kept under sedation most of the time."

"I hope you're right."

"I have to be, don't I?"

"The world could turn on us if you—we—aren't."

"Only initially. Remember, Katherine, more boys will be born and grow into men to act as hosts. The species will continue. Mothers will cradle babies in their arms once again. Fathers will play ball or humble themselves to enjoy tea parties. The public will get over any collateral loss. After all—"

"Women have been doing it for generations."

Agatha nodded. "Indeed."

***

We took necessary precautions with our infant boy, which included keeping the specially prepared nursery room impeccably sterile. Everyone who entered the room wore a mask and gloves.

We gave him round-the-clock attention and kept him under a heat-radiating lamp the first two weeks. He breathed well, ate well, and eliminated with no problem. Despite this, we carefully watched for symptoms of persistent ductus arteriosis, hemorrhaging in the brain, and intestinal inflammation—all conditions infants born four weeks early have the potential to experience.

Six weeks later, once we were certain the infant was in excellent health, I arranged for Sasha Aspen to interview me at the medical facility, in a private office near the lobby. I insisted the interview last no more than five minutes. Connie and two others of her team stood offside in the room. Ten others stood watch outside the door. Additional security positioned themselves inside and outside the building.

We'd made certain Sasha and her crew were in good health, and to time the interview after the infant was fed, burped, changed, and bathed. I held the sleeping infant in such a way that the camera, stationed three yards away, on my orders, could zoom in on his face. I'd deliberately left one of his arms free of the swaddling.

Sasha's gaze fixed on his face. "Is he okay?"

"He's in perfect health in every way."

She slid a finger into his curled hand. His tiny hand instinctively curled around it. Turning tear-filled eyes to the camera, voice choked, she said, "He's beautiful." Her eyes focused back on me. "May I hold him?"

"Of course." I transferred him into her arms.

Numerous times, she attempted to ask questions but struggled to get the words out. Half-sobbing, she faced the camera. "I'm sorry, viewers. Someone with my professional experience should be able to—" She took several seconds to swallow hard more than once. "Should be able to ..." She cuddled the infant to her and rested a wet cheek on his downy blond hair. Her shoulders moved up and down as she sobbed.

I smiled like an ecstatic saint and placed an arm around her. My gaze drifted to the clock on the wall. I whispered in her ear, "You have a minute left."

She nodded, sniffed several times, straightened her posture and said, "What is this precious treasure's name?"

I looked into the camera. "Kane. K-A-N-E."

She shook her hair, vivid orange this time, from her face. "Is the K part for Katherine?"

"No." I let go of her and said, "Time to get him back to his usual routine."

She handed him back to me reluctantly and said, "We can expect more such miracles?"

"They're happening as we speak."

I left her and the cameraman to pack up under a security team's supervision, relieved she'd asked no questions about the male host. Neither did the warden or governor question the host's death when our report was made to them.

As Agatha had said, our result held more significance.

CHAPTER 101

By the end of August 2017, we'd delivered two girls and a boy. The male hosts survived, and once fully recuperated, returned to their former, permanent residence uterus-free.

We hated losing the uteruses, but it wasn't feasible for the prisons to do what it would take to maintain them in the hosts. Nor could we recycle the organs. We saw the writing on the proverbial, future wall about this, but we'd deal with that at a later time, especially as we still believed we could reverse the lack of conception in women matter.

As with Kane, the infants had their moments in front of the camera with an emotional Sasha. Also as with Kane, we waited another month then turned them over to the couples who'd contributed the eggs and sperm. Our sperm bank raid had been mostly for nothing. Still, I asked Connie to keep the containers on ice, in case needed for the future.

When the last infant left us, Agatha and I met in my office to sip tea and discuss how to proceed. We debated whether we should continue using prisoners for another period of time or whether it was time to train select medical professionals so as to expand this service to the public. We decided it was prudent to handle procedures for the first general public males ourselves. However, we'd use prisoners for another year or two, to establish a standard for procedure.

"How is your other research going?" I asked.

"I'm excited about the prospects."

"What are you doing that hasn't been done?"

"I had the thought to use heat on cancer cells."

"That's a new one. How'd you come up with that?"

"Sort of a two-plus-two, I-wonder-if idea while reading something about infrared treatment for diabetic patients. We did a number of tests on mice we gave cancer to and saw that cancer cells began to die off when the tumor was heated to somewhere between 104 and 106 degrees."

I grinned. "That explains the purchase of the far infrared sauna unit. I thought you ordered it so you and the other scientists could relax, which would have been fine. So, your results are satisfactory?"

"To a point. We added other protocols to amplify results. Filtered water, organic foods, which we amped up with beetroot and chlorophyll, vitamins, and so forth. Basically, anything that would detox their furry little bodies and boost their immune systems. The results pleased us so much we've moved to rats. So far so good. However, in at most a month, we'd like to use one of the chimps."

I nodded. "Any but Mada or Michael."

"That goes without saying."

***

By the end of October, four new prisoners were recovering from transplants. As for Agatha, she wasted no time moving from rats to a chimp, which she'd given cancer to at the end of September. She'd escalated the cancer's speed of growth for a month then began her protocol. By May 2018, the chimp was cancer-free.

I asked her if she wanted to make a public announcement. She declined, stating she wanted to test the result on at least three more chimps and a few humans first.

Two weeks passed, and I received an envelope sent overnight, handed over to me after security X-rayed it and ran it through a variety of scans.

I looked at the sender's name, which was unfamiliar to me, and began to read.

> *Dear Dr. Barnes,*
>
> *My wife and I are in urgent need of your help. Please allow me to give you a brief, candid summary of our situation.*
>
> *I was wrongly incarcerated at Sands Correctional Facility in Massachusetts. Let me clarify—I was guilty in part, but not of what led to my imprisonment. I faced unfathomable situations during that time and, thankfully, the truth came out and I was released around this time last year.*

While incarcerated, my wife, Kayla, was diagnosed with uterine cancer, listed as terminal, and given only months to live. I believe her strong-willed nature (I used to call her stubborn) has allowed her to survive as long as possible for the sake of our three children.

It seems that with your proven solution to the conception matter, and now this new treatment in what I would call a stellar oncology department, you and your team are miracle workers.

I'm a wealthy man, Dr. Barnes. I'd happily make a generous donation to your organization. I beg you to help us. The status quo she's had so far is beginning to falter. She desperately wants to live. Our son's birthday is in several months. Please help us celebrate it without a death sentence hanging over our heads.

Sincerely,

Frederick Starks

I remained in my desk chair, staring at the letter for several moments. Ignoring my ringing phone, I grabbed the letter and envelope, and hurried down to Lavender.

She read the letter and said, "Hmm."

"Indeed. I don't know that you can find out how he knows about the oncology work, but I want you to find out everything you can about him. How fast can you get something to me?"

"Faster if I start now."

"His awareness of what's what here makes me uncomfortable."

"I hear you. It may be tomorrow before I have results for you. I want to be extra thorough."

"I'll leave you to it." I started to walk away, turned back, and rested a hand gently on her shoulder. "Thank you."

"Thank Patricia."

"I do. Often."

I've found that work is the best way to cope with stress at times. This was not one of those times. I couldn't get Frederick Starks's letter out of my mind.

***

Just after four the next day, Lavender texted to see if we could meet in my office. I waited on the sofa and jumped when the wall panel opened. She entered carrying a far larger stack of material than I'd anticipated. I stared wide-eyed at the thick folders in her arms. "Who *is* this person?"

"Relax." She pushed the panel closed and joined me. "I looked up more than him. Sometimes it's a good idea to research the people closest to a person." She placed the folders between us on the sofa.

"You're extraordinary."

"Back at you." She pulled the weighty top folder from the stack and handed it to me. "Frederick Starks. I've got info on him, starting with his birth, and, of course, everything I could find since then."

I opened the folder. Lavender tapped the top sheet and said, "Included in there is everything I could get on his criminal case—arrest, trial, incarceration—anything related to that time. This guy's something else, and I'm pretty sure I didn't see everything."

"What do you mean?"

"I kind of read between the lines about him. I'd bet anything someone protected him at that prison and didn't include some of the *finer* details."

"Should make for interesting reading."

"Behind those papers are his assets for the last ten years."

"He said he was wealthy."

"Did pretty good for a guy behind bars for almost two years."

I placed the file on the floor.

She handed the next folder to me. "That's the file on his wife. I don't know whether I like her, want to give her a good shake, or commiserate with her."

"Her husband called her strong-willed."

Lavender snorted a laugh and handed me a third folder. "This one's about his business."

"Tendum Enterprises. Never heard of it."

"It's on its way to being worth almost a billion dollars. Value dropped a bit when he got sentenced, but started back up with the help of this guy."

She handed me the last folder. "Jeffrey Davis. He increased revenue through acquisition of some major contracts and several firms. He's also a lifelong friend of Freddie-boy. You might say they used to party hearty together."

"This is a lot to read."

"It has a certain level of entertainment value."

"I'm impressed with your efforts."

"I hope you don't mind, but I used some of the other techs so we could cover more ground faster."

"I don't mind. Give them my thanks."

She stood and stretched. "What's the next step with this guy?"

"The next step is to pour over this information."

"You gonna reach out to him?"

"I don't know."

***

Frederick Starks proved he was both impatient and persistent. Not that I could fault him for this. But I not only wanted to learn as much about him as possible, I also had no idea how I'd respond to his request or if I even would.

I read for hours each night, once Lauren was asleep. It took twelve nights to read every word. Two days later, I received another overnight envelope—certified—with a letter from Starks requesting an in-person meeting. The last man who'd entered our headquarters building had paid with his life for doing so. Of course, he'd been uninvited.

I wanted to read the material in the folders again before making any decision about his request. This time, I'd go through it more slowly, carefully. I wanted to read between the lines as Lavender had done.

Once again, as soon as Lauren slept soundly, I read and made notes as needed in the margins. By the time I completed this task, it was the end of May. I didn't hear from him during that time.

That left me both unconcerned and concerned. The last thing I wanted him to do was show up and attempt to barge in to see me.

I reminded myself not to worry about this. If he managed to put a toe onto the grounds, that would be as far as he got.

CHAPTER 102

Early June, the top women threw a surprise party for my scientists and me. They'd waited this long to do so, wanting to make sure there was cause to celebrate. Four babies delivered, four more on the way, plus Agatha's other success, seemed reason enough for them. We'd all been working so hard, it was time to do something fun.

I smiled and acted as graciously as I could, but couldn't shake what was bothering me. First was my concern about which of these women might be the mole, who seemed to have gone into a long period of hibernation. The second was how Frederick Starks knew anything about what we were doing, other than the conception matter, that is. There was one other thing, but I preferred not to think about it.

Brenda joined me. "Why so pensive?"

I relaxed my face and gave her a small smile. "Sorry. I have a lot going on. This party, lovely as it is, wasn't on my schedule."

"I think it's more than that."

I faced her. "What do you mean?"

She shrugged. "Just that you're under a lot of pressure to perform and succeed in significant matters. Added to that is the intensive involvement and responsibility of running such a massive organization."

"I have a great deal of help with all of it."

"My dear friend, this is me you're talking to. Something else is on your mind."

I gave her another small smile. "You're right. But it's nothing I can't—"

"I'm free at three tomorrow. A session will do you good." She placed her hand on my forearm. "Three o'clock sharp. I'll expect you then. Now, relax and enjoy your party."

"You're right."

Brenda checked her watch. "Please make my goodbyes, if anyone even notices. I have a session starting in fifteen minutes. I like to prepare for several minutes beforehand. Remember, three o'clock."

"I'll be there."

***

Mug of tea in hand, I rested back on Brenda's office sofa. "It's nothing to do with anything or anyone here," I said. "It's Abigail. She's been on my mind. Best friends since middle school, though that friendship has dwindled. I guess I'm noting her absence."

I glanced at Brenda, who watched me with an especially attentive expression. She said nothing, so I continued. "There are many reasons I feel betrayed by her, including the lack of any contact from her after the announcement about Kane and so forth. I realize I could have reached out to her, but I suppose my disappointment and pride got the better of me. Along the way, I've convinced myself that our relationship is worth saving, mostly because of its longevity. Perhaps I'm fooling myself about that. We've had no contact, not so much as an exchange of Christmas cards, in a few years. Total silence on both sides."

"As upsetting as that understandably is, I still feel there's something else. I'm here for you, Katherine. Let me help you, even if just to listen."

I exhaled hard and walked to the window that looked out on the grounds and pond. Brenda remained silent. It took several moments to build the confidence to say what I did want to say but hesitated to. I took another deep breath, turned, and leaned against the wall. "It's only happened infrequently, but enough times to get my attention. My attempts to dismiss it are failing."

"What's happened?"

"I'll be somewhere—the first time was at the Haven—and I'll hear someone say Abigail's name. My pulse races and I look around to see if she's there or at least who might have said her name."

She nodded. "It's a common enough name."

"That's what I've told myself each time. But it really isn't. It's a name from another generation and seldom used now.

"A couple of times, I've heard it here, as I walked through head-quarter halls. And with the same results. Maybe my mind is playing tricks on me because I miss her. Because we used to share so much. Because I loved how she was always ready to celebrate my successes and didn't begrudge them."

I returned to the sofa and faced Brenda. "What do you think? Is it a simple matter of wishful thinking influenced by a need for more sleep than I usually get?"

Brenda's eyes welled and her lips trembled. She took my hands in hers and kept eye contact with me, like someone about to say, "My condolences for your loss."

Her behavior startled me. I tried to pull away but she gripped my hands tighter. "What is it?" I asked.

She stared intently into my eyes. "My dear, dear friend."

"You're frightening me."

"That's the last thing I wish to do. Not to you. But needs must, I'm afraid."

"What aren't you saying?"

"My dear, it pains me to tell you …"

My heart thumped against my ribs. "Tell me what?"

"*You* are Abigail."

CHAPTER 103

I stared, mouth agape, at Brenda. One tear spilled onto her cheek. I slid my hands from hers and stood. "I think we need to get you to the clinic immediately and let Agatha run diagnostic tests. Have you experienced any symptoms of dizziness, headaches? Any recent, extraordinary confusion?"

"I'm not the one who's confused."

"Any recent insect bites? Head injuries?"

"You've heard people say the name Abigail, mostly in passing and never to your face, because they were referring to you. Many of them have met *her*, quite to their surprise, though I dare say they're used to it by now."

I reached to test her forehead for fever. She gently pushed my hand away.

"Please sit, Katherine. It'll be easier to explain if you do."

I did so. Tentatively.

"It happened during your sixth session."

"We never had a sixth session."

Her eyes welled with tears again. "We've had a number of them."

I shook my head. "Brenda, something is very wrong. You need to let us do a thorough examination."

"Your manner, your facial expressions, even your speech patterns altered. When I asked what you were thinking, and said your name, you told me you were Abigail. The remainder of our session, and subsequent ones, were with Abigail, not Katherine."

My blood pressure dropped, dizziness filled my head. "Do you realize what you're saying?"

"Better than anyone. Whereas you, as Katherine, have spoken of Abigail, Abigail has never mentioned you. In fact, she claimed she doesn't know you exist. I asked her once. She stated emphatically that she doesn't know anyone named Katherine."

I studied her eyes. "Perhaps it's the onset of an aneurysm."

"She spoke at length about her promiscuous behaviors and en-counters with men. She's quite proud of it."

I got up and paced. "This is all wrong. I don't know what's going on here, but Abigail is a real person. She's been my friend for ages. Helped me cope with every turbulent situation that came up for me, at least while we were still close."

"You're proficient when it comes to matters of the body, but I'm the expert regarding matters of the mind. What you have is known as dissociative identity disorder."

"You're saying I have a split personality? I don't accept that. But as for you—"

"Formerly called multiple personality disorder." She sighed. "It's a complex psychological condition believed to be caused by a number of factors. These can include severe trauma during early childhood. Often extreme, repetitive physical, sexual, or emotional abuse. You know as well as I that you've experienced each of these.

"There is Katherine Barnes and there is Abigail Wright. Both exist in the person I'm looking at."

I shook my head. "Abigail exists. She's a separate human being— annoying at times, but a living, breathing individual. She sat next to me in class. I helped her with her studies so she could pass." I went to the window and focused on Caitlin's laurel tree. "Caitlin's conception was a result of her perfidy."

"Was it?"

I increased my volume, as though that would drown out her words and my thoughts. "None of this makes any sense." I faced her. "And that's because you're the one who has something psychologically or physiologically off, not me."

"Have you noticed Abigail shows up for you, in your mind, that is, after painful and emotional times in your life? This explains why you haven't heard from her about your recent success."

"You're wrong. I've heard from her whether events were positive or negative. We've always been there for each other. At least, we used to be."

I resumed pacing, all the while listing such times. My steps halted and I faced her. "I survived my mother's death because of her. And what about her husband, mother, and the other people we know in common?"

"That's how it works. But it doesn't erase the fact that it happens solely in your mind."

"In my mind, huh? I'll prove to you she's real." I grabbed my phone from my pocket, scrolled to the numerous text messages from Abigail, and handed the phone to her. "Look. Look at all the messages from Abigail. They may be old now, but they're as real as she is."

Brenda took the phone and scrolled up and down. She shook her head and handed it back to me. "As you can see, there's nothing there. The text messages you believed you've seen and kept are also in your mind."

I grabbed the phone from her and stared bewildered at the blank screen. "I don't know what you did, but she's in my contact list."

"Check it. Let's see if her information is there."

It wasn't.

CHAPTER 104

I collapsed onto Brenda's sofa. "Something is very wrong."

She smoothed her unwrinkled skirt. "That's what I'm trying to tell you."

"I'm going directly to Agatha and ask her to verify what you've told me. She'll know, if anyone does. Or Connie. I'll talk to both of them. Then we'll collect you, sedated if necessary, and get you to the clinic."

"It doesn't matter who you ask. They won't confirm it."

"They'll confirm you've gone off the deep end."

She shook her head. "Patricia made it plain, made them swear that even if you brought it up, they'd deny knowing any such thing. She understood, as we all did, the need to protect you. You're brilliant, as you know, and the last thing she or any of us wanted to do was disrupt that."

"You're disrupting me now. Why?"

"I can tell it's beginning to affect you more than it has in the past."

"I don't accept any of this." I pointed at her. "My scientists. Patricia was gone when I hired them. I'll ask them."

"They were warned. They had to be. You see that, don't you?"

"Why have I never been aware of any discrepancies in my behavior? Never seen anything out of place?"

"The technical term for the transition is switching. It can take seconds, minutes, or days. Under hypnosis, the person's different—what we call alters—or identities, are responsive to the therapist's requests. However, it doesn't always require hypnosis for the personality to manifest. It didn't the first time Abigail made her appearance. Something had triggered you. The change was dramatic and nearly instant, catching me quite by surprise."

"Did I blurt out, 'Hi, I'm Abigail. Who are you?'"

"As I said, there was a dramatic shift. Each personality presents his or her own postures, gestures, speech, age, even race or sex at times.

One personality may be allergic to something and the other not. One may be nearsighted and the other with perfect vision. Some unfortunate souls switch into animals, but that's exceedingly rare."

"I don't recall you ever hypnotizing me."

"I'm not surprised."

"So you're saying I'm schizophrenic."

"No. The two conditions are different, though people confuse them. Schizophrenia is a psychosis. People with it have hallucinations and delusions."

"That's what you're saying I do."

She shook her head and leaned forward. "They don't have multiple personalities, which is what you have. Whether you have more than just Abigail?" She shrugged. "So far you haven't revealed that to me."

My breaths came short and rapid. "I have to get out of here. I need air."

"Please stay. We need to talk more about this. I need to help you understand—"

"Not now." I sped from her office, down numerous hallways, and then into my own. Once inside, I leaned against my closed door and fought the bile rising in my throat.

She didn't want me to ask anyone about my supposed condition.

But she didn't say I couldn't look up Abigail. I double-checked my phone for her number. Not there. I rushed to my computer and looked up my backup data. Abigail's number, the one I knew as well as my own, was listed.

Finger poised over the keypad on my phone, I hesitated. Chided myself about the importance of getting to the bottom of this, of proving the problem was with Brenda, not me.

I couldn't touch the keypad.

Terror had gripped me.

Unfit to focus on work, I called the landline in my private lab. Gretchen answered. I said, "I won't be back today, but will be there first thing in the morning."

"Ah. Forgive me, but are you feeling unwell?"

I gripped the phone tighter and said with a tone sharper than I'd intended, "Why did you ask that?"

"Forgive my nose where it does not belong, ja? We see you in the morning. You rest. You feel better."

I ended the call without another word and made my way to our quarters. Outside the door, I called the head of the security team inside and said they could go; that I was home for the remainder of the day. I waited for them to come out, listened to their brief report, said goodbye and entered.

Irish Too scrambled to me. More out of habit than conscious attention, I patted him on the head.

Lauren swiveled on one of the stools at the counter as she did her homework. She glanced at me and smiled. "Hi, Mommy. The aunties said you're home early. Yay!"

"After your homework is done, maybe we can play Scrabble or one of the other games."

"Okay."

Trance-like, I walked with heavy steps to Lauren and touched her, starting at the top of her head then down her arms.

Speaking over her shoulder, she said, "What are you doing?"

"Just making sure you're real."

She placed her finger on the paragraph she was reading, looked at me and said, "You can be really weird sometimes."

She turned her focus back to her studies, leaving me even more disquieted.

How much of my life was real?

How much of it was lived in my mind?

If Lauren proved to not be real, I'd shatter into unrecoverable shards.

Just as, according to Brenda, Patricia had feared.

I was close to doing that as it was.

CHAPTER 105

I left Lauren to her studies and plunked onto the sofa yards from where she sat. Occasionally I'd glance at her to make certain she was still there rather than blinking in and out of existence. Or was she and other aspects of my altered reality like quarks in the laboratory, appearing where and when the physicists looked for them?

She had to be real. Otherwise, it would require an extraordinarily elaborate collaboration to maintain such a charade. According to Brenda, such a charade already existed in some measure.

But if Brenda was right, who had been Caitlin's father? Had I had sexual relations with both Jared and Clyde? Was it me having the disgusting sexual escapades that night, and at other times, rather than a person I knew as Abigail, who not only reveled in such activities, but liked to brag about them?

Bile rose in my throat. Every inch of my skin turned clammy. I made it to the bathroom in time to lose the contents of my stomach.

Lauren knocked on the door. "Mommy? You okay?"

"I'm fine. Must have been something I ate."

What that statement might actually mean sent another ripple of nausea through me. Finally, only dry heaves remained.

I rinsed my mouth and splashed my face with cold water mingled with tears, sobbing as silently as possible. Moments later, I stood straight and looked at my mirrored reflection.

What about cosmetics? Abigail practically slathered them on.

I checked the medicine cabinet, the cabinet under the sink, every inch in the bathroom where cosmetics might be hidden. Nothing.

I found the purse I seldom carried and dumped the contents onto my bed. Nothing there.

Lauren touched my shoulder and I jumped.

"Mommy, you're really not acting like yourself."

Weakened by her statement, I propped a hand on the bed to keep myself up.

314

"Did you lose something? I can help you look."

"No. I'm sorry I keep disturbing you."

"I'm not the one acting disturbed."

I stood and grabbed her by the arms. "What are you saying?"

Fear filled her eyes. "What's wrong, Mommy? Should I call Auntie Agatha?"

"No." I pulled her to me. "Oh, Lauren, I'm sorry. Maybe I need to rest. Go back to your studies. I think I should lie down."

"Okay. If you need me to, I'll call someone to help."

I nodded, kicked off my shoes, and crawled into bed fully clothed.

The next morning, I left the bathroom, having decided to act as normal as possible—whatever that now meant.

Lauren looked up from her cereal. "Are you better?"

"Much. I suppose it was a matter of getting the toxins out of my body and getting a good night's sleep."

"*I* didn't sleep."

"Were you worried about me?"

She chewed her bottom lip for a moment then said, "You talked in your sleep. A lot."

My arms hung limp at my sides. "What did I say?"

"You mumbled. And moaned."

I patted her on the arm. "I'm sorry. It'll be okay tonight."

The call came to alert us that Lauren's security team was about to enter. I waited a moment to answer.

"Don't tell anyone I was unwell yesterday, okay?"

"Why?"

"Please."

She grinned. "Supermommy can't have sick days?"

"Promise."

Her smile faded. "I promise."

I answered the phone. The team entered. Each fixed their eyes on us. The leader said, "Any problems?"

Lauren answered. "I couldn't sleep. Tummy ache. But I'm all better."

I kissed her cheek and wished her a good day.

The door closed behind them, leaving me alone in the sound-proofed space.

My nine-year-old daughter had lied on my behalf.

Had she done it before?

CHAPTER 106

I continued the search for cosmetics in my office, to no avail. Wherever I'd hidden them, only *Abigail* could find them. If they even existed, I reminded myself.

Exhausted, I plopped into my desk chair and sipped the coffee that had gone cold.

A knock on my closed door was followed by it opening and Connie sticking her head in. "How's it going?"

"Why do you ask?"

"I was told you and Lauren didn't sleep well."

"Lauren explained why."

"Just double-checking. Mind if I grab half a cup of java from you?"

"Help yourself."

Connie poured liquid from the carafe into a cup and positioned herself on a corner of my desk. "I'm happy to report I've made each of our facilities as secure as possible. But I'll keep up with innovations. Can't afford to let our guard down for a millisecond."

"Your efforts seem effective."

She knocked on the desk. "So far, so good."

"Was there a reason you never asked me to carry a gun?"

Connie's eyebrows shot up. "Where'd that come from?"

"What's the answer?"

She shrugged. "You didn't seem like the type. Besides, you have me and any number of others around all the time. Why are you asking now?"

"Just wondered if you had a specific reason."

"Like I said ..." She drained the coffee from the cup and placed the cup on the credenza. "Time for me to do my thing. You heading down below?"

"Of course. Why wouldn't I?"

"Man, are you cranky when you don't sleep." She strode to the door, waved without turning around, and said, "Later."

This situation had me on a precipice of utter confusion. I reminded myself I'd always been someone who did what it took to overcome adverse circumstances.

My mother had named me as she had for whatever her reasons were. The purity of Katherine hadn't lasted. However, I'd clung to the meaning of my middle name while growing up.

I did something I hadn't done since I was a child—I looked up Eris, the Greek goddess of strife and discord. On the monitor I read how there were two types of strife on the earth, not one. That man would need to understand her—Eris, that is—in order to praise her.

As though I'd ever need or seek praise from any man.

The other aspect of her was worthy of blame, it said. Maybe I was worthy of blame, but only because I, as had she, had been forced into taking specific actions.

The next sentence sent my pulse racing again. *The two types are different in nature.*

I rejected the obvious thought about what this could refer to if Brenda had her way. Instead, I dwelt on the two types of strife aspect. It was a thread in my mind and I chose to follow it.

I continued to read, snorting at the next bit. The writer of the description had it wrong about Eris having a side that was cruel, fostering evil and war, and that no man loved her. A misinterpretation of actions, for which blame had to be placed on men.

It wasn't me who'd started this fight. And they could keep their kind of love.

Then I read the last sentence claiming that through the will of deathless gods, and though she was cruel and harsh, men paid the honor due her.

Any cruelty or harshness toward a man expressed by me had been earned. And it wasn't any deathless god that would cause men to respect me, it was my own efforts that would achieve this. Some might argue that the word respect was overstating it. Whatever anyone chose to call it didn't diminish the desired outcome.

I nodded at the words on the screen. Whatever was going on, I was nowhere near ready to give up the fight.

Any fight.

I drafted an e-mail and sent it to the top women at headquarters.

It was time for a meeting.

CHAPTER 107

At two that afternoon, I entered the conference room, nodding at the seated women as I stood at the head of the table.

I gave them a summary update on the conception process, most of which they already knew from news reports we'd set up.

"We're making a difference," one of the women said.

Others murmured their agreement and approval.

I held up a hand. "Where we are now, you might say, is the beginning of the end."

The same woman spoke up. "But isn't this a new beginning rather than an end. After all, you and your team created a viable solution."

"I refer to man's egregious treatment of women. I refer to the fact that more and more men will finally begin to grasp what it's like to be a woman."

Another at the table said, "They'll never fully understand that. Not until they deal with periods every month."

I waited until the comments and laughter settled down. "True, but this will be a humbling experience for them. Along the way, as we continue to take control of everything, as our beloved Patricia not only intended but knew was necessary, we'll teach them how to be more like us—better, kinder, more humane."

"You think they'll go along without a fight?" another woman asked.

"They'll have to. Too many of us have sacrificed too much, including our lives in some measure, for us to give a moment's thought to failing. Patricia, for one." Nearly silently I added, "My mother. And Chloe."

"Excuse me, Dr. Barnes."

I held up a hand for silence and scanned each woman's face. Connie wore an expectant expression, as did many. Brenda's expression was one that even days ago I would have read as compassion. Now it annoyed me.

I straightened my posture and said, "From this moment on, I'll be using a different name."

Brenda visibly paled. Her lips parted, her eyes widened. She gave a subtle shake of her head.

It was time to yank on the thread I'd followed earlier that morning. "I will no longer be known as Dr. Barnes. From now on, I'm Katherine Eris."

Agatha said, "You're switching to your middle name?"

I glanced at Brenda, who sat as silently apoplectic as one might when not alone. "I'm not switching anything," I snapped. "But call me Dr. Eris. I want all stationery to reflect this."

As they muttered among themselves and Brenda looked anywhere but at me, I reminded myself of something Buddha said. "The worlds originate so that truth may come and dwell therein."

I studied the face of each woman in turn.

Welcome to my truth.

And I'm just getting started.

ABOUT THE AUTHOR

Nesly Clerge received his bachelor's degree in physiology and neurobiology at the University of Maryland, and later pursued a doctoral degree in the field of chiropractic medicine. Although his background is primarily science-based, he finally embraced his lifelong passion for writing. Clerge's debut novel in The Starks Trilogy, *When the Serpent Bites*, received the Gold Medal Award from Readers' Favorite 2017 International Book Awards. The second book, *When the Dragon Roars*, received Readers' Favorite 2017 International Book Awards Silver Medal. The newly released *When the Phoenix Rises* is the third trilogy book. The trilogy books explore choices, consequences, and the complexities of human emotions, especially when we are placed in a less-than-desirable setting. *End of the World: The Beginning*, is the first book in a new serial, and became an Amazon #1 Bestseller two weeks after publication. Clerge's other novel, *The Anatomy of Cheating*, has also been well received by fans of his novels. When Clerge is not writing, he manages several multidisciplinary clinics. He enjoys reading, chess, traveling, exploring the outdoors, and spending time with his significant other and his sons. For more information regarding his books, please visit Clergebooks.com.